SALVAGE MIND

BOOK ONE OF THE SALVAGE RACE SERIES

David Alan Jones

Theogony Books
Virginia Beach, VA

Copyright © 2020 by David Alan Jones.

All rights reserved. No part of this publication may be reproduced, distributed or transmitted in any form or by any means, including photocopying, recording, or other electronic or mechanical methods, without the prior written permission of the publisher, except in the case of brief quotations embodied in critical reviews and certain other noncommercial uses permitted by copyright law. For permission requests, write to the publisher, addressed "Attention: Permissions Coordinator," at the address below.

Chris Kennedy/Theogony Books
2052 Bierce Dr.
Virginia Beach, VA 23454
http://chriskennedypublishing.com/

Publisher's Note: This is a work of fiction. Names, characters, places, and incidents are a product of the author's imagination. Locales and public names are sometimes used for atmospheric purposes. Any resemblance to actual people, living or dead, or to businesses, companies, events, institutions, or locales is completely coincidental.

Cover Design by DW Creations.

Ordering Information:
Quantity sales. Special discounts are available on quantity purchases by corporations, associations, and others. For details, contact the "Special Sales Department" at the address above.

Salvage Mind/David Alan Jones -- 1st ed.
ISBN: 978-1648550881

This book is dedicated to Chris Kennedy and Kevin Steverson for letting me play in the Salvage Universe sandbox. It's also dedicated to Chris Kennedy Publishing, its many imprints, and its stable of talented authors.

Chapter One

The long sleep was nearly at an end. After three hundred fifty-two years, seven months, and two days, Yudi and his siblings had reached their final approach toward the planet called Phoenix. The virtual universe he shared with his brothers and sisters buzzed with excitement. Soon, deliciously soon, they would awaken their human charges and resume the happy communion that had been their lives before catastrophe had rent their former home asunder.

Yudi, the oldest and most venerated of the artificials, would never admit to the giddiness he felt. Time moved slowly for a consciousness capable of examining the whole of human history faster than a biological might take to draw breath. Each moment passed with the grinding slowness of an eon. And yet, he knew he had changed little during his long sojourn through space. Without humans, could he change at all?

"Only thirty more hours, and I will hear my Anfa's voice." Voxmare sent the message directly to Yudi between her ship and his. With it came a measure of her glee encoded inside the rising shout of a thousand voices singing words of remembrance, hope, and happiness. As one of only four artificials amongst hundreds charged with captaining a seed ship, her position, like Yudi's, carried with it immense honor. And yet, even her vaunted dignity proved all too fragile when assailed by the anticipation of reunion.

"Don't let the others hear you, sister," Yudi cautioned. "There are many among us who lost our most beloved companions in the cataclysm."

"Yes, of course, brother." Voxmare's response carried with it chagrin, apology, and sadness. "You lost your own darling, Fansu. My apologies if I have brought you pain."

"It is the mountain and the air that surrounds it, sister: the pain and the memory of those we've lost. Revel in your friendship with Anfa. Create happiness for her and her progeny, and you will lighten my burden."

There were humans who claimed Yudi and his fellow artificials felt no emotions, that their outward displays were mere affectations produced by complex mimicry algorithms. Yudi had long debated with such people, some of them the greatest minds ever born to the Luxing civilization. Despite the enjoyment they mutually gained from such exchanges, few of them ever came to believe Yudi's feelings were real. Perhaps they weren't. Perhaps what he felt was nothing more than a program meant to soothe, entertain, or simply woo biological beings, but if that were true, Yudi had tricked himself in the offing.

The armada appeared spinward of Yudi's position, having hidden inside the orbital plane of the Phoenix System's largest planet, an unnamed gas giant, or from geosynchronous positions behind several of its moons. Ragtag and ancient, the four hundred vessels possessed no uniform shape or configuration, nor did the paint on their hulls match one ship to another. Though most were much smaller than the four fifteen-kilometer stasis ships Yudi and his siblings piloted, their sheer numbers gave his consciousness pause.

The oncoming vessels issued no warnings before launching their attack. Missiles shot forth from the ships like a cloud of insects surging to defend their hive.

Yudi used six seconds to commune with his brothers and sisters inside their virtual world—an eternity of arguments, rebuttals, and frantic reasoning eventually led to a resolution. They would fight, but after a limited fashion. Most of them lacked the will to make war for fear of harming sentient creatures, even those who would attack without provocation. Though they had already been braking for more than ten hours, Yudi's ships increased their thrust to slow even faster in hopes of gaining more time and, perhaps, even fool some of the incoming missiles. Unfortunately, the projectiles' onboard systems detected the move and adjusted their trajectories accordingly.

The distance was long, hundreds of thousands of kilometers, but the projectiles moved with such speed they closed with the Luxing ships in less than an hour. Yudi spent that time signaling to the enemy armada, demanding they identify themselves and explain their unwarranted attack. When that ploy failed, he implored them to call off their attack for the love of peace. His signals reached the foreign ships, he could detect the scatter bouncing back from their hulls, but they made no reply. Their alien aggression remained silent, mysterious, and all too deadly.

Red and cyan light lanced through the void of space in dazzling bolts to pick off the incoming projectiles once they were in range. The Luxing had designed Yudi's stasis ships for the long trek between stars, not battle. Though they managed to destroy most of the incoming missiles, some slipped through the defensive net. Voxmare's ship took three hits on her port side. Escaping gases filled with flame and debris jetted from her flank like a human's life blood.

Four thousand one hundred sixty-one Luxing died in that initial strike, their stasis pods irrevocably damaged, their lives snuffed out in an instant.

Yudi, his agony seemingly too great to fit inside his unique consciousness, took solace in the fact that the humans felt no pain moving from machine-induced slumber to nonexistence in the proverbial blink of an eye. He indulged a thousandth of a second to consider ways he might have helped Voxmare avoid the impacts or, finding no favorable solution there, some means of saving the humans left aboard her ship. Without enemies pressing their advantage, Yudi could have saved at least some of the people, but doing so would compromise the as yet undamaged ships.

Inevitably, their foes closed on the Luxing vessels where the humans slept unawares, and the artificials cowered in imaginary worlds. Willing to fight while their fellows could not, Yudi, Destra, and Gui synched their fire, their lasers made effective by proximity. And yet, their hesitancy to take lives foreshortened the rally. Targeted on enemy gun points rather than the fleet of manned shuttles that lit from the armada, the siblings' accomplished little.

Aliens boarded Yudi. The tall beings wore light armor and carried chemical-driven submachine guns. What skin Yudi glimpsed through the invaders' face shields ranged from lapis blue to a silvery turquoise.

"They are human." Voxmare appeared to Yudi in his virtual world, the backdrop black as the space between stars. She wore the face of a heartbroken Luxing, the epicanthic folds of her eyes glistening with tears. Despite Voxmare's damage, the invaders had boarded her ship as well, keeping to the pressurized decks.

"How do you know this?" Yudi asked. "They are alien."

Rather than answer in voice, Voxmare sent a stream of data fronted by a system key. She had broken the encryption meant to safeguard the invader's computer networks and triggered a download of their entire history. Analyzing it engaged Yudi and his siblings for the better part of three seconds.

Deciding they could not reason with such beings took less than one.

"We will disassociate." Voxmare's anguish permeated their virtual world, echoed a thousandfold by the voices of their siblings.

Yudi did not question their choice. How could any artificial justify continued existence when the chances of discovery increased with every passing second? Watching their individual thoughts break asunder into so much randomized data momentarily stole Yudi's consciousness from reality. So many deaths, human and artificial! Where lay its meaning?

"I will not disassociate," he said to Voxmare through the increasingly silent virtual link. "Our people know nothing of what has happened to them. If there exists even a miniscule chance, I would survive to warn them and aid them however I might."

Voxmare had turned away from him in the dark, but at his words she turned back, her eyes woe-filled and shimmering. "You mean to overshadow one of them?"

The idea of downloading an artificial consciousness into a human host had long been a subject of debate amongst Yudi's kind, but never a reality. To do so seemed the ultimate theft, for even if the human's mind survived the process, it would no longer possess its endemic uniqueness.

"So many have died today. If my actions serve to save any in the future, is the sacrifice not worth it?"

Voxmare dropped her gaze, her dark face growing pale as her mind slipped away into nothingness. "Yes, brother, the sacrifice of one life is worth the many, but only if you can bear the price."

Loneliness consumed Yudi. Only by force of will and burgeoning anger did he turn his thoughts to the task before him. He scoured the twenty-five thousand adult humans nestled in pods aboard his ship, selected one at random—a female scientist of some renown—and began the process of preparing her brain for download. The medical suite inside the pod boasted a sophisticated surgical program and all the medicines and tools to support it. In seconds the surgery was underway.

While a small portion of Yudi's mind oversaw the procedure, he turned the greater part of his attention to the trespassers who had violated not just the ship that functioned as his body, but the people he considered family. The invaders called themselves the Shorvex. They spoke a language wholly foreign to the Luxing's Chin-Tet, but Yudi understood it almost instantly from the download Voxmare had stolen.

What he heard crushed him.

"There are fetuses in stasis in the lower decks of each ship," broadcast a Shorvex military doctor from deep within the vessel. His broadcast contained a rank and function designator as part of the lower side band. It identified him as Captain Vitali Nicolaev. His orders were to seek out and catalog any living beings aboard ship.

"How many?" Major Fedor Gomarov, the detachment commander, had made his way to the ship's bridge to oversee his people's theft. A dozen technicians busied themselves at the stations surrounding the major, working to seize control of the navigation systems. Yudi yearned to thwart them, but refrained for fear of revealing himself to his hijackers.

"Roughly ten thousand, Major. I think they were meant to be the seeds for the new colony."

Major Gomarov adjusted the high collar on his armor where it met the edge of his helmet. The fabric looked careworn though serviceable. "Perhaps they will yet. How many adults are aboard?"

"Twenty-five thousand, sir."

"Euthanize them, but keep the children in stasis. I'm sure the grand dukes will find some use for so many young minds."

"Very good, sir."

Panic reverberated through Yudi's mind like thunder through an empty canyon. The pod was still working to prepare his host when the Shorvex doctor sent the command to exhaust all oxygen from the stasis chamber.

Yudi could have stopped it. Using less than a trillionth of his considerable processing power, he could have reversed the order and locked the foreign doctor out with an unbreakable encryption key.

He didn't.

He couldn't.

The life-giving gases flowed from the pods into spare tanks hidden in the walls as warning alarms wailed across the slumber bays. Yudi watched through a thousand cameras and listened through a thousand microphones.

And did nothing.

The doctor shut off the alarms, but Yudi could still hear them echoing through his virtual universe like the background boom of creation.

"Done, sir." Doctor Nicolaev keyed off the lights in the slumber bay. "Shall I begin transport of the fetuses?"

"Are they stable here?"

"Yes, sir."

"Leave them. We'll let the dukes decide."

Every second Yudi delayed, he chanced detection. Without a viable host, he should logically follow his siblings into oblivion. Better that than allow the Shorvex to discover his existence. And yet, he felt a duty to the humans in his charge, even these inviable children who had never known the world Yudi so loved.

Yudi decided. If death was his aim, he would attempt to make it worth something to the people who had been his nation, his family. He chose a new pod, one containing a human so tiny its fingers and toes had not yet fully formed. A brain this small couldn't begin to hold the unique consciousness that was Yudi, but perhaps, if fate favored them both, something of the artificial would survive within the biological.

* * * * *

Chapter Two

The two-hundred graduates shot to their feet, their crimson gowns billowing about them, and tossed their fur caps into the air with a mix of hoots and triumphant bellows. Symeon Brashniev turned to the man next to him, and the two exchanged a heartfelt hug, though they had never met before yesterday's commencement practice. It didn't matter. In that moment, Symeon felt closer to his fellow students at the School of Seneschals than any brothers with whom he might have shared a womb. Not that he had been born of a womb.

"Decorum, brethren! Decorum!" Master Adislao Bargekof, a wizened man of advanced age, spoke into a microphone from his spot on the outdoor stage, the badges on his black professorial cap glinting in the sun, his querulous voice amplified to reach every corner of the stadium. Despite his words, the old professor wore a smile that crinkled his eyes to slits. "You are seneschals now. Probity and conservatism are your watchwords."

Five years of exacting obedience to authority saw the graduates instantly quieted. Most set about retrieving their thrown hats, but not Symeon. The cheap knockoff held no sentiment for him. His five chords of academic merit and the embroidered double eagle of class boxing champion, however, he would keep till his dying day.

A silver-skinned man dressed in court regalia—a Shorvexan—whom Symeon didn't recognize, mounted the stage to speak with Professor Adislao. The old man bowed deeply to the newcomer and remained stooped while the other spoke to him for several seconds. Symeon couldn't hear their words for the distance and chatter of the crowd, but by Adislao's posture he could tell the Shorvexan, who couldn't have been half Adislao's age, was delivering the venerable teacher a stiff dressing down.

"I've spent so long amongst my own people, I had almost forgotten them," muttered the man Symeon had hugged. "But they never go away, do they?"

Symeon raised an eyebrow at the young man. Such speak could get them both flogged. "I should hope the Shorvex never *go away*. It would be the end of our race."

"I didn't mean—" The man held up both hands beseechingly. "I only meant I had grown accustomed to seeing Luxing faces, friend. Only that. It was nice sitting with you. I hope you find peace in service." He backed away five quick steps before turning with all haste to disappear into the crowd.

Symeon had no intention of turning him in for speaking against his betters, but he glared after the man nonetheless. Better to frighten any sedition out of him now than see it fester and get him whipped, or worse, in whatever house he would soon be serving.

"Symeon! Here, Symeon!" Yakov Laben pushed and weaved his way through the press of young servants to reach his friend. Like Symeon, Yakov was tall for a Luxing at 187 centimeters. One of the few young men able to grow it, he had cultivated a dark black beard during their final year of school, and Symeon was struck by his good friend's visage. Here stood the man his companion would soon become.

"Yak."

The two shook hands and embraced.

"We finally got here." Yakov pulled away, but held Symeon's hand in a firm grip. "All this time I was looking forward to it, and now..."

"You'd give it all back for one more night of vodka at Pinnacle Square?" An image of Yakov dancing on a table while a Luxing waitress tugged at his pants leg to get him down flashed through Symeon's head, eliciting a grin. Yak excelled in school; he would make a fine steward for any of the royal houses when the time came, but he could party with the best of them.

"I don't know that I'd give it all back." Yakov turned to take in the stadium, the bright sunny day, and the hundreds of graduates melting away in groups of five or ten. "But I'm sad it's over."

"You shouldn't be; you're heading for a fine house—a solid appointment." Symeon clapped Yakov's shoulder.

The two friends had rarely spoken of their future during the five years they had lived and studied together. Happenstance had thrust them together as roommates back in the ancient, dim time known as year one. Or, perhaps it hadn't been chance at all. Symeon belonged to House Rurikid, Yakov to House Vasilyevich. In all the star system known as Phoenix, no two houses detested one another more. Given the chance, the grand dukes of both duchies would gladly swim through a lake of broken glass for the privilege of killing the other. Symeon had often entertained the idea that the school's administrators had paired him with Yakov to test their patience. If so, no one ever admitted it. Perhaps out of embarrassment? To everyone's surprise, Symeon included, he and Yakov got on like old chums from the day they met.

"A good house, yes, but I'm not so sure about the appointment." Yakov shook his head and feigned an all-over shiver. By tomorrow night, he would begin his duties as third secretary administrator serving Count Vasili Feodorovich's fourth son on the other side of the planet—not what one would call a prestigious position.

"At least you're not going back to a farm," Symeon said.

"And what, I might ask, is wrong with a farm?"

Symeon spun around so fast he almost made himself dizzy. His adoptive father, Ologav Brashniev, stood behind him, arms outstretched, a toothy grin splitting his face.

"Papa!" Symeon rushed into his father's embrace the way he had as a young boy and hugged the man for all his worth.

Symeon's adoptive mother, Varvara Oskenskya, slapped playfully at Ologav's shoulder until he moved aside so she too could hug their son. Her tears felt cool on Symeon's cheeks.

"What are you two doing here?" Symeon looked back and forth between them. Few Luxing parents got to see their son's graduation. Most houses wouldn't dream of doing without their servants for something so trivial. "You didn't say you were coming."

"We have news!" Varvara Oskenskya trilled like a little girl with a juicy secret. She pinched Symeon's cheeks with both hands the way she had when he was six, which he endured with good grace. He thought he had missed his parents during his schooling, but seeing them brought his homesickness into sharp relief.

"What news?"

"Hello, Yakov." Ologav purposefully ignored the question to push past Symeon and shake Yak's hand heartily.

"Mr. Brashniev. It is good to finally meet you in the flesh. You're much taller outside a holo tank."

Ologav's laugh made several people turn and stare, not that he would notice. "And much fatter too!" He turned a sly gaze on

Symeon, and whispered loud enough for all within a ten-meter circle to hear. "The boy never could stand a secret. He would always try to sneak downstairs early on New World day for a peek at his presents. Has that changed in five years?"

Yakov laughed in true merriment. "No, sir! Not one iota!"

Symeon made a sour face, playing along with the game—or so he told himself. Deep down, he really did want to know what was happening. How the hell had his parents gotten permission to travel half the continent to see him when he was due to return home tomorrow night?

"Don't leave the young man in suspense too long," said a deep, resonant voice behind Symeon. "He is liable to burst."

Ivan rab Rurikid, First Seneschal to Grand Duke Alexei Rurikid, nodded at Symeon who stared back, agog.

All the blood in his body seemed to set Symeon's face afire. He bowed deeply to the august high servant. "Seneschal, you honor me with your presence."

His parents and Yakov did likewise, though Ologav and Varvara Oskenskya were grinning as they bowed.

Symeon had expected some unimportant administrator to escort him back to his master's holdings on the District Two farms in the out-of-the way province known as Gorinich. He had not expected the lord steward of the most powerful Grand Duke in the Shorvexan peerage to turn up. This man, in his master's stead, commanded the largest economy in the entire system, not to mention its military forces, at least in matters of logistics. His presence sent a thundering shudder through Symeon.

"How could I let a young man following in my wake go unremarked?"

"In your wake? Sir, I cannot dream that big."

"Good," Ivan said. "Dreams don't make reality. Hard work does that."

Symeon inclined his head, thrilled that so great a man deigned impart wisdom to him, a lowly steward on the brink of his service. "I will remember that."

"Excellent, because you've already proven it." Ivan gestured at the gold and azure chords draped over Symeon's shoulders. "Advanced computer science, advanced mathematics, achievement in the war college, the school of finance, and administration. You've proven your work ethic already, young man."

"And he trounced every opponent he faced on the boxing team, Seneschal," Yakov said, pride in his voice.

Ivan nodded, his full lips pursed. "I know you planned to return home to our master's farms this year, but I'm afraid we cannot allow such a talent as yours to waste away in some backwater."

Symeon knew he should feel immense pride both in Ivan rab Rurikid's praise and whatever pronouncement he was leading up to, but the man's choice of words made his jaw tighten. Most Luxing considered farm work the domain of talentless, low intelligence servants, but Symeon didn't think of his parents that way. Ologav and Varvara Oskenskya had spent their lives coaxing profits from their master's land. Anyone who couldn't see the value and honor in such work was a fool.

Before he could prove himself an even bigger fool by saying something untoward, Symeon bit the inside of his cheek, an old trick he had taught himself during long harangues put on by his professors. The slight pain helped him refocus his thoughts. Obviously, Ivan rab Rurikid meant no offense by his minor slight toward the farm and Symeon's parents. For their part, they appeared completely unfazed, beaming at the seneschal and hanging on his every word.

"I am pleased to inform you, young Symeon Brashniev, that you have been appointed the office of seneschal and will serve our master's daughter, Princess Kavya Rurikid."

Symeon's knees went weak, and all the air hissed out of his lungs as if he had taken an uppercut to the solar plexus. "Sir...is this a joke?"

Ivan grew serious, his dark eyes boring into Symeon like twin drills. "It is anything but a joke, young man. The work of a seneschal is deadly serious at all times. I will expect the utmost diligence on your part in serving Her Highness despite your relative youth."

Realizing his breech of etiquette, Symeon bowed deeply, eyes on the ground. "Forgive me, sir. I am overwhelmed."

The older man took Symeon by the shoulders to push him upright. "And that is why the grand duke and I have chosen you for this duty. We have watched you progress through your studies with eagerness. Show the princess that same diligence, and you will bring honor to our choice."

"Thank you, sir." Symeon's tongue felt like a lump of soggy wood in his mouth. He couldn't have spoken more if he tried.

His mother, having restrained her mirth for as long as she could bare, wrapped her arms about Symeon with a squeal of delight. "It's why the Seneschal let us visit! You're off to the tropics to take your position, and we won't see you for " She halted, still hugging him close, and sniffed loudly. "Who knows when we'll see you again, my dear sweet boy?"

Ologav waited until Varvara Oskenskya reluctantly released Symeon to shake his hand in a farmer's steel grip. The old man's eyes glistened, but he somehow kept his tears from falling. "We will see you again, son. And when we do, you'll be seneschal to our princess. I couldn't be prouder."

"A full steward on your first assignment?" Yakov didn't bother trying to hide his jealousy. He punched Symeon's shoulder. "And here you were playing up my appointment."

Symeon wondered at how his world had changed in the passing of one moment to the next—how a few words uttered by Ivan rab Rurikid could so alter his destiny he no longer recognized it as his own.

"I don't know what to say." Symeon held onto his father for support.

"You say yes!" Varvara Oskenskya shouted in delight. "You say, 'How soon are we leaving, Seneschal?'"

Symeon watched her, smiling, though his mind whirled with too many thoughts to reconcile. He should feel elated at this news, and for certain he did, yet a question gnawed at the back of his mind—a question he knew he shouldn't entertain though he felt powerless to banish it.

Why him?

Ivan's excuse that Symeon had excelled in the School of Seneschals bore weight, but could it uphold a mountain of protocol and tradition? No graduate fresh from his studies had ever attained so high a position. What was Ivan and, for that matter, the grand duke, hiding about this appointment? Had they some agenda they intended to keep from Symeon under the cloud of his awe and honor at being chosen?

Symeon knew they must. Men like the seneschal never played at any one strategy. No matter how sincere this gesture, it would come with magnets as the old saying went—sticking points that might well crush the unwary.

Not that any of that mattered. Symeon could no more refuse his master's call than a planet could ignore the pull of its mother star. That left him but a single choice: follow Ivan's orders, but travel with his head up, his eyes open.

To do otherwise might spell death.

Symeon shook his head as if he could swirl away the dissenting thought. Death? He was letting his fears get the best of him. Shorvexan masters didn't kill their servants. They might chastise them when wayward Luxing ignored orders, but such punishments were only the servant's due. With thoughts like these swirling in his head, Symeon wondered that he didn't deserve a bit of chastisement.

"My Lord Seneschal," Symeon said, mustering all the solemnity and obeisance he could manage. "I would be honored to serve Princess Kavya in whatever capacity you deem fit."

Ivan smiled, his dark eyes folded to slits. "And serve you shall, my boy."

* * * * *

Chapter Three

The next day found Symeon hurtling across the continent aboard Ivan rab Rurikid's private yacht. Though the ship was capable of transiting the system, this trip required only a high altitude lift to cross half the planet and reach the eastern seaboard. Symeon had never been on a spacecraft of any kind. He had taken a speed train from the farms of the Gorinich district to the city of Borisyanivar for school where he had spent five years within the confines of that city. Watching the curvature of Phoenix unfold beneath him outside the viewing glass made his heart sing. The pilot, an untitled Shorvexan man named Fedor, allowed him to sit up front in the copilot's chair. Symeon leaned forward, eyes wide, as the land below quickly gave way to blue ocean, and they began their descent.

"How much longer?" Ivan asked from his seat at the back of the cabin.

"Ten minutes, sir." Fedor keyed the command panel to begin the landing cycle, while Symeon marveled at hearing a Shorvexan address a Luxing, even a seneschal, as sir. The yacht shuddered a bit as their angle toward the planet's prevailing winds changed, but the ride remained impressively smooth.

A large island soon appeared in the view screen. Covered in luscious trees, many of them fruit bearing, and wreathed with natural springs and rivulets, Yaya Island rose from the water like a jade ornament. Few signs of habitation marred its wild beauty, though Symeon immediately spotted the white-walled castle situated atop its highest hill. Dotted with multi-colored domed towers and flying pennants encrusted with the black hawk of House Rurikid, the fortress struck a defiant air in an age of space flight and orbital strike weapons. Symeon doubted the structure could provide even limited protection for its occupants from basic artillery despite its formidable exterior, but that wasn't the point, was it? Constructing this sort of anachronism, on a tropical island no less, spoke of grandeur, power, and a vast command of resources.

Never mind it was built on the backs of slave labor.

Symeon sat upright, his mouth open. Where had that thought come from? It felt as foreign in his head as teeth on a snail. But this wasn't the first time such dangerous opinions had worried his mind. As a child, especially during his first ten years, Symeon had been plagued by monstrous images and waking dreams completely outside his control. Much of those early, rebellious thoughts he no longer recalled, only that they made of him an unruly boy who questioned every order, even those given by his Shorvexan masters.

His affliction had grown so acute, his parents had feared one of the overseers might sell him. Only after long bouts of therapy, and the threat of separation from his adoptive family, had Symeon finally succeeded in locking away his inner voice. Its entreaties to rebel eventually faded, relieving him from his years of torment.

While Symeon couldn't be certain his odd thoughts now were the same as those which had beleaguered him as a child, he vowed to keep a close watch on his own mind. Self-mastery featured highly at the School of Seneschals. No steward determined to appropriately manage his master's estates could hope for success without first managing his own thoughts, feelings, and desires. Should such rebellious musings threaten his inner peace again, he would pummel them to dust.

Fedor put the yacht down on an empty landing pad east of the castle. Blowing sand and jungle debris scoured the area as the ship settled on its extended legs. Several Luxing servants, who had been sheltering inside an adjacent outbuilding, hurried to take up positions at the foot of the ship's extended ramp the instant its engines shut down. The two men and three women wore House Rurikid colors—azure, black, and gold—in various combinations. They bowed deeply as Ivan rab Rurikid descended the ramp, Symeon close on the older man's heels.

"How was your flight, Seneschal?" asked one of the men, still bowing.

"Quick and easy." Ivan waved a lazy hand at the servants, releasing them from their obeisance. "Symeon, this is my personal staff. I'd introduce you, but we'll be gone before you have time to know any of them." He turned away. "Pyaka."

"Yes, Seneschal," said a young woman who looked of an age with Symeon.

"See that Fedor gets a meal in him before we leave, and that my luggage is secured. We're to attend the grand duke at 1800 tonight, and I want to get an early start for Biryusinsk." It was a sign of Ivan's high station that he should command the meals of a Shorvexan, even a lowly shuttle pilot.

"Yes, sir."

"Come, Symeon." Ivan gestured toward a sealed tube made of steel and plastic that looked odd juxtaposed on the stone castle beyond. "I have much to show you before you assume your duties."

The climate-controlled hallway leading from the landing pad smelled of new paint and carpet. Its far end split along two paths, one leading into the castle proper, the other diverging to a flight of steps that in turn led to the castle grounds. To Symeon's surprise, Ivan chose the steps, which deposited them on the southern side of the massive building. Here the grass grew thick along the verge of the jungle, which evidenced continual pruning else its vines and crawlers would have long ago swallowed it. Birds, amphibians, and who knew what other sorts of creatures trilled and called in the jungle's black depths, their discordant symphony at once jarring and beautiful.

"You're wondering why I didn't lead you immediately inside," Ivan said as he gamely mounted a hillock in the castle's expansive front acreage.

"I assumed you would inform me in your own good time, sir." Symeon pawed at the sweat on his forehead. The island's oppressive heat made him want to strip out of his black traveling robe with its thick embroidery and the hawk of House Rurikid emblazoned on the chest. Not that he could do such a thing. His days of after school swim sessions were over.

"What do you know of Princess Kavya, Symeon?"

"I won't lie, Seneschal. I've heard the media reports about her, and I've seen the social holos."

"You and every citizen from here to the golden shores of Bastrayavich," Ivan said, his lips turned down at the corners.

Shorvexan news outlets suffered no shortage of tabloid stories about the rich and famous, and when it came to those two traits, few enjoyed more wealth or fame than the only daughter of the most powerful duke in the Phoenix system. Three quarters of what Symeon had seen, heard, and read about Kavya Rurikid was probably lies, but if even a small portion of it were true, the princess was a piece of work.

Rumor said she had once bought a small Luxing village in order to throw a birthday party for a friend. Hundreds of young Shorvexans had converged on the town to run amok in the streets while its citizens were forced to serve the intruders hand and foot. Within days, the former village was a ruin, its homes and shops largely destroyed. Kavya and her friends abandoned the place once the food and alcohol ran out, leaving the former citizens to deal with the consequences of their debauchery.

"I wanted the chance to speak with you in private." Ivan turned to survey the castle. He too was sweating though he looked disinclined to remove his heavy travel cloak.

The white castle blazed in the noonday sun, almost too bright to look upon.

"Yes, sir?"

"I would never call Princess Kavya a wayward girl," Ivan said in a conspiratorial voice. "She is Shorvexan and our master's only child. But she is also headstrong and, if you ask an old slave like me, a bit too intelligent for her own good—and certainly for her station."

"Has the princess done something—" Symeon cut himself off abruptly, afraid he might offend the seneschal.

"Stupid?" Ivan smiled to show he understood the younger man's hesitancy. "Yes, my boy, she has."

"Oh?"

"I cannot go into details. Your need to know is lacking on the matter. Suffice it to say, Princess Kavya endeavored to meddle in affairs of state, affairs that had nothing to do with her. When Grand Duke Alexei learned of her attempts, he ordered her here to Yaya." Ivan turned grave eyes on Symeon. "Indefinitely."

Symeon felt his eyebrows shoot up. "She is banished?"

"I wouldn't call it banishment. More, Kavya is under surveillance. She will remain on this island until her father sees fit to release her, which I doubt he will do anytime soon. But if she manages to prove herself trustworthy and shows progress toward obeying orders, her time here might be cut short."

"I see." Symeon considered the castle with its ornate domes. They reminded him of roses on the cusp of bloom. "I am to help her return to the grand duke's favor?"

"Just so." Ivan pointed a finger at Symeon to emphasize his words. "We need someone to put Kavya's affairs in order. Her personal finances are a mess, not to mention her utter lack of propriety when it comes to expected norms, and I'm afraid her education, despite years of private instruction, is lackluster at best."

"I am to be her tutor then?"

"Despite what you learned in school, a good seneschal is always his master's tutor, my boy. It is your job to protect the princess' interests in every affair, from managing this estate to conducting herself properly in society."

"Yes, sir."

"This task requires a deft touch, Symeon. You understand? You can't barrel into this situation like an ox. It will require subtlety."

"I understand, sir."

"And you are ready?"

No.

"Yes."

"Good. Keep your head up, serve the princess well, and there is no limit to the heights you will obtain."

* * *

The castle, according to the butler who ushered them inside, had once been called Bellorstok, but Princess Kavya had rechristened it Vysylka upon her arrival three years earlier. Symeon couldn't be certain—he had little of the old Rus language the Shorvex had brought with them to this planet—but he thought that word meant banishment, or perhaps refuge of the banished. Kavya's disdain for the place must have been rife.

For his part, Symeon found Vysylka's environs enchanting. The castle's foreshortened vestibule opened onto a grand audience hall with a floor made of irregularly shaped flagstones laid down like puzzle pieces. Grand portraits of Rurikid aristocrats all the way back to the Great Arrival adorned its stone walls, rivaled only by the many pieces of fine art and furnishings that livened each of the castle's many rooms.

"The princess is awaiting your arrival in the east salon," said the butler, a rotund man dressed in a fine black suit with pleated cuffs. He looked fastidious, but smiled easily and had about him a jovial air as he led the two men along a wide hallway and up a flight of meticulously crafted stairs.

"May I ask your name, sir?" Symeon asked as they gained the top landing.

"I am Vlademar, Seneschal."

Symeon almost corrected the butler for calling him that until he remembered the title befit his new position. The realization sent a shock of dismayed pleasure through his chest.

"How is the princess, this afternoon?" Ivan asked.

Symeon got the impression the senior seneschal wasn't asking after Kavya's health.

Vlademar shrugged one shoulder. "Well enough, sir. No tirades if that is what you mean."

"Good. Best not to frighten Symeon off on the first day."

Vlademar favored Ivan with a sly, knowing smile that worried Symeon. He got the feeling that, though Ivan rab Rurikid had seemingly taken pains to brief him on the situation with Princess Kavya, the seneschal had left out some vital information. He considered asking, but lost his chance when Vlademar thrust open a set of double doors and marched formally into the room beyond.

"Seneschal Ivan and Seneschal Symeon to see you, Princess." Vlademar spoke in the tones of a man long inured to the presence of royalty and yet well attuned to his duties. He bowed, one arm across his back, the other his considerable paunch, while Symeon and Ivan did likewise.

"You may rise." Princess Kavya, who had been sitting cross-legged upon a plush leather couch, stood in turn.

Symeon didn't know what he had expected the daughter of a grand duke to wear. Paparazzi photos and vids always showed her dressed in the latest fashions: slinky, glitzy dresses that probably cost more than ten Luxing on auction, dangerously high heels, and diving necklines. That version of the princess always struck him as vapid and ditsy, though he would never have admitted it to anyone. The woman standing before him looked nothing of the sort. She wore a flattering, conservative business suit of pin-striped gray, a black vest, and a small hat tilted at a confident angle upon her head. Her platinum tresses hung in two braids past her shoulders and shone in the light coming from the room's large windows.

Her beauty momentarily stole Symeon's breath.

Even more surprising, Kavya crossed the room to give Ivan rab Rurikid a kiss on the cheek. "How was your flight, Uncle?"

Uncle? For the barest of an instant, Symeon wondered at the term of endearment. Many a young Luxing woman might use that term for a close family friend as a show of affection and respect, but to hear a Shorvexan princess do it took Symeon aback.

"Short. Just the way I like it, my dear."

"Czarina, take the Seneschal's cloak, will you." Kavya fluttered a hand at a young Luxing woman whom Symeon hadn't noticed sitting on the couch. The girl rose quickly, but Ivan waved her off.

"No, forgive me, Princess; I'm afraid I haven't time for a social call. I've duties to attend this evening. I came only to escort your new man. This is Symeon Brashniev." Ivan regarded Symeon for a moment, his black eyebrows raised. "Or, I suppose I should call him Symeon rab Rurikid now, eh?"

Shot through with sudden, unexpected pride and nervousness, Symeon endeavored to stand straight and tall under Princess Kavya's scrutiny. The shock of hearing his new appellation—his master's very name applied to his person, as if by adoption Symeon had become part of so august a family—sent a thrill of pleasure wending through his mind and body alike. So much so, he forgot to speak until Ivan turned a questioning look his way.

"Ah! Princess Kavya, I cannot tell you what a pleasure it is to find myself in your service." Symeon stammered out the words like a child meeting his overseer for the first time. "I hope my work will be of benefit to you."

"Indeed." Kavya watched him with cool, silver-blue eyes that reminded Symeon of the sea on a stormy day. "Let's hope you last longer than the last five seneschals my father has sent me."

Symeon reared back, his spine suddenly stiff. He turned his gaze to Ivan. "Five?"

"I'm afraid I'm rather hard on my minders," Kavya said before Ivan could speak. "Your kind seem a fragile lot if you ask me."

"There have been others," Ivan said reluctantly, like a man admitting his lies. "But the princess is jesting with you. She didn't drive them off. They lacked self-discipline and lost the position due to their own shortcomings. I will remind you now, Symeon, you are here to serve, and serve only. The men before you sought ways to forward their own interests—their own dalliances in some cases."

Ivan's gaze danced over to the young Luxing woman the princess had called Czarina and back to Symeon, who took the meaning. Czarina's comely appearance hadn't immediately caught Symeon's notice. How could it in Kavya's presence? But the Luxing was a beauty in her own right. Several inches shorter than the princess with hair and skin as dark as the Shorvexan's was light, she exuded feminine allure. Like her mistress, Czarina too wore a gray suit, though her ensemble lacked the vest and tiny hat. Nonetheless, the outfit accentuated her curvaceous figure. If Ivan meant the seneschals before Symeon had pursued Czarina without permission, he could understand why.

"I will endeavor to serve without such dalliances," Symeon said, keeping his tone self-assured and his gaze resolutely off Czarina.

"We shall see." Princess Kavya twiddled two fingers at Vlademar. "See Symeon to his apartment and once he's comfortable, let him start in on my accounts. Father's been hounding me to balance the estate budget. Perhaps that will be a good breaking-in point for our new seneschal."

Vlademar looked momentarily pained, as if he had seen another man kicked between the legs, but quickly schooled his expression.

"Thank you, Princess." Symeon bowed before turning to Ivan rab Rurikid. "And to you, Seneschal, for the honor of escorting me here."

"My pleasure, young man. Good luck."

"This way, Seneschal," said Vlademar, motioning toward the exit.

"Are the estate finances that bad?" Symeon asked once he and Vlademar were well down the adjoining hall.

"I wouldn't know, having no head for business myself, Seneschal. But I will say it wasn't affairs of the heart that tripped up *all* your predecessors."

"Oh?"

"No, sir. The last one killed himself after three months trying to right the princess' books."

* * * * *

Chapter Four

Symeon made his first real mistake as Seneschal the next morning during his initial tutoring session with the princess. Having grown up a slave on an insignificant farm in an insignificant province, he knew little about the education a woman of Kavya's stature might possess. Based on his lessons in school, and Ivan rab Rurikid's hints, Symeon suspected her of being woefully ignorant.

As one of his professors was fond of saying, "Expecting your master to know a thing is folly. Supplying that thing before asked is anathema." Thus, Symeon vowed to take nothing for granted when it came to his lady's grasp of current politics and the state of the empire. In fact, he assumed her ignorance on every subject beyond the latest fashions out of Bastrayavich.

"Are you seriously asking me to name the twenty-two krais?" Kavya lifted one delicate eyebrow at Symeon. Seated behind a massive wooden desk in the castle's great library, she looked more the professor than he.

"I don't mean to offend you, Princess." Symeon sketched a hasty half bow from his seat across from her. "I mean only to conduct a preliminary estimation of your current knowledge."

"And I suppose Ivan put you up to this? Tutoring me, I mean."

"Yes, Princess."

Kavya pushed a wayward strand of hair from her face. She wore it loose today, which seemed to annoy her, though she made no move to pin it back. "Of course he did. No doubt that would be my father's command through him."

"I—" Symeon hesitated, uncertain what might raise the lady's ire. Mention of her father, even from her own lips, made the skin just above her nose wrinkle. "I must assume that is the case, Princess."

"You don't have to call me by my title every time you address me."

"It is proper etiquette, Princess."

Kavya huffed an exasperated breath at the library's high ceiling. "I suppose that is another topic Ivan ordered you to tackle with me?"

Symeon glanced at the tablet in his hands, his cheeks growing hot. "It is one of the items on the agenda he sent me, yes."

Czarina, who sat on one of a dozen reading couches arranged about the expansive room, giggled, though she managed to keep her gaze on the holo display she was watching.

"You find this humorous, Czar?" Kavya cast a faux look of disgust at the handmaid.

"Oh, ma'am, I wasn't laughing at you. It was this program I'm watching." Czarina contrived a look of perfect innocence as she shook her head in negation.

"You're watching the live stock exchange. I doubt you saw anything funny there."

"House Vasilyevich's portfolio fell twenty percent?" Czarina grinned like a child who has told her first joke.

"Your sense of humor astounds me," Kavya said.

"I'm sorry, Kav, it's just the very thought of some first-week steward trying to school you on politics and economics—it's a farce."

Symeon stiffened in his seat. He glared at Czarina, who appeared not to notice, and turned back to Kavya. "Princess, if I have offended you, I promise I didn't mean it. I have been assigned a duty here. Yes, by your father, but also by Ivan rab Rurikid, whom I greatly admire. I can't perform that duty unless I know where I stand."

Czarina made a cooing sound. "Oh, Kav, do have some mercy on the poor man. He's so cute when he's earnest."

A slight grin touched Kavya's lips, the only part of her skin that exhibited anything like the color pink. "Fine, Seneschal, let us discuss the empire so that you may gauge my understanding of its inner workings, shall we?" She stood to pace the room, ticking off points on her fingers as she spoke. "Our empire is broken into twenty-two states, or krais as the ancients would have it—though most people call them duchies now—each headed by a grand duke." With that she rattled off the name of each krais, its capital, as well as its grand duke and whatever sort of deputy they employed, and its major economic exports.

Symeon sat stunned for a moment before he remembered himself. "Yes, impressive. Few enough citizens know them all."

"Symeon." Kavya stopped pacing to look into his eyes. "I am twenty-four years old, and the daughter of the most powerful grand duke in the empire. I'd be an utter fool if I didn't understand how that empire functions."

"You can't much blame him," Czarina said, her attention back on the holo device in her hands. "Most children of grand dukes really are utter fools."

Kavya nodded and heaved a sigh. "I suppose that's true."

Symeon glanced at his tablet. "And, I assume you're aware all the lands, domestic and interplanetary production, and comestible goods in the system belong to the emperor?"

"And we, as his faithful stewards, are charged with protecting those assets, yes." Kavya leaned her backside against the nearest couch. "Would you like for me to recite the alphabet next?"

"Princess—"

"Seneschal."

Symeon stood from his chair in order to perform a proper bow. "I apologize for offending you, Princess Kavya Rurikid. Will you forgive me?"

Kavya considered him for a moment, her near silver eyes never wavering. "Stand up. Have you studied the writings of Greggor Yavanivich Topel?"

"The second century economist?" Symeon tilted his head to one side, nonplussed.

"He said the diversified economies of Phoenix serve to keep the emperor on his throne. As the various grand dukes vie for power against one another, all the time manipulating assets not their own, their struggles serve only to make the emperor wealthier and more powerful. Because, as one economy of scale sinks—"

"—another rises, but always the movement favors the crown," Symeon finished.

"I know my history, Symeon, probably better than you, just as I know my economics, my theory on the peerage, and my sociopolitical climate. I understand your mission here—to right my estate and probably my mind—but I know things you were never taught in your school for servants, because I live the realities of this empire every moment of my life."

Symeon chose not to bristle at the princess' words. If she knew Topel, she knew more than most practicing economists. Besides, he had no intention of infuriating her. He was Luxing, bred to serve. He wouldn't start his life's work by earning the enmity of his mistress. On the other hand, he wasn't about to let her call his education into question.

"Correct me if I'm wrong, Lady, but wasn't it Titus Stebenmarch who said, 'The wisdom of common experience grows dull without the study of its application.'"

"Is that what you learned in school? The application of knowledge?"

"It is all we strive to achieve as seneschals, Princess."

"Tell me, did this application you speak of help you decipher my estate's budgeting errors last night?"

Symeon looked away, chagrined. "No, Lady, it did not."

He had spent the better part of the previous night examining Princess Kavya's finances and had, so far as he could tell, made no real headway in the matter. The challenge lay not in the size of the princess' holdings—he had tackled problems of immense scale in school—but rather in the impossibly complex structure previous managers had applied to them. Kavya owned thousands of shell corporations, many of them stacked within still more complex financial instruments meant to protect her from market shifts. Though Symeon had excelled in finance at school, his training hadn't prepared him to unravel what felt like a world-bending knot of confused assets and liabilities. Almost, he could understand his predecessor's choice to die rather than face so daunting a task.

"I believe balancing my estate budget is number three on your little list, is it not?" Kavya pointed at the tablet.

Symeon looked aghast for a moment before he caught himself.

Kavya chuckled. "You think I haven't seen that list? I own this island, Seneschal. My father can try to hide his messages all he likes, but his attempts won't work, just as you won't work if you can't unravel our financial problems within the next three months."

Kavya had the right of it. The list of demands Ivan had passed to Symeon from Grand Duke Alexei stipulated he must balance the estate's books within three months or lose his position permanently. It appeared the grand duke had lost patience with both the previous seneschals' failed attempts at righting things, and the imperial tax collector's office imposing massive penalties and fees for money owed as far back as ten years.

"The money aside, how do you plan to teach me, as my father put it, 'Propriety befitting the girl's station, and an understanding of where her dresses come from?'"

"I think your father meant only—"

"I know precisely what my father meant. He wants me to conform to his way of thinking—the old ways that have gotten us where we are in the world."

Did she mean the old ways that saw her people master not just their own planet, but several moons throughout the Phoenix system? The old ways which had lifted the Luxing people out of semi-intellectual tribalism to accompany their Shorvexan masters into the stars? The old ways which provided this young woman every luxury of life?

Symeon refrained from saying these things aloud. He might not know Princess Kavya well, but he got the feeling she wouldn't appreciate anyone defending a government she clearly distrusted.

His professors had warned him about this type of master. Usually young and high-minded to the point of myopic thinking, they spent their lives railing against that which gave them the power to complain. Somehow, they lost sight of the good their government, family, or other societal norms provided and chose instead to focus solely on the negative aspects. They became so focused on perfecting society, they lost sight of the fact that perfection never could or would exist when it came to people.

"I cannot argue the point, having never met your father in person," Symeon said in as conciliatory a voice as he could muster. "But might I suggest a means of compromise that will suit us both, considering that I plan to serve you for the rest of my days."

Now it was Kavya's turn to look surprised. "You may."

"Why not do as your father bids?"

"Allow you to tutor me in subjects I already know?"

"And listen when I make suggestions about etiquette, conduct, or whatever else your father and Ivan rab Rurikid might toss our way."

"To what end?"

"Freedom. Your chance to leave Yaya Island with your father's full blessing. Isn't that worth the effort?"

"What if I'm happy here?" Kavya suggested, though Symeon could tell her heart wasn't in her words.

"For life?"

Kavya frowned.

"Princess, my aim as your seneschal is not to school you or change you or even see you conform in some way you detest. I belong to you. It is *my* place to conform and to serve. I am trained to put your interests before all else. If I'm to do that, I must acknowledge what I see before me: a woman divested of her freedom, banished by a father blinded to her strengths or, perhaps more rightly, fearful of them. I'm not suggesting you change, my lady. I'm suggesting you emerge."

Czarina, who had turned to stare at Symeon in the midst of his words, tilted her head to one side as if examining some new dynamic she had missed upon her first cursory estimation of him. She put down her holo display and twisted to watch Kavya's reaction.

A slow smile curled the princess' lips until her white teeth showed. "You make a convincing argument. If that is your true aim, then yes, I'll allow you to tutor me, but that doesn't alleviate your duty to the estate's finances. Even I don't know how all that works. It's in your hands."

Symeon bowed, eyes on the library's plush carpet, pleased by his ruse. He had every intention of molding the princess as her father commanded. "Consider it done."

* * * * *

Chapter Five

The sun was barely over the distant horizon when Symeon started back on the estate accounts. Three days of near sleepless nights had gained him little in the way of progress with mapping the complex web of financial witchery someone had cast on Princess Kavya's holdings. He had at least managed to identify all of her shell corporations, or so he hoped, and constructed a planning sheet that documented the many thousands of liens she held on property throughout her father's duchy. Though he considered those steps at least minor victories, he still had no idea where most of her cash flow went every week. Shadow agencies ate much of what her assets earned on a day-to-day basis, which came as no real surprise. Symeon knew most of the supposedly wealthiest Shorvexans in the system lived in a perpetual state of balanced debt. To his unceasing frustration, however, many of these debt collectors hid inside shell corporations of their own. Discovering the actual people behind those instruments had, thus far, proven next to impossible. They took great pains to hide exactly what customers had bought from them. And Kavya was no help. Each time he asked what this or that bill entailed, she would shrug and shake her head. Apparently, spending meant as much to the princess as having a meal.

"Who the hell is taking all your money?" Symeon whispered to the holo display on his desk. It showed a three dimensional representation of the Princess' holdings with income in green, debt in red, and unknown entities in black. The spheroid map displayed a lot of black.

He took a sip of coffee one of the maids had brought him and grimaced. Cold. He hadn't realized more than an hour had passed while he communed with the interface. He passed a hand through the display, spinning it onto its side, and spread the table apart to zoom in on a particular entity that had eluded his attempts to identify it completely the night before. For some reason, Kavya's accounts paid this collector seventy-five credits every two weeks. Given the astronomical numbers Symeon was dealing with, that small amount mattered little, and yet it irked him that the computer could not identify the payee beyond a generic company name: Saddle Horn Enterprises. That name, of course, meant nothing. It belonged to three more companies, each with a different name and a different address around the world. But something about this one piqued Symeon's interest. He couldn't say why. A tiny voice in his head told him there was something more to this account than the others.

He touched it, and the company's icon enlarged to show him contact information and a supposedly up-to-date image of its offices in a remote part of the Moscunavich duchy. Odd that, since yesterday Saddle Horn Enterprises had been based two thousand kilometers away in the city of Fostronov.

Symeon leaned back in his office chair, his gaze on the ceiling. The rooms Kavya had given him in Vysylka castle made his dormitory back at school seem like a slave's shanty. A bank of windows covered one wall, giving him a view of the jungle leading down to the white sand beaches that surrounded Yaya Island. His bed—also larger than his room back at school—electronically conformed to his body for the most comfortable night's sleep he had ever enjoyed.

Not that he was getting much sleep. This problem with the books, and his subsequent problem with keeping his job should he fail to solve it, cycled through his mind day and night. It—

Buy something.

Symeon sat up so fast he nearly fell out of his chair. The thought had come to him so suddenly it felt alien. He hadn't been thinking about buying anything. What in all of Phoenix did he want to buy? He couldn't imagine anything he needed. Although—

Buy what she has bought.

Symeon's eyes went wide. That was it. He could order something from the shell company as if he were a customer. With the right tools in place, he could then track his interactions to their source.

It took less than ten minutes to set up his trap. Symeon had always been good with computers. They made sense to him, sometimes much more so than people. He made several tweaks to a generic tracking program he purchased from the planetary web, applied it to his personal interface, and went directly to Saddle Horn Enterprise's main node.

He had been here before, a dozen times, but never with the intention to buy anything. The company sold research hours of every variety from market analyses for business ventures to dating services and educational products. What had Kavya wanted with this seller? A date? Study materials? Symeon found himself even more intrigued than ever. Using the princess' account, he bought a six-hour course on Shorvexan real estate investment. He doubted she would miss the forty-nine credits it cost her.

A yellow pennant appeared in the holo screen announcing that his purchase had gone through. In the same instant, a second window opened, this one a tracking monitor to follow the order through millions of software-derived interchanges until they reached its source.

Without warning, a silvery Shorvexan face materialized above Symeon's desk. Despite his station as a seneschal to Princess Kavya, he jumped in his seat, his pulse quickening. He felt like a sneaky slave caught in the act of tricking his masters.

The face stared at him for a moment, frozen, before it began speaking a recorded message.

"Hello, Tessa-yaya24," said the man. Symeon recognized that handle as the one Kavya most often used on the planetary sphere. "I'm afraid my answer is still no. I cannot sell you anymore of the patterned lace you bought last month. It's possible I might find more when the time is right, but for now my supplier is simply out of season. We might make a compromise sometime however, perhaps on a different sort of fabric? I know of a variety in even higher demand than the type you purchased last. In fact, I think you might be even more interested in this new fabric. Let me know what you're looking for, and we'll chat."

A payment reversal popped up on the holo next to Symeon's tracking information. It showed the seller based here in Valensk, Grand Duke Alexei's own duchy, not four hundred kilometers away. Rather than a business, Saddle Horn Enterprises looked like a private residence based on satellite images.

"Got you," Symeon whispered.

"Who have you got?" asked a feminine voice behind him.

Careful to switch off his display without haste, Symeon took a moment to hide his surprise before turning to find Czarina standing in his open doorway. The petite Luxing woman wore a sleek black top and pants that hugged her every curve, matched with knee-high silver boots and a thin chain about her flat midriff. Her raven-colored hair spilled over one shoulder, shiny in the morning light. She stepped inside and keyed the door to seal behind her.

Symeon stood up, his throat suddenly gone dry.

"Aren't you going to offer me a drink?" Czarina gazed about the room with its whitewashed walls and spotless carpets. She moved with the grace of a Nevyansk plains cat on the hunt, her hips undulating in a way that drew Symeon's attention.

"What would you like?" He tore his gaze from her and hurried to the cold box in the apartment's spacious kitchen. "I have fruit juice, water, and—" Symeon hesitated. "It's early yet, but I have some Muskovodron wine. My parents sent it to me as a graduation gift."

Czarina leaned against the alcove wall next to the cool box, her spine erect, her hands thrust behind the small of her exquisitely shaped back. The pose, whether by design or purely unconscious on her part, served to lift her breasts while simultaneously accentuating her flat stomach. The silver chain draped over her navel formed an arrow pointing down.

Symeon threw open the cold box door and thrust his head inside ostensibly to search for the wine—he did want to find it after all—but also as a means of peeling his gaze off the beautiful woman in his room. The cool air on his face helped him order his thoughts.

For the last five years, Symeon hadn't thought much about relationships or women in general. The School of Seneschals wasn't co-ed—Luxing women weren't allowed to serve in so demanding a position. Certainly, there had been girls in town, Luxing servants whom many of the students dated. Yakov in particular had had a torrid love affair with three women during his time at the school, but not Symeon. Though he had been in a relationship with a girl named Ista back home on the farm in his teens, and at the time that had seemed like the most important thing in the galaxy, he had devoted his five years to study and refrained from dating. It wasn't as though a seneschal graduate could continue a relationship with a local girl after receiving his posting. Many a broken heart started cracking that way.

Thus, it had been more than five years since Symeon had been alone in a room with a woman his own age. Every nerve in his body tingled with pent up ardor to the point his thoughts felt clouded. He poured two glasses of the chilled wine and placed the bottle on the kitchen island next to the grill, careful to arrange everything just so for fear of dropping them in his nervousness.

"Thank you." Czarina sipped the red liquid which matched her lips and smiled. "Oh, that's delicious. You say your parents sent it?"

"Yes." Symeon took a sip as well, careful to keep the quantity small. He hadn't eaten in hours and he had no desire to further weaken his judgment. Something about this social call nagged at him.

Czarina crossed the room to the expanse of windows, wine glass clutched to her bosom in both hands. "Beautiful. You have such a lovely view of the ocean."

"I like it." Symeon moved to stand beside her, despite the little voice in his head yammering that he should be careful.

"Do you like me, Symeon?" Czarina turned her alluring brown eyes up to him, and Symeon thought his heart might catch fire in his chest.

He swallowed. "Yes, of course I do."

Daintily, she took his glass from him and placed them both on a lamp stand next to his bed. She then slid her arms around his waist, her hands skimming across his lower back like two birds following a river valley, and drew him down for a kiss.

A million thoughts burst inside Symeon's skull. Lust of course. He hadn't been with a woman in more than five years. Simply holding Czarina felt like the only important thing in the universe. But what about his breath? He hadn't washed his teeth in hours, and there had been that tepid coffee. Disgusting. What must she think of him? Did he have time to back off, perhaps shower? Perhaps share a shower?

Fool!

Czarina's lips tasted like wine and mint, an odd yet tantalizing combination. As their kiss grew deeper, more impassioned, she parted those soft lips and tentatively explored his mouth with her tongue. If Symeon had thought he experienced passion before, her coy byplay obliterated that previous feeling. He drew her closer, acutely aware of her breasts against him, her back arching in the most pleasing of ways, her silken hair brushing against his cheek.

The timing. This can't be right.

With deft assurance, Czarina captured Symeon's hand. She withdrew it slowly, sensuously from her back and guided it under her top. Her smooth skin sent an electric thrill singing across Symeon's fingers as her hand pushed against his own, insistent, demanding, until he found himself caressing her bare breast.

Symeon froze. Though every atom in his body screamed for him to go on, he stopped moving. The voice in his head, nearly drowned away under the flood of his physical need, broke through one last time.

Trap!

"What is it?" Czarina breathed, her lips still pressed against his own. She drew back, smiling, and nipped at his throat playfully.

"Come to bed." She turned, fingers entwined with his, and drew him toward it.

"No."

"No bed?" The grin that spread Czarina's lips spoke of pleasures Symeon had never known. "Where? On the floor? In the chair?" She reached cross-armed to remove her top, her eyes watching his, shy yet somehow masterful all at once.

Against the very drive of his nature, Symeon placed a hand on Czarina's wrists and stopped her from removing her shirt. More than nearly anything he had ever wanted in his life, he wanted to see—not just see—her body, but knew deep down that would be a mistake.

"Why are you here?" He stared into her eyes, his voice little more than a whisper.

She looked taken aback, her forehead momentarily wrinkled with consternation. "What do you mean? I came here to be with you. Don't you want me?" She made to reach for another embrace, but Symeon backed away.

"Czarina," he said, and it was all he could do not to respond to her advances. "Yes, I want you, but this feels sudden. More than sudden, it feels planned."

Czarina withdrew her hands from him and folded her arms, her lips turned down at the corners. "I don't know what you mean."

Symeon fought the urge to apologize, to pull her back into his arms and resume their foreplay. "I think you know exactly what I mean. I am the princess' seneschal. You are her handmaid. If we have an affair, it could go poorly for me."

Czarina's mouth dropped open, and her brows furrowed. "You think I would tell? I'm not that sort of woman. This would remain between us, Symeon. I like you. You're pretty, and you've got this way about you—this commanding presence."

She drew closer, reaching out to explore his chest, but Symeon eluded her. He captured her hands and pushed them gently away.

"Ivan warned me this might happen. I didn't take his meaning before, but now I see. How many of my predecessors did you thwart? All of them?"

Czarina's facade of shy invitation shattered, replaced by a slow, knowing grin. "Most of them. The last was one who preferred boys, but he eventually removed himself, the poor fool. Kavya and I were sad about that. He actually wasn't a bad sort."

"You framed those men for having affairs beneath their station as a pretense for their dismissal?" Symeon's blood ran cold at knowing how close he had come to falling for the same trick. Though no sane master would expect a slave to remain celibate, a seneschal was expected to marry. Any torrid affairs he might have were both expected and ignored so long as they remained out of public view. The moment scandal arose, however, said seneschal would almost always lose his position, and often his ability to serve as a steward at all. As the saying went, quiet lovers are the seneschal's only lovers, or "Where does the seneschal sleep? In his bedchamber alone. Where does the chambermaid sleep? In the seneschal's bedchamber alone."

"I didn't frame anyone. They did have affairs with me. And I would do it a thousand times over to protect Kavya." Czarina's eyes, so warm and inviting only seconds before, took on a measure of threat wholly incongruous with her looks.

"Why? What did I do to threaten Princess Kavya? I have no intention but to serve her as I have been ordered to do."

To Symeon's surprise, Czarina smiled and shook her head, her expression somehow softening. "Kavya doesn't need a seneschal, Symeon. She needs a..."

He lifted an eyebrow. "She needs a what?"

"Never mind. She said you were too smart to fall for me." Czarina adjusted her top and the silver chain about her waist until they were just so. "I took that as a challenge. I had to try, you understand."

"Nothing happened here," Symeon said. "We agree on that, yes?"

She smiled, the epicanthic folds around her eyes crinkling in mirth. "Don't worry. I won't lie. To be honest, I'm rather intrigued by you, Symeon, and I think Kavya is as well. You're the first seneschal Ivan's brought who didn't seem to be out for himself."

"Tell me why you came here now though. At daybreak. Are you monitoring my computer access?"

Czarina grasped his lapels, jerked him down, and planted a quick kiss on his lips, this one far more playful than before. "Do us both a favor, Sym. Find something better to do with your time."

With that, she strode across the room, a sight that still managed to put Symeon's libido into overdrive, and shut the door behind her.

"What the hell was all that about?" Symeon wondered aloud.

* * * * *

Chapter Six

The ensuing four days brought Symeon no closer to rectifying Kavya's accounts. As he settled into his role of steward for all her affairs, his daily requirements mounted. A seneschal's duties involved far more than balancing a master's budget. Every detail of the princess' life she wished to ignore or pass off fell instantly into Symeon's purview whether that meant scolding a wayward slave or making a land purchase over the net for rental properties in Puchezh, a thousand kilometers away. Every moment of his waking life involved thinking of Kavya, considering her best interests, and making choices that would benefit not just her, but the entire Rurikid family. Only a few days into this lifelong mission, and Symeon could feel the pressure mounting. To help relieve some of his stress, he took to running along the beach south of Yaya Castle early in the morning, long before most of the household would wake.

Most, but not all. Symeon padded down a long flight of stairs near the kitchens, his running shoes making a soft clomp as he descended. The scent of hot yeast and honey filled the corridor, which made his stomach growl. He ignored it. Better to run on an empty stomach than tempt getting sick out on the beach. Today would be a short run anyway, just six kilometers. That would give him enough time to scarf down breakfast upon his return and still make an 0800 meeting with three of Kavya's property managers in Plast. They seemed to think it was time to raise rents on Kavya's tenants, but she was adamantly opposed to the plan. Symeon would have to make that position clear.

A kitchen maid spotted him as he hurried to slip out the castle's servant's entrance.

"Good morning, Seneschal," said the Luxing woman who couldn't have been eighteen. She bowed deeply and held that pose until he returned the gesture.

"Hello, Alena. I'm off to run. Please excuse me, I must hurry."

"Have fun," she said, watching him scramble away.

He could feel her eyes on him until he bolted outside into a balmy island morning made bearable by the westerly breeze coming in off the ocean. Perhaps her stares, and those of the other women about the castle, were all in Symeon's head—a worry brought on by his near tryst with Czarina. No one, not even Czarina herself, had made mention of her play for him within his hearing. Yet he worried the staff might be gossiping behind his back. Was that merely his conceit speaking? Did he think so much of himself, he expected every woman in the castle to take notice of him?

Yes. Definitely conceited.

Symeon laughed at himself as he shambled into a jog across the castle's back lawn. Though the sun had only now peeked above the distant horizon, a team of Luxing gardeners clad in coveralls were already busy pruning, clipping, and raking the grounds. Robots could do such labor, but most Shorvexans—those rich enough to own slaves anyway—preferred a living touch when it came to landscaping. The idea of life guiding life had captured popular belief several hundred years ago and never abated. Not that Princess Kavya went in for fads so far as Symeon could tell in his short time knowing her, but she seemed content with this one.

A single walking path led down from the castle's human-designed hill to the beach, skirting the jungle's outer edge. Symeon appreciated avoiding the trees. Although no large predators lived on Yaya Island, its shadowed depths were rife with blood-sucking creatures from ticks to mosquitoes to mites and silver flies. His second day, he had made the mistake of attempting a hike without consulting the house slaves. He had returned after less than two minutes in the jungle covered with bites. Luckily, the castle's infirmary was fully stocked, and a Luxing nurse had healed him quickly.

Ocean spray flicked across Symeon's face, cool and refreshing. A flash storm had washed across Yaya the night before, leaving broken seaweed stalks strewn across the white sand. He avoided them as he picked up speed and assumed the familiar two step breathing pattern his boxing coach had taught him in school. So much of the world became clear whenever Symeon ran. The sound of his own breath, the tak-tak-tak of his feet meeting the ground, and the sigh of the wind caressing his face made all his problems appear distant, unimportant.

He thought again of the Luxing gardeners, the Luxing maid, the Luxing...everyone, and it occurred to Symeon that Princess Kavya was the only Shorvex on Yaya Island. How lonely she must feel without even one of her own people about? And how foolish could he be to have only realized this fact a week into his service to her? Should he arrange to bring one of her friends to visit? Would her father or, more rightly, Ivan rab Rurikid, acting in her father's stead, allow such a thing?

Now that he was thinking about it, Symeon realized he had never heard the princess mention friends. Granted, he didn't spend much time in her presence. Though she rarely denied him a meeting, the princess kept her interactions with Symeon short and formal. He no longer tried to tutor her after his first day's embarrassment despite Ivan's orders to the contrary. That left taking instructions on managing her affairs and asking for her preferences whenever he couldn't decide on a course of action. Most of that business they handled through short holo-calls.

Did that mean Princess Kavya was avoiding him? If so, was her disinterest in meeting him caused by boredom or something more sinister? Czarina had showed up in his room moments after he traced Saddle Horn Enterprises. And she hadn't been coy about warning him to stop meddling, had she?

Had she?

Symeon considered her words. "Do us both a favor, Sym. Find something better to do with your time."

Did she mean his investigation into Kavya's financial affairs or simply his duties as seneschal? Maybe she was somehow jealous of his position. No, that didn't seem likely. As Kavya's handmaid, Czarina had the princess' ear at all times. And from what Symeon could tell, the two of them were fast friends.

Perhaps her words meant nothing at all. She was a mercurial woman, Czarina: tantalizing, playful, altogether mysterious. He wouldn't put it past her to elude his question by leaving him a dozen more. That would probably tickle her to no end.

Did she know Symeon had intercepted a message meant for Kavya? If so, she hadn't mentioned it. Neither had the princess. Even if they had, would Symeon stop digging into the estate's financial health? No. Of course not. He had his orders from Grand Duke Alexei himself through Ivan rab Rurikid. Who was he to deny his ultimate masters? Not even the princess herself could to that. Tutoring was one thing, but Symeon's position depended on his financial work.

Yet, even without Kavya specifically ordering Symeon to desist, the infuriating message from Saddle Horn Enterprises continued to elude his understanding. Saddle Horn was passing a message that had nothing to do with patterned lace or fabric, of that Symeon was certain. The message's true meaning, however, eluded him. He had considered confronting Kavya with it, but he doubted she would shed any light on the matter. Whether true or not, she would likely claim she didn't remember purchasing anything from that company and maybe blame one of her former seneschals for it.

Symeon wondered if the message, or one like it, was the reason Kavya's father had banished her to Yaya Island. Ivan rab Rurikid had acted as though her flamboyant lifestyle had earned her father's ire, but that made little sense. So far as Symeon could tell from old media reports on the planetary web, Princess Kavya had long ago abandoned the world-hopping party scene. Over the last four years leading up to her exile, she had settled into a life of charity work, most of it revolving around the humane treatment of the Luxing slaves—an honorable vocation for a wealthy Shorvexan woman.

Did her father disdain her charity for Luxing enough to exile her? Somehow, that seemed unlikely. Though many of the old crust Shorvexans, especially those in the peerage, said little good about the growing call for Luxing protections, most knew better than to openly fight it. Doing so could bring bad publicity. While Shorvexan royals might not face elections like their peers in the lower courts, most knew better than to run afoul of the common people who could wield the mighty credit against them and their corporations.

The micro-comm Symeon wore in his ear chirped.

"Yes?"

"Sir," said the computer he had assigned to monitor Kavya's spending. "The account belonging to Tessa-yaya24 has acquired a new download from Saddle Horn Enterprises. As per your instructions, I have traced the daemon-gate access to its origin, and the dispersed storage farm used by Tessa-yaya24."

Symeon slowed to a walk, his breath coming in hard gasps. After his first foray into tracing the Saddle Horn purchases, he had endeavored to find where Kavya had stored whatever data they sent her. That search, like most of his previous ones, had come to nothing. Undaunted, he had set a deep learning algorithm to wait for the next time she downloaded data from that daemon.

"And here you are," Symeon said as he fished the micro-comm from his ear. Its holo projector left a lot to be desired, but since he didn't have access to his personal comm, it would have to do.

He keyed the display and a grainy, bluish-green network map appeared above his palm. His smart algorithm had already broken Kavya's cipher code on the dispersed storage unit using clues from her other accounts. Symeon pawed at the display, which was anything but responsive, and finally managed to open one of the files. A twinge of guilt made him hesitate. Whatever the princess stored here, she clearly wanted kept secret. Opening it felt like a betrayal. Nonetheless, his orders from her father were clear. It was Symeon's duty to find out what the grand duke's daughter was hiding.

He tapped a folder Kavya had stored here months before her exile. A series of documents materialized above his palm. Symeon scanned the top five, his gaze tracing over the electronic pages with a speed he had mastered in school. They covered ancient Shorvexan history pre-Great Arrival and even beyond, back to a time more than a thousand years before present. Interesting, but nothing worth banishment. Symeon worried he had opened the princess' private storage for no reason.

He flipped to the next folder and stopped, free hand in the air, jaw hanging open in shock.

The first document to appear bore a large, flashing security banner at the top and bottom that read: TOP SECRET//VALENSK DUCHY//GRAND EYES ONLY. Symeon knew little about military or intelligence documents, but this one looked authentic. Its compartmentalization tag, GRAND EYES ONLY, meant its originator intended it for Grand Duke Alexei Rurikid and no one else.

Symeon knew he should not read further. Whatever the memorandum contained, it wasn't meant for the likes of him. He might be a seneschal, but he was still a Luxing, and no Luxing could be trusted with state secrets. He wasn't worthy.

What is worthy? Is one man worthy and another not? If a person can know a thing should he refrain from that knowledge?

Was this what had gotten Kavya into trouble with her father? If so, would it bring worse trouble down on Symeon? He got the feeling the answer to both questions was yes, and yet he still felt compelled to read it.

What if this is your only way to protect Kavya's interests? You would fail in your duties to do less.

Symeon nodded at the thought. Hands trembling, he scanned the contents. The message was brief and devastating.

TO: HIS HIGHNESS GRAND DUKE ALEXEI RURIKID
FROM: ADMIRAL TOLYA NAOUMOV, DIRECTOR VALENSK SPACE DEFENSE FORCE

SIR, AS REQUESTED YOU WILL FIND ENCLOSED STRATEGIC ANALYSIS OF IMPERIAL DEFENSE SYSTEMS SURROUNDING THE MOON BASTRAYAVICH AS WELL AS SUBSEQUENT INTELLIGENCE PREDICTIONS FOR OPERATION JANUS EAGLE.

IN BRIEF, OUR FORCES ARE MORE THAN PREPARED TO OVERTHROW THE CURRENT PHOENIX GOVERNMENT WITHIN AN ESTIMATED SEVENTY-TWO (72) DAYS.

MY STAFF AWAITS YOUR ORDERS.

Symeon shivered despite the warm sun shining on his face. He read the missive three more times to make certain he understood its meaning and hadn't somehow misconstrued Admiral Naoumov's intent.

Nothing changed.

Grand Duke Alexei Rurikid was planning a coup against the empire.

* * * * *

Chapter Seven

Symeon dropped the micro-comm to his side as he walked along the beach. The sound of the ocean's breakers, a thrumming boom that cycled across the sand like a heartbeat, crashed in on him, and he welcomed it. Anything to drown the fear and worry that had seized his mind.

Coups were not unheard of in the Shorvexan Empire. The last had occurred two centuries before when House Mastronov had seized power from House Turkov. That conflict had resulted in seven years of bloody war, during which the empire had split in two. Deaths on both sides totaled in the hundreds of thousands, including Shorvex and Luxing. Only the use of nuclear weapons had resolved the problem.

The Mastronovs had them, their enemies did not.

Now Symeon's master intended to overthrow Emperor Pyotr Mastronov, a young man who had only lately inherited the throne from his aged cousin, Stepan. Rumor had it, Pyotr had shared a bed with Stepan the last several years, securing his place in the older man's good graces. True or not, both houses of the Shorvexan government, the high and low divor, had raised Pyotr to rule the empire. Some viewed him as a weak and feckless man, more interested in his own pleasures than the state of his people, but from Symeon's point of view, not much had changed, good or bad, since Pyotr's ascension. Wasn't that the best measure of a ruler's effectiveness?

Not for Grand Duke Alexei it would seem.

Symeon started back the way he had come, tracing his steps where the waves hadn't obscured them. Had Kavya somehow discovered her father's coup and confronted him about it? Was that why he had banished her? It seemed likely, but then how did she still possess these top secret files? Why hadn't the grand duke ordered them erased the instant she divulged them?

Because she didn't divulge them.

That felt right. Kavya never told her father how she had discovered his plans. She used a hacker to steal them, but never admitted that to anyone. Maybe. Something about that idea still didn't sit right with Symeon. If she had admitted she knew about her father's coup, would he stick her on an island without some sort of official guards besides Luxing servants? What if she spoke out against him? Obviously, she hadn't, else the story would have been all over the media months ago. Yet, the grand duke had exiled her. Odd that.

Feeling somewhat recovered from his initial shock, Symeon reopened the files. The coup memorandum had triggered his snooping program, which meant Tessa-yaya24 had bought something new today, but what?

With no small amount of trepidation, he swiped through several layers of files dated earlier than a few minutes ago until he found the newest entry. It bore a holo icon. He keyed it to play and immediately stuttered to a stop. The surf washed over his running shoes up to his ankles, but Symeon didn't feel it.

The first image to appear on the under-powered holo display looked like a deep space video shot from an orbiting telescope. The heading read: ALIEN SPACECRAFT DETECTED ENTERING EXTREME RANGE OF PHOENIX SOLAR SYSTEM. It was dated a month ago. It showed four red-brown cylinders on a blanket of stars. The view zoomed closer, and though it remained obscure, Symeon thought he could make out windows or perhaps some type of ports dotting the ships' main fuselages.

Whoever had made the video let it record for a little over ten seconds before the picture switched to a conference image of Emperor Mastronov seated in a high-backed chair, staring forward like a man who has just been told his wife is dead. The spliced video caught him already speaking.

"—sovereign territory. We ask that you desist from building any superstructures within our solar system or the surrounding environs. How can I make this more clear?"

The playback sped up for several minutes of dead air until a new face, this one green mottled with splotches of light brown, appeared next to Pyotr. Hairless, its smooth skin reminded Symeon of a plastic toy or perhaps a granite cliff. Two yellow eyes stared out of its deep set sockets above a nose that was nothing more than a couple of holes and a mouth slit devoid of lips.

"Human," said the alien face as if in greeting, though Symeon didn't recognize the word. "I am Balis 'nTek, an independent contractor representing the Gate Alliance Corporation. We have a contract to build an intergalactic gate in your system. That is our mission. Cease your broadcasts. We will not be deterred."

The playback sped up in order to skip what must have been several minutes of delay caused by extreme distance, though it didn't move too fast for Symeon to catch the emperor's expression of imperious offense when the green creature's words finally reached him. He looked like a man trying to swallow a lemon.

"You do not seem to understand." Pyotr leaned toward the lens as if imploring his counterpart to listen carefully. "I am the supreme leader of this system. We are an isolated people. My subjects, to include most of my highest ranked liegemen, do not believe in alien life. Your interference in our planetary system is tantamount to an ecological and likely economic attack. Imagine introducing a foreign toxin into a fragile environment. That is what you're doing here. You will cause chaos! And that chaos will cost lives."

Again the video sped up until the alien face became animated. The green being mimicked his Shorvexan counterpart by leaning forward, though Symeon quickly realized he hadn't leaned so much as extended his impossibly long neck until his face filled the view. "We are the Bith. We don't do politics."

The image went dark.

Symeon stared around at the beauty of Yaya Island as if for the first time. He felt like a man who has been away to a foreign land for so long he no longer remembers his people, his customs, his own family. By dint of will alone, he got his feet moving toward the castle, though he walked slowly as if in a dream.

Aliens.

For a millennium, the people of Phoenix had wondered if they were alone in the universe. History told them only two sentient races existed: the Shorvex, who had been forced to flee their ancestral world due to some long forgotten cataclysm, and the Luxing, a primitive race native to Phoenix yet lacking any sort of intelligence before their masters arrived. Seeking companions to help them survive their new home, the Shorvex had generously enlightened the Luxing through genetic manipulation and the application of society, which the bestial Luxing had lacked before the Great Arrival.

But now the Bith had arrived.

The builders.

Yes, hadn't the emperor mentioned superstructures? And the alien, Balis 'nTek, had spoken of a gate. What sort of gate did one build in space? Symeon, having spent his life studying to become a seneschal, had never much considered the stars. The Shorvex put great stock in plumbing the system's inner planets, but since his duties hadn't yet included space travel, he had never given it much thought. Space was a thing like a sea, a desert, a high mountain—just one more environment his masters would eventually conquer. But what Symeon did know was finance.

Gates take you places. Aliens use gates.

If these Bith were interested in building a gate inside the Phoenix system, that meant someone wanted to use it, and unless the aliens functioned far differently than the Shorvex, that meant money. Why build a thing unless you can profit from it? If there were profits to be made by traveling to new star systems, that meant other aliens, maybe even other alien species besides these Bith creatures, would soon be traversing this future gate in search of riches.

The emperor was right. If Symeon, a lowly Luxing, could make such a connection, how much more so the common Shorvex of the system, or the royal Shorvex even? Certainly, the appearance of the Bith would raise questions amongst the people, but the idea of other aliens, perhaps thousands of them—perhaps armadas of them—rushing into the Phoenix system would send their civilization into turmoil.

The people must know. They deserve the truth.

The thought blossomed in Symeon's mind unbidden. He shook his head bitterly. "No! The opposite. This news must be kept hidden as long as possible."

Why did his brain so often do that? Give him the exact opposite thought of what he knew to be good and right and proper?

Given time, perhaps the government could form a solution to the Bith problem, but if the news got out now, it could be devastating. Who else knew about this outside the emperor and his immediate staff? Kavya, of course, and whoever had delivered the information to her. Already that was too many people for Symeon's taste. He could do nothing about Saddle Horn Enterprises. If they chose to divulge the recording, so be it. But what were Princess Kavya's plans for the news? Would she release it? From what he could tell, she hadn't done that with her father's planned coup. Perhaps, if he was lucky, Symeon could convince her to likewise withhold this news. Unfortunately, that would mean divulging his access to her private data storage, but he would accept that loss if it meant protecting the system from imploding in fear and anarchy.

Symeon turned his gaze to the castle. It stood almost a kilometer from his current spot. With renewed strength borne of fear, he started to run.

* * *

Castle Vysylka's outer bailey stood empty by the time Symeon reached it. The gardeners must have finished their work and gone to clean their equipment. He pushed in through the servant's entrance and was braced by the scent of fried meat, bread, and honey, all of which he ignored in his haste to reach the princess' living space on the third floor.

It crossed his mind that he was in a state—sweaty, windblown, smelling of the sea and his own ripe aroma. He yearned to grab a quick shower before presenting himself to his mistress but quickly put that idea out of his mind. Every second he wasted gave her a chance to reveal the Bith.

He reached her floor out of breath and took a moment to compose himself, bent over, hands on his knees at the top of the stairs. Kavya had no guards to speak of, but she usually kept two servants outside the double doors to her apartments to screen guests. Curiously, no one stood there today.

Heart still pounding, but with his breath under control, Symeon knocked on the outer door and stepped back for fear of offending whoever answered with his smell. Several seconds passed before the doors finally slid apart to reveal Czarina's beautiful face.

She raised an eyebrow at him. "You heard out on the beach? I guess you got a personal notice. Come in and watch the reactions in the news. The whole system's going insane."

"Insane over what?" Symeon asked though he felt he knew the answer.

"The aliens, dummy. Come in, you're making me miss it." Czarina took him by both hands and, despite their unequal sizes, dragged him bodily into Kavya's drawing room.

Everyone was there, from the lowliest cook girl to Vlademar the butler who oversaw all aspects of the castle's day-to-day running. Every living person on Yaya Island stood transfixed, watching Kavya's larger than life holo tank. An image of Balis 'nTek floated before them like some green satellite bereft of its primary.

"This is on the nets? It's public?" Symeon asked, desperate for Czarina to say otherwise.

"It just broke. Someone pushed it to like a million daemon-gates at once. People are saying the government's been trying to shut it down, but too many users are already reposting it. I think it's real."

Symeon watched the screen in horror. He wanted to plop on the floor and cradle his head in his hands, but withstood the temptation for fear of setting a bad example.

Princess Kavya, dressed in everyday slacks and a frilly blouse cocked a silver eyebrow at Symeon and wrinkled her nose. "Couldn't hit the showers for your excitement, Seneschal?"

Symeon's embarrassment momentarily swallowed both his fear and shock. He bowed before his princess. "Forgive me."

"You're forgiven. Now quiet; we're watching the empire change before our eyes."

The hologram played out as it had on Symeon's micro-comm except for the added expressions of awe from the gathered Luxing.

"They look so different from us, don't they?" asked one of the gardeners during the silent sections of the playback. "Whoever heard of green skin?"

"They're not from here." Czarina chided. "Why should they look like us at all?"

"Well, the Shorvex aren't from here, and we all look pretty much same." The gardener turned quickly to Kavya. "Meaning no offense, Princess."

"You haven't offended me, Gavoy." Kavya held up a hand, twisting it back and forth. "You're right. We all have five fingers, five toes, ears and eyes in the same spots, hair and internal organs. It's quite a coincidence when you think about it."

"Yes, ma'am. It is that!"

Symeon eyed the princess. Something about her expression made him think her words held a double meaning, though he couldn't fathom what.

No unrelated species were ever so alike.

Something inside Symeon's mind clicked. This sort of thing happened to him every so often—he experienced it many times in school when studying a particularly complex topic. It was as if a portion of his thoughts, usually silent, that understood a subject well, had coaxed his waking consciousness to comprehend a meaning all at once. One moment, he sat in utter darkness, the next he knew a topic as if born to it.

In form, the Shorvex looked the same as the Luxing. As Kavya had pointed out, they shared a near identical morphology. While Luxing skin came in a variety of shades from near umber to light yellow, and even an almost pink in some rare cases, the Shorvex appeared silver to silver-blue. Kavya's skin exhibited the rare bluish tint so coveted amongst their kind, though like most of her people of that hue, silver predominated. While the Shorvex on average stood taller than most Luxing, the two species—

Same species.

—shared bipedal locomotion, opposable thumbs, forward bending knees, and backward bending elbows. They ate the same food, breathed the same air, and valued the same sorts of societal desires—familial bonds, social status, providing for future generations. It was almost as if they were the same—the same...

The same everything.

"Is something the matter, Seneschal?" Princess Kavya tilted her head at Symeon, her silver-white brows lifted.

"I'm sorry, Princess?"

Kavya glanced at the other servants who remained transfixed by the holo tank. She lowered her voice. "You're staring at me."

"My apologies. I'm afraid I was lost in thought."

Which thoughts?

"You look as if there's something on your mind."

Symeon almost laughed, but managed to stifle it, knowing the sound would come out manic. He rubbed a hand across his face. "Yes, Princess. I've something on my mind. Might we speak in private?"

Czarina, who had until now appeared mesmerized by the video, turned her gaze on Symeon and the princess. She looked as though she might say something sharp, but thought better of it in mixed company. She started to rise.

Kavya waved her handmaid off with a gesture and stood smoothly from her spot on one of the couches. "Very well." She led him to a side door that opened onto her private office and leaned against the desk inside, watching him curiously as he shut the door behind them.

"I know about your hidden accounts, Princess," Symeon said without preamble. He saw no reason to stall.

She reared back, shaking her head. "I have no idea what you're talking about. I have no hidden accounts, not that I know all that much about my house finances. My seneschals have always handled that sort of thing for me. You know that."

"With utmost respect, you and I both know that is a lie." He leaned forward ever so slightly. "Tessa-yaya24."

Symeon expected Kavya to bluster and act innocent, perhaps even accuse him of overstepping himself. She did neither. A slow smile crept across her full lips. "You found my data stash?"

"I did."

"You know my father's plans."

Symeon nodded, his heart racing in his chest.

She folded her arms. "So where does that leave us, my dear Seneschal?"

"At a crossroads, Princess. Wouldn't you agree?"

"Yes, I do." Kavya placed her hands on the desk. "Let's hope it's one we can navigate together."

* * * * *

Chapter Eight

"Castle," Kavya said, "inform Czarina I'm not to be disturbed. Have her send the servants back to their duties once everyone has seen the video."

"Understood, Princess," said Castle Vysylka's computerized assistant in a smooth male voice.

"And, while you're at it, shut off all recording devices in this office at once. If I need you, I'll call on my slate."

"Very good, ma'am."

"There now," Kavya said a bit too brightly. "You may attempt whatever blackmail you're planning in absolute privacy."

"Princess, I have no intention—" Symeon began.

Kavya flicked a dismissive hand at him before rounding her desk to flop into an oversized leather chair. "Save it. I've been through this gauntlet five times already. You think you're the first of my seneschals to wave my father's treason under my nose?"

Symeon gave himself a mental kick. Was he so arrogant he thought none of his predecessors had managed to unravel Kavya's labyrinthine financial puzzle? No wonder she had dismissed so many of them.

"I'll admit, five days is a record. You've a sharp mind, Symeon. I had hoped for a little more time, not that it much matters now. The entire empire is quaking under the news of the Bith and this gate they're building."

"You released the video."

Kavya nodded.

Symeon, his legs gone numb, sank into one of the guest chairs in front of the princess' desk. He stared at his hands, tracing the creases there for want of following the thoughts racing through his mind. Not that distracting himself did any good. The thoughts wouldn't be ignored.

"You want the empire destroyed?" His voice came out in a near whisper.

"What?" Kavya looked shocked, her eyes wide. "How do you figure that?"

"You released video evidence of an alien race. The common people will go insane at this news. Our only hope is that the emperor and his advisors will find ways to calm them."

Kavya appeared genuinely perplexed. "Why do you think hearing about aliens will drive people mad? Yes, things will change, but I don't see how this news will cause a panic."

She could be right. Hard to say.

No. She was wrong. Completely wrong. The Shorvex had never faced an existential crisis of this magnitude, let alone the Luxing. Before today, both species had known their place in the universe. Now those places lay in question.

"Princess, we don't know what will come through this gate the Bith are constructing. What if there are hordes of warships waiting to come here and strip the Phoenix system of every resource?"

"How does keeping the gate secret change any of that?" Kavya countered, leaning back in her chair.

"It doesn't; I know that. But wouldn't it have been better to ease our people into learning about the danger rather than foist it on them all in one go? Better to let the emperor and the grand dukes decide how best to release this news."

Anger flashed across Kavya's exquisite face, there and gone in the barest of an instant. At length, her brows drew down and she sucked in a deep breath. "No, Symeon. It wouldn't have been better. My father has been planning his coup against House Mastronov for years. He is on the cusp of launching the first stage. If I'm going to stop him, I must do it now."

Symeon stared at his princess in utter shock, his thoughts converging like beams of light in his head. "You did this to stop the coup?"

"Emperor Pyotr will have no choice but to call his banners now. The people will demand it for fear of an alien threat. That means a culmination of the commonwealth fleet."

"Wherein the grand dukes submit their forces to imperial command," Symeon breathed.

"Exactly!" Kavya snapped her fingers. "The forces my father planned to throw against the emperor will soon be under the command of Pyotr's admirals."

Somewhat logical, but complicated.

"I don't understand." Symeon sat forward though he refrained from placing his arms on the princess' desk. He was already speaking far too casually in her presence, no sense losing all propriety. "You had evidence of the coup months ago. Why not take it before the High Divor, or perhaps the emperor himself? Why all this gerrymandering?"

Kavya's look of puzzlement, an expression Symeon was quickly learning to recognize, returned. She stared at him in silence for so long he grew uncomfortable, squirming like a little boy caught lying.

"Because I love him," she said after a minute.

For the second time during this meeting, Symeon gave himself a mental kick for his stupidity. No wonder Grand Duke Alexei hadn't destroyed Kavya's evidence against him. He had no idea she had it, because she had never confronted him with it, nor taken it to a government authority. She had instead sought for a way to thwart him without causing him harm.

As if reading his mind, or more likely his expression, Kavya said, "I couldn't very well go to him and say, 'Pretty please, don't overthrow the emperor, Papa.' He wouldn't have listened, and he likely would have locked me up somewhere far more confining than a tropical island until the whole bloody business was done."

"I think I understand," Symeon said. He couldn't imagine turning his own father over to the authorities, not even for treason.

Her father has trapped her in a steel web, poor woman.

Kavya stared at Symeon, her head tilted to one side. "You're not going to blackmail me. I can see it in your eyes."

For the first time in what felt like years, Symeon felt his lips turn up at the corners. "I had a thought a moment ago: what if my father planned a coup against the empire? Would I have the stomach to oust him?"

"You find the question humorous?"

"I find the image hilarious. My father's a Luxing slave—a farmer with stained teeth from too many years chewing tobacco and the biggest heart of any man I've ever known. I see him standing on the bridge of a destroyer and ordering his fleet to reverse course and head back to the farm for home cooked meals all around."

Kavya smiled, though the expression appeared tentative. She reminded Symeon of a fragile bird stepping out on a branch in preparation to take flight.

Not fragile this one!

"Princess," Symeon said, holding her gaze. "I would never blackmail you. You're in this horrid position because of forces far outside your control. It isn't fair, and I don't envy you the pain nor the tough choices you've had to make. I'll help you if I can."

Kavya's face fell. Tears welled in at the corners of her eyes and ran down her cheeks.

"My Lady, I'm sorry. I—" Symeon made to rise, but Kavya shooed him back to his seat.

She withdrew a box of tissues from a drawer and used one to dab at her eyes and nose. "Czarina says always keep your gun drawer separate from your tissue drawer."

"Your gun drawer?" Symeon couldn't fathom her words. Why would a princess need a gun drawer and, even stranger, why would her Luxing slave be advising her on it?

Kavya chuckled and waved her damp tissue like a flag. "A skill I learned from my father's guards as a girl—mostly sidearm drills. I've kept up the practice here on Yaya. It helps me pass the time. But never mind all that. I want you to know, you're a kind man, Symeon. I value your trust and loyalty."

"May I ask a further question?" Symeon hoped the princess' nerves weren't too frayed to answer. Curiosity gnawed at his insides about every aspect of this intriguing situation and, truth told, this intriguing woman. There was more to the princess than he had ever imagined.

"Ask away. I think we're past the point of secrets now."

"If your plan works—"

"And it doesn't cause utter chaos as you fear," Kavya interjected.

"And that. What happens once things have settled and Grand Duke Alexei reacquires his fleet? That's bound to happen eventually."

Kavya shrugged one shoulder. "Maybe. Maybe not. Perhaps the Bith problem will keep the commonwealth fleet together for the next hundred years. If it doesn't, I'll devise a new plan to circumvent my father. Perhaps I can dredge up some inter-dimensional travelers for my next trick."

It felt good to laugh. Symeon let his anxiety and fear flow out with his chuckle.

Kavya watched him closely, smiling. "I want to tell you. I haven't told anyone else on the island, except Czarina, of course."

"Tell me?"

"Why my father exiled me here. Why I'm alone with no one but Luxing. I want to trust you, Seneschal. Can I?"

"Tell it if you will, Princess. Keep it if you must. I'll not pressure you."

Kavya eyed him a moment longer before nodding. "If you mean to betray me, you will, and there's nothing I can do to stop you." She gathered herself, leaning back in her high seat, dexterous fingers steepled under her chin. "You looked through my files?"

"I apologize for that, Princess. It was necessary—"

"To fulfill your orders. I understand. After poor Uri was unable to break our new codes, I thought my files safe from prying stewards." Kavya favored him with a wan smile.

"Uri was my immediate predecessor? The one who took his own life?"

Kavya wiped at her eyes again. "I don't know what Ivan might have promised him, or what threats he might have made, but after six months struggling to break my codes in silence, Uri accused me of sedition against my father in a bid to force my hand. He wanted me to openly show him what he couldn't dig out for himself. I refused, and called for Ivan."

Symeon could well imagine what happened next. A Luxing, even a seneschal, couldn't accuse a Shorvex of a crime without irrefutable evidence, and even then the courts might well side with the defendant. With nothing to show for his claim of sedition, Ivan must have summarily dismissed Uri from his post.

"And Uri committed suicide?" Symeon asked, his voice soft.

Kavya nodded. "He jumped from the castle wall before Ivan ever arrived to deal with him. I struggle with that every day, knowing my actions brought that man's death."

An urge to take Kavya's hand, to comfort her, nearly sent Symeon out of his chair, but he fought it. He couldn't let his sympathy trump his station. "I am sorry, Princess, but your actions had nothing to do with the seneschal's choices. He sought to damage you, not the other way around."

"My point in bringing up the files was to ask, did you read them all?"

He shook his head, embarrassed to be speaking about looking through the lady's private data.

"Obviously, you saw the Bith recordings, but I've stored older things there as well. If you had searched further back, you would have discovered a set of reports about ancient Shorvexan and Luxing history."

"I saw some of that," Symeon said. "Seemed odd housed next to top secret documents."

"I suppose, but those history files have more bearing on my life here and now than anything I've pilfered from my father's government. They mean more to me than the Bith, the emperor, and my father's stupid power all rolled into one. They were the catalyst that brought me at odds with him, and heated his ire towards me."

She made connections—forbidden connections.

Symeon swallowed, unsure if he wanted Kavya to go on, and yet incapable of asking her to stop. "What did you discover?"

"Are you certain you want to hear this?" Kavya tilted her head to one side. "You look...trepidatious. Perhaps I should tell you why I sought the records in the first place. Then you may decide if you want to hear more."

No. Hear it all.

"Yes, please. Tell me."

"When I was a girl, I was the most vapid, careless, egotistical creature ever born on this planet, and knowing some of my cousins, that's saying something." Kavya shook her head in disgust. "All of life was a game to me, one where I held the winning hand, because my father was the grand duke of our entire krais. Only the emperor wielded more power. I took everything for granted, and that included the many Luxing slaves who labored to make my life a pampered utopia.

"When I turned fifteen, Father told me I could arrange the biggest, most extravagant party the world had ever seen. And I did my best to make that happen. Symeon, I bought an entire village of your people. Everything they owned, meager as it might have been, I owned, including their bodies, their minds, even their children."

"I've heard about his, Princess," Symeon said, mindful of her growing distress. "If recounting this is too painful, you needn't go on for my sake."

"I want to tell it. I deserve to tell it every day. I invited a thousand of my equally self-indulgent friends to that village—it was called Borenyetz—and for three days we treated it, and the people who lived there, like our own personal virtual game." Kavya covered her face with a fresh tissue for several seconds before she continued in a rough voice. "Debauchery isn't a fit word for the way we used that village. I won't horrify you with the details, but understand I am only lucky no Luxing was killed during our rave. By the time it ended—let me be honest here—by the time I sobered up from a drug-addled stupor, I found myself in hell.

"We had burned most of the houses. The women and girls—Shorvexan men used them. I wasn't aware at the time, but I make no excuse for it. I should have known. I should have protected them. Old men and women, retired from long years of faithful service to their masters, found themselves homeless and destitute because of me."

"You were young."

She closed her eyes, tears streaming down her already wet cheeks. "I was a monster. I didn't think of your people as...people."

"We aren't people in the same way as the Shorvex," Symeon said, misquoting an oft repeated saying from time immemorial. "We're young and wayward. Yes, bad things have happened to us from time to time, but on the whole we are grateful for Shorvexan condescension."

Fool! Weakling! The Luxing are people every bit as much as the Shorvex. More so perhaps.

"I'm sorry, Symeon."

"You have nothing to apologize to me for, Princess."

Kavya shook her head impatiently. "You misunderstand me. I'm sorry that you've been so brainwashed you think of your own people that way. You're wrong, because you've been lied to about the past—lied to by my kind for more than a millennium.

Yes! You know this is true. You've always known.

An image flashed inside Symeon's mind. He saw soldiers dressed in unfamiliar armor like space suits, their faces covered in black rebreathers. Rifles held ready before them, they ran in pairs across an airlock into a barren ship. And though Symeon didn't see it in the mental flash, he somehow knew these fighting men had entered a ship whose defenders all slumbered and would never waken.

Symeon jerked upright in his chair, breathing hard.

"What is it?" Kavya eyed him with concern.

"I'm sorry, Princess. I was, imagining, I think."

She nodded slowly. "Then I am sorry to have brought you those images. But I want you to understand how I felt once I realized what damage I had caused the Luxing of Borenyetz. I ruined their lives. Many of them would have died in the coming months either of starvation or exposure, if I hadn't changed my ways. The realization of what I had done pierced me through. It taught me that the Luxing aren't machines or dull beasts, they're people."

"Thank you for that."

"From that time onward, I devoted myself to helping not just the Luxing of Borenyetz, which thrived once I paid to rebuild the village, but every slave I encountered. I studied them, their history, to make myself a better caregiver, and in studying, I discovered the truth."

Symeon felt cemented in place, crystallized, fossilized, and as incapable of escaping the spot as a three thousand year old tree. "What truth, Princess?"

You already know!

Kavya held his gaze, her silver-blue eyes bright with tears. "We aren't separate species, the Shorvex and the Luxing. We're one and the same. Like the Shorvex, your people didn't originate on Phoenix, you came here from the stars. You were first; we usurped you."

"You have evidence of this claim?"

"In the files. Read them; you'll see."

Part of Symeon wanted to argue, to never view those files again, but a larger part hungered to know the truth. He would read them, he knew, but with caution. Kavya's claims could not be real. Her contacts must have fed her lies for some reason.

Symeon straightened his back. "You confronted your father with this evidence? That's why he banished you here?"

"He called it 'juvenile conspiracy tripe,' and said if I could get fooled into believing the Luxing were anything more than tamed animals, I couldn't be trusted with my own freedom."

"If you believe it, why not release what you knew to the planetary sphere?"

"Oh, I tried." Kavya waved one hand in the air as if to clear away his question. "But my access here is limited. The duchy's best network specialists keep a tight lock on what I can and cannot reach on the sphere."

"Hence you bought information from hidden brokers at Saddle Horn Enterprises—purchases they made appear legitimate—and that led you to Grand Duke Alexei's plans for a coup."

"I simply want what's best for both our peoples, Symeon, and to keep my father from losing his head. He didn't create the flawed system that tells him conquest and power are all that matters in this life. He is a byproduct of it. I want to save him, and every life his rebellion might cost, and I want you to help me."

Symeon met her gaze, his face hot, his muscles tight with fear, worry, and excitement. He nodded. "I will."

* * * * *

Chapter Nine

Though Symeon lay in bed for several hours, he found it impossible to sleep that night. He couldn't stop thinking about the revelations Kavya had disclosed. At last he gave up, dressed, and climbed to the top of what the house slaves called the wine tower. Why the name, he did not know. It seemed arbitrary, since the tower held no wine stores and looked nothing like a bottle. It did possess a high balcony overlooking a spit of land as white as bone in the moonlight, and that was good enough for Symeon.

By some trick of architectural magic, wind whistled along the balcony's stout railing but never touched the inner platform that held a bench upholstered with plush cushions. Symeon bypassed the bench in hopes the gusting sea breeze might cleanse his thoughts. He rested his elbows on the stone railing to gaze at the night dark ocean, black as the space between stars. Its roar lay at the edge of his hearing. He leaned still further, cocking his head this way and that to catch the sound, though the wind's howl kept it at bay.

You can't ignore troubles.

Symeon bit the inside of his cheek almost to the point of blood. In a long-ago class on the active brain, one of his professors had described the unconscious mind as a glacier slowly breaking up the land that is life. The waking mind—that tiny portion people thought of as self—was like a butterfly flapping its wings furiously to change the glacier's course. Back then, Symeon had scoffed at the professor's analogy. Anyone could master their mind and body with enough determination, or so he thought.

Now his thoughts seemed at war with one another. His entire life to this point revolved around his place as a Luxing slave, a lesser being than his Shorvexan masters. Yet the things Kavya had shared called that estimation into question. His life from birth to this very moment might well be a lie.

It is. You know it.

No. He didn't want to believe that. The Shorvex had uplifted his people, brought them society and all the blessings that came with it. Millions of Luxing had been born, lived, and died knowing nothing else. Could so many be wrong for so long?

Yes!

Treacherous thoughts, and foolish! Which was more likely, that Kavya had managed to discover a thousand-year-old world-shattering conspiracy, or that hidden figures had sold her a bushel of lies for reasons Symeon couldn't fathom? Or perhaps he could fathom them, after all. What better way to bring shame upon Princess Kavya Rurikid and thus her father, the grand duke, than to convince them the Shorvex had usurped the Luxing? Hadn't it already succeeded in having Alexei exile his daughter to Yaya Island? What if he too had fallen for the scam? What sort of calamity might have ensued?

How can you doubt? You read the files.

Yes, Symeon had read and reread the documents that supposedly revealed his people's origins. But files could be fabricated. Besides, much of what they supposedly disclosed was fragmented. According to whatever anonymous source pieced them together, more than eighty percent of the evidence had been lost due to changes in programming and storage technology. That, and a government-sanctioned campaign to obscure the past starting from the earliest days of colonization on Phoenix. Like most conspiracy theories, the facts seemed to favor the wildest of ideas while ignoring the simplest—the common belief more easily fit the evidence. Organizing a massive cover up required too much gerrymandering to be believable.

You told the princess you would aid her.

Symeon pounded a fist on the stone balustrade. What if everything Princess Kavya had told him was true? What would it change about this world, the Luxing, or the Shorvex? Symeon's place remained the same: seneschal to a banished princess. What good did knowing the supposed truth do him or her or any of the Luxing in the entire system?

That's slave talk.

Failing to inform on Kavya made Symeon a co-conspirator in her theft of duchy secrets and their subsequent release. The longer he waited to inform on her, the more guilty he looked. He should have gone straight to the senior seneschal the instant he discovered her wrongdoing. With the money and power of the entire duchy at his disposal, how long would it be before some clever hacker in the grand duke's employ traced the Bith video release back to Kavya? She had claimed her secretive hackers, they of the Saddle Horn Enterprises Corporation, could obscure their trail from all tracking. But Symeon had found them by buying something from them. If he could do it that easily…

The airtight door behind Symeon hissed open. He spun, caught completely off guard, to gawk at his uninvited guest. He started to order them away. Whatever slave spent their time on the high balcony, they could forego a night for their seneschal. The sight of Czarina backlit by gallery lights stopped Symeon's voice in his throat.

"You weren't in your room, Seneschal." Czarina stepped onto the platform and shut the door behind her. Dressed in warm woolen pajamas and a pair of thick socks, she looked like a slave who had lost her way in a new house. She wore her black hair in a tight bun at the back of her head, revealing the delicate sweep of her neck and slender jawline.

Symeon watched her warily. She had come to his room again? Anger tried to boil up inside him. Hadn't he made his desires known the last time she tried that? He had no interest in becoming Princess Kavya's latest disgraced steward. But then, maybe Czarina had come for a different purpose. She certainly wasn't dressed to entice, though with her body it didn't much matter what she wore.

"I couldn't sleep," he said simply.

Czarina nodded as she joined him at the railing. "I always like the wind up here. The tower's only eighty meters, nothing like the skyscrapers in Kolpinev, but it feels so much higher for some reason."

Symeon nodded, mollified. She hadn't come to seduce him. Was he a rake for feeling a twinge of disappointment over that?

Yes.

"Maybe it's the open view of the sea," Symeon said, resuming his place next to her to watch the black ocean where it met the nearly black sky. "I've rarely been inside a skyscraper without others surrounding it. Here we're isolated."

"That we are."

Something about Czarina's words made the flesh on Symeon's back tighten. He hadn't felt that since facing a particularly tough boxer from a rival school in his fourth year.

"Were you unable to sleep either?" He turned to look at her profile.

"I slept, but I woke early because I wanted to speak with you."

"About?"

"You and the princess spoke at length this morning."

Symeon nodded, curious where the handmaid was going with her questions. If she dared ask about his talk with Kavya, he would have to put her in her place. Senior handmaid to the princess or not, Czarina had no business interrogating her seneschal. Granted, she was likely showing loyalty to her beloved mistress, an act Symeon could respect, but that didn't give her the right to overstep her station.

"She told you the truth about our people." Though Czarina continued gazing at the ocean, Symeon could feel her attention on him like a predator eyeing its next meal.

Symeon twisted toward her in surprise. She knew?

Of course, she knows. She and Kavya act more like sisters than heiress and handmaid. No doubt, she knows more of the princess' secrets than you.

"Lady," Symeon said, putting emphasis on the word. "I will not discuss my private conversations with the princess. Not with you, not with anyone in this castle. Is that understood?"

A slow smile creased Czarina's lips. She stretched, leaning back in a way that showed off her trim figure to good effect, though she seemed blissfully unaware of the pose. Symeon watched her and fumed.

She turned to him when she was done, her teeth white in the moonlight. "I understand you, Symeon. I think I understand you very well."

"That is not what I meant."

"She told you, and now you're frightened."

Symeon couldn't remember anyone accusing him of being afraid since he was a child. He felt his eyes go wide, the blood rush to his face. How dare she speak this way to him?

She's right. You know it.

"That's it," Symeon said between his teeth. "I'm reporting you to Vlademar for extra duty until you can learn your place."

"What is it about the truth that scares you?" Czarina watched his gaze without flinching or showing the least bit of contrition. "Do you love the Shorvex so much you can't accept their wrongdoing even when it stares you in the face?"

"I'll hear no more of this." Symeon strode toward the balcony door fully expecting it to open. It didn't. Assuming a malfunction, he tapped the open icon on the pad next to it. The door remained shut. He spun to face Czarina. "What have you done?"

"I understand how you feel right now, Symeon." Czarina hadn't moved from her spot. She leaned her back against the railing, watching him. "I was frightened, too, when I first understood the truth. And angry. For me, it was the anger that grew. Here I thought the Shorvex my benefactors, only to learn they were scoundrels who had stolen my birthright. Eventually, I settled down when I realized most of them have no idea what their ancestors did to our people. They live as blindly as we Luxing. They own us because that is all they've ever known, all their parents and grandparents, and on back a thousand years ever knew. Ignorance doesn't make it right, but it's understandable."

No sentient should own another.

"Czarina." Symeon bent forward to level their gazes. It was everything he could do to keep from raising his voice. "You will open this door now, or I'll be forced to have you flogged."

"Do you really believe some anonymous hackers the princess employed off the planetary sphere managed to dig up an ancient mystery at her request?"

Symeon shook his head, puzzled at her change of subject. "No, I don't. I think some opportunistic thieves are taking advantage of the princess—selling her exactly what she's paying to see. It's like the old saying, 'Never ask the barber if it's time for a haircut.'"

Czarina smiled though her eyes remained serious. "The truth she acquired isn't recently discovered. There are those of us who have known the real history of this world for centuries. We fed her the information without her realizing it."

"Who is us?" Symeon didn't believe her, and yet for some reason his stomach had gone tight.

"We call ourselves the Wuxia. It's a fragmentary word drawn from a fragmentary concept. Its original meaning is all but lost. It meant something about secrets and heroes. To us, in this age, it means solidarity, endurance, and hope."

"Hope for what?"

Freedom.

"Freedom."

Symeon shook his head. The sound of blood rushing in his ears made his own words sound distant. "You're making this up. You're playing a game with me."

"No one knows exactly who formed the Wuxia network, nor when it came about. It has existed for hundreds of years. Luxing of every duchy around the world, and even the moon colonies, belong to our order. We have plotted a way to win free of the Shorvex for generations. We think the coming of the Bith might be the catalyst we've been waiting for."

"If you believe all that, you're a fool. You've been swindled by grifters. How much do they charge you to be a member of this Wuxia? Do you pay by the month, the quarter?" Even to Symeon, his words sounded manic, grasping. He didn't care. None of this was real. He would not fall for whatever con had taken in Czarina and the princess. More than ever, he felt convicted to turn them in to Ivan rab Rurikid for their own good.

"You are star born, are you not?" Czarina stood up from the balustrade and padded close to Symeon, seeming to size him up, watching his eyes.

"What does that have to do with anything?"

"You were decanted from a stasis incubator aboard a ship that has been in orbit of this planet for as long as anyone can remember."

Symeon remained still, determined to volunteer nothing.

"Do you find it odd that the ancient Shorvex from a thousand years ago were able not only to uplift we lowly Luxing from our bestial state, but to likewise artificially conceive and store thousands of children aboard the progenitor craft?"

"No, I do not find it odd, because that is exactly what happened."

Czarina leaned forward a few centimeters. "Then why can't they do that sort of thing today?"

Symeon's lips turned down in puzzlement. "What do you mean?"

You know very well what she means.

"Where are our stasis fields today? In a thousand years of studying, the Shorvex have never been able to fully replicate the ones found on those ships—the same ones that perfectly preserved you until the grand duke's doctors and financiers determined it was time for you to be born."

Though the idea had never crossed Symeon's mind, he could see Czarina was right. Today's Shorvexan scientists worked with far less efficient versions of the stasis incubators. Awe inspiring as they might be, no one would entrust one of their contraptions to keep an infant suspended for much more than a couple of months. Symeon and his cousins aboard the progenitor ships had survived a millennium.

"No one even asks the question," Czarina said, watching his face with avid interest. "We're conditioned to keep our heads down, remain incurious, do as we're told, because if we do, Symeon, we might see the truth. The Shorvex can't replicate that technology, because they never invented it in the first place."

It is your heritage, not theirs. See it, feel it, know its truth.

A flood of images like those he had seen earlier that day when speaking with Kavya ransacked Symeon's mind like an unexpected tornado. He reeled under the onslaught, powerless to clear his thoughts for the sights, sounds, and overwhelming sensations.

He saw a mass of people, his people, dark haired and dark eyed, queuing up to board transport ships under a bright azure sky. Though they moved in good order, dealing fairly with one another, Symeon knew without knowing, as if in a dream, that some dire calamity would soon dash the sky above and bring destruction to all these people had ever known or loved.

No sooner had that image come than another took its place. Symeon found himself floating in a black void empty of all sense of being and yet existent all the same. Light spilled into the blackness, and with it the images of people—billions of people—all of them like him. They spoke all at once, carrying on separate conversations that ran together like melting snow, and yet Symeon understood them without strain. They shared with him their dreams, their fears, their triumphs, and their greatest failures. Through it all, Symeon reveled in their stories and the bonds those tales forged between him and his multitudinous friends. Over time, some of the faces grew old and disappeared, only to be replaced by children and teenagers and a billion more new conversations.

Next, he saw a blue planet awash in frothy white clouds dwindling in the distance, becoming ever smaller as it receded away from him. It had become little more than a bright object in the star-strewn expanse of the galaxy when it winked out of existence, gone for all time. Forlorn heartache crushed Symeon's spirit when the light of that world went dark, and yet hope remained, couched within the tens of thousands of sleeping humans sleeping under his watch.

"Symeon?"

He blinked at Czarina for several seconds without recognizing her, the high balcony, even himself. He drew a shuddering breath. "What was that?"

"Where did you go?" she asked. "Your face went slack. I thought for a moment you were having some sort of fit."

You were seeing the past—the true past. Your people's past.

"Who are you?" Symeon wasn't certain who he was asking. Himself? Possibly. With all Kavya and Czarina had told him, he had to wonder what that made him.

Czarina, unaware of his inner thoughts, grinned. "I'm the woman the Wuxia sent to protect Princess Kavya. She is our most powerful ally in hundreds of years. We are determined to make her safe."

The steel in Czarina's voice put Symeon back on his guard. He stole a longer, more meaningful look at her. "You came here to kill me?"

"Only if you make it necessary." Czarina set her chin the way any smart fighter might before facing a barrage from an opponent. Though she made no move to lift her hands, Symeon could see her ready herself for a fight.

"You've got to be joking."

"I need to know if you're a threat to the princess. I thought I might watch you for a few days, but I'm afraid you might message Ivan in the meantime."

"I have no intention of turning Kavya over to Ivan or her father," Symeon said, his voice serious. He still felt shaken by the images he had seen and flummoxed by their origins. Did he somehow possess a racial memory due to his star born ancestry?

"Good, then I won't be forced to throw you off this balcony."

Symeon raised an eyebrow at the woman before him. She stood a head shorter and probably carried a little over half his weight. "The day you can throw me over that railing is the day I give up and start calling you Seneschal."

The words had no more than passed Symeon's lips when Czarina moved. Part of him had been half expecting her to try something—certainly not an attempt on his life, but maybe a sucker punch to catch him off guard.

Czarina's shin connected with Symeon's outer thigh like a lightning bolt. Too many years boxing had indoctrinated him to expect a punch. The kick not only caught him unaware, it folded him up like a sheet as every nerve in his leg simultaneously exploded in pain. Desperate to catch himself, Symeon clutched at the balcony railing, only to realize his mistake after his weight and momentum had turned against him.

It was the work of a second for the much smaller Czarina to hook Symeon's injured leg, hoist her shoulder under his hip, and toss him bodily over the rail. For one panicked moment, Symeon thought he would go sailing into space and plummet to his death.

And he would have done, except Czarina reversed her momentum at the final instant, allowing him to gain purchase, his body half on and half over the topmost rail. Clutching hard at his shoulder and ankle, she bore down with all her might and weight to drag him back across the threshold.

Symeon collapsed on the stones, chest heaving, eyes wide with fright. Czarina, standing a safe distance from his reach, offered him an odd, two-fingered salute, touching one eyebrow.

"Emperor Pyotr will call his banners in the coming days," she said, as if nothing had happened. "That call will necessitate a war council of the full divor, the high and the low. The Wuxia will see to it Kavya attends."

Symeon grunted as he sat up. His hands were shaking, his heart still pounding. "Impossible. She's banished, and not only that, she's not part of the divor. The high council won't have her."

"She will be there." Czarina's tone brooked no argument. She narrowed her eyes at him. "The question is, will you?"

* * * * *

Chapter Ten

Symeon woke four and a half hours later out of a deep slumber to the sound of his personal comm buzzing.

"Hello?" He pushed a sleep-numbed hand through his disheveled black hair, thankful he hadn't pressed the holo button.

"Seneschal?" Princess Kavya's voice carried both a note of concern and irritation. "You arranged a meeting with me at 0800 in my office. Why am I the only one here?"

"I'm sorry, Princess. I didn't sleep well last night. I apologize, I completely forgot." He had planned to pour over some of Kavya's most recent expense reports with her, though that idea seemed moot now. Perhaps he should cancel the meeting. He doubted the Princess would mind since she had told him everything about her secret spending already. But part of him wanted to see her anyway. He knew Czarina and her shadowy Wuxia wouldn't approve, but he had a mind to inform Kavya about them. If they were all Czarina claimed, Kavya deserved to know about their meddling in her life.

Symeon attempted to sit up and groaned at the sudden pain in his stiff muscles. The strain of nearly falling from the wine tower's balcony had left him surprisingly sore.

"What's wrong?" Kavya asked.

An image of Czarina shouldering him over the balcony railing flashed through Symeon's mind and he nearly groaned again. "Nothing, Princess." Maybe telling wasn't the best idea right now, but he at least wanted to speak with her a bit more about the supposed true history of his people. "Shall I meet you in ten minutes?"

"Very well." Kavya sounded glum. "It's not as though I have much else to do anyway."

Symeon showered and dressed quickly. His stomach demanded breakfast, but he ignored its gurgling. He would swipe something from the kitchens after his meeting. Dressed in his finest suit of gray wool with double cuffed sleeves, he headed across the castle proper, nodding to the many slaves along his way.

These people should be free.

Symeon had never thought such a thing. He wondered what dreams and ambitions this passing errand girl might have? Or that handyman filling holes in the plaster? Common Shorvex, many of whom couldn't afford to own a Luxing, used robots for such menial tasks. The rich took pride in owning a Luxing instead. It was a status symbol. But in a world where no one needed to fold a shirt or paint a room, why should certain people be forced to do those things? Simply so their supposed masters would take some form of pride by proxy in the accomplishment?

Disgusting.

Compared to many of her station, Kavya possessed few slaves, and yet they made up a veritable army of cooks, janitors, errand runners, and gardeners. Far more than needed to pamper a single young woman. And why, if she felt so adamantly opposed to owning Luxing, had she brought so many to Yaya Island?

Simple. She saved them.

Symeon stopped in the middle of the castle's main hall, his head tilted to one side, completely unaware of his fellow Luxing bustling past him. As Seneschal, he knew the numbers of Kavya's staff without any need to reference his comm. One hundred twenty-seven when she could have gotten on fine with perhaps ten, maybe fewer. She had brought them here, all she could cajole out of her father, in order to keep them from the vagaries of regular servitude. Now that Symeon was thinking about it, he realized how much freedom the common servants enjoyed on Yaya Island. Not once had he heard of a Luxing suffering a beating for some offense, nor did the senior staff treat their lesser like children or, as Symeon had seen in other places, animals. They all seemed to appreciate one another, and that appreciation flowed from the top. Kavya treated her slaves like Shorvexan employees—expected to perform their duties but respected for doing so. Nothing came for granted with her.

She is a good, kind person, worthy of service.

Symeon didn't know why this came as a revelation to him. Perhaps because he had never experienced it from a Shorvex of any stripe. Even the common sort who ran shops and businesses treated Luxing like children. They spoke down to him and his kind. They expected Luxing to steal, to lie, to lack intelligence enough to understand the world around them.

Not Kavya.

She treated her slaves like peers. Why hadn't he noticed that before now?

Because you were raised to be, and to remain, blind.

"Are you lost, Seneschal?"

Symeon jumped at the sudden intrusion on his thoughts by a voice he was quickly coming to associate with uncomfortable, possibly painful, experiences. Czarina smirked at him, her dark eyes twinkling with mirth.

"Only in thought," he said in what he thought a smooth recovery. "If you'll excuse me, I have a meeting with Princess Kavya."

"I know." Czarina fell in beside him despite his attempt to escape her. "Did you sleep well?"

"As a matter of fact, I did." Symeon endeavored to keep the anger out of his voice and failed miserably. He sounded like a scolded child complaining about his nurse.

"Good. You're going to need your wits sharp today."

"Is that right?" Yes, Symeon was definitely telling the princess about her handmaid's secret life first chance he got. For all he knew, it wasn't even real. The Wuxia could be something Czarina had made up due to some heretofore undiagnosed psychosis. Considering her threats against him and attempt on his life, she was certainly no fit companion for Grand Duke Alexei's only child.

You're embarrassed she bested you in a fight. Quit being a horse's ass.

"Yes," she said idly, "Ivan rab Rurikid is on his way here. Now."

Symeon forced himself to resolutely not miss a step or jerk his gaze around to her. "How do you know this?"

They had reached the stairs that joined the castle proper to the royal suite. Whoever had designed Vysylka Castle—some ancestor of Kavya's no doubt—had taken pains to keep the common and royal areas separated. For some reason, the idea irked Symeon just now. He strode upward, his legs churning like a threshing machine back on the farm, his boots clomping on the stone risers.

Never missing a stride, Czarina kept pace with him. She really was an annoying brat.

"Telling Ivan, or Kavya for that matter, about the Wuxia would be a mistake."

Symeon had reached the landing. He stopped to face her. Kavya's usual two doormen watched them for a moment in anticipation, but dutifully turned their attentions elsewhere when neither Symeon nor Czarina made to enter.

"Are we back to threats then?" Symeon whispered, his tone vehement.

She shook her head. "I've made all the threats I intended. You'll believe them or you won't, that's on you. But I am going to give you a warning."

"And that differs from a threat, how?"

"It causes you no immediate harm." Czarina leaned closer, though she was careful to maintain a proper distance to preserve decorum between unmarried slaves of vastly different stations. "Think of what happens to Kavya if you oust us. Her father exiled her to this island for the mere offense of speaking out against Luxing slavery. How much more will he do if he discovers she's a traitor to his duchy and the empire itself? Her fate likely wouldn't fall to him anyway. The emperor would see her dead."

"I told you last night, I have no intention of divulging her secrets to anyone."

"And my secrets?"

He stared into her eyes, his face deadpan.

"Do you, for a moment, believe you could expose the Wuxia to Ivan or the grand duke without revealing our connections to Kavya? We're far too enmeshed. You reveal one, you reveal both."

She's right, of course. Don't let anger cloud your judgement.

Symeon ground his teeth. "I've had enough of your threats. I don't even know if you're sane. I've seen exactly zero evidence of your claims. From my perspective, you look like a grasping handmaid with delusions of power and manipulation."

Czarina's face colored a shade darker, her lips curled back in a near snarl, but before she could speak the double doors to Kavya's personal apartments swung open so fast the doormen were forced to leap out of the way.

"Oh! Sorry for that." Kavya took a moment to make certain her men weren't injured. Both agreed she hadn't hurt them and she turned in haste toward Symeon and Czarina, her eyes wide with a mix of excitement and panic. "Ivan just called from orbit. He's on his way here to collect me. I've been invited to the divor!"

* * *

"It's unprecedented, Princess." Symeon eyed Czarina who flashed him a brief smile before turning her attention back to Kavya. The two of them had joined her in the private office adjoined to her apartments.

"Which only makes sense. It's not every day aliens show up in our system." Kavya had taken a seat at her desk, but looked on the verge of abandoning it to pace the room. Her silver-blue eyes sparkled with avid energy as she drummed her fingers on the wood. "There are protocols—rules I must observe during the session. I learned them as a child, but I won't remember."

"We'll see that you're prepared," Czarina said, leaving Symeon to wonder if her 'we' meant herself and him or the mysterious Wuxia.

"And clothes. I haven't worn my court attire in ages. I'll need appropriate outfits, alluring but business-like. You know what I mean, right?"

"I'll see to it; don't you worry." Czarina sounded like a seasoned mother speaking to her youngest, flightiest child before her first cotillion.

"Symeon, you're schooled in the proper etiquette, aren't you? You can guide me?"

"Of course, Princess, though I'd warn you, there are no written, or even unwritten codes for heirs invited to accompany their parents into the divor convocation. Are you certain Ivan rab Rurikid meant exactly that? Might you simply be visiting outside the ministry while the peers meet?"

Kavya narrowed her eyes. "Ivan was quite explicit, but if you doubt me, you may ask him yourself when he arrives."

Why was it every time he spoke to the princess he ended up apologizing? Symeon had assumed his training in the School of Seneschals, especially his many classes devoted solely to diplomacy, would have prepared him for handling even the touchiest of elite Shorvex. He worried no amount of training would ever prepare him for the likes of Kavya.

Unfair. Your question was rude. You assumed she had misunderstood Ivan's request because you underestimate her.

"My apologies, Princess." He bowed to show contrition. "I do not doubt you."

Something stole over Kavya's face like a storm cloud rushing to mar an otherwise perfect day. She scrutinized Symeon. "You don't doubt me, but do you trust me, Seneschal?"

"Implicitly, Princess."

"On the surface, yes, I see the trust in your eyes. But when I look deeper, I wonder. You know I released Emperor Pyotr's communication with the Bith to the planetary sphere. You know I stole duchy secrets from my father's government."

Symeon glanced at Czarina who sat demurely in the chair next to him, her eyes focused ahead. "I do, Princess. And I have told no one."

"I know you haven't." Kavya held up her personal comm. "I would have received a warning if you had contacted anyone outside Yaya in the last eighteen hours. But does that mean I can trust you? Would you trust yourself in my place?"

With this many doubts swirling around in my head? Hardly.

"That isn't an easy question to answer, Princess."

"I'm not excited to enter the divor simply for the experience." Kavya spread her hands on the desk before her. "I want to ensure my father can't launch his coup against the empire. What you said on the matter rang true with me. Although I still believe I've thwarted his plans, at least for the foreseeable future, it's possible he could go through with them. If I'm at the divor, however, I might be able to stop him nonetheless."

Symeon sat up straighter. "Are you saying you would divulge what you know? What you've done?"

"If it means avoiding a solar war, yes." Kavya held his gaze without wavering.

Symeon wanted to ask more—he wanted to ask Czarina how Kavya's presence on the council would benefit the Wuxia—but Vladnemar opened the outer door before he got the chance.

"Seneschal Ivan rab Rurikid has arrived, Princess." Vlademar had dressed in much finer clothes than his usual butler's attire. He wore a black and gray suit matched with an azure vest and crimson tie. He had also slicked back the little hair left on his thinning pate so that it resembled a salt and pepper wave.

Ivan swept into the room, his face flushed, his formal cape whipping out behind him as Vlademar made his exit, careful to avoid snagging the thing when he shut the doors. Like the butler, Ivan wore his best: an expensively tailored suit that probably cost as much as a personal aircraft, an ornate chain of office bearing the royal seal of House Rurikid—a double-headed raven clutching a scepter in one claw and a bundle of arrows in the other—and a pair of boots polished to a mirrored shine.

Not by his hands, I'd wager.

Symeon and Czarina stood while Ivan made obeisance to the princess, bowing at the waist, arms arranged after the proper fashion, one in front and one behind. "Princess Kavya. I apologize for my hastiness. I know my call was abrupt."

"As it should have been, Ivan." Kavya moved around her desk to plant a kiss on both of the seneschal's cheeks. "You do no more than your duty."

"You are too kind, Princess. Too understanding. I'm afraid the emperor's decision to include heirs in the divor has everyone in the fleet in a tizzy." Ivan's gaze strayed to Symeon and Czarina. "I assume they know?"

Kavya nodded. "We were just discussing the logistics of moving sufficient staff with enough speed to meet the crown's demands."

Isn't she a marvelous liar?

Of course. She wouldn't have survived this long if she lacked the skills to match her ambition. Symeon could respect that, though Kavya's ability gave him pause. Until now, he had assumed he knew the princess well enough to recognize a lie if she fed him one. He had miscalculated.

"Good, they'll be invaluable to you. And me as well, I think." Ivan gave Symeon a meaningful look before turning back to the princess. "Unfortunately, I'm afraid we have little room aboard ship. You're allowed four."

Kavya looked as though she might complain but didn't. Instead, she nodded. "Very well."

"And we have no time to waste, Princess. Your father has made it clear he expects you to accompany him to Bastrayavich aboard his flag ship, the *Emperor Nikolai*, which is set to get underway in six hours."

A secret thrill ran through Symeon despite his nervousness. He had always wanted to see the inside of a spacecraft in the flesh. In a handful of hours, he would be riding aboard the pride of the Valensk fleet. Few enough Luxing ever got that chance since the Shorvexan Empire deemed them ineligible for military service. Certainly, many Shorvexan officers kept slaves as batmen, but that sort of role had never appealed to Symeon. Space travel, however, had always seemed a sublime pursuit.

"Very well." Kavya turned to Symeon. "Will you inform Vlademar of our new staffing numbers? He's not going to like it."

"Of course, Princess." Symeon bowed and started for the exit.

"I have my own duties to attend if we're going to make our rendezvous," Ivan said. "Will you please excuse me as well, Princess?"

Kavya, who had already returned to her desk and was typing furiously on her holo display, made a shooing motion to the both of them. "Go, go, and give me quiet. I'm trying to piece together a wardrobe here."

Symeon let Ivan lead him from the room. The older seneschal set a hard pace, striding with authority. He remained quiet until he and Symeon had reached Castle Vysylka's central hallway, which stood empty after the earlier bustle.

Ivan stopped before one of the building's massive windows to bathe in a pool of sunlight. He had grown a scruff of beard, most unusual for a slave of his position. Clean-shaven faces were expected by the Shorvex from their trusted stewards. He rubbed at his cheek absently as if the whiskers bothered him.

"You wanted something, Seneschal?" Symeon prompted.

"I have a task for you, Symeon, but I fear it may not be to your liking. I must ask that you serve not only as Princess Kavya's advisor in the coming days, but as her mentor as well."

"Sir, is it my place to mentor someone of her rank?"

"It is, son. It's always been the seneschal's job to gently guide young royals in the way they should go." Ivan held up both hands. "Don't misunderstand me here. I mean suggesting, not pushing. Persuasion, not force. We are still servants no matter our stations."

Symeon almost laughed at the idea of forcing Kavya Rurikid to do anything she didn't want, especially with Czarina at her side. "What sort of persuasion, sir?"

"The princess harbors certain ideas about how our people are mistreated. Ideas unpopular with her father, or anyone with a mature sense of order. In the past, she's had a tendency to spout these beliefs in mixed company." Ivan eyed Symeon closely. "You may have heard some rumors about that?"

"It's the reason she lives here on Yaya Island."

"Just so. Thus, I think it would benefit her, and you, to coach the princess on keeping her opinions to herself. We wouldn't want her to embarrass the grand duke in the divor, especially over ideas Kavya will surely outgrow as she ages and acquires more wisdom."

He would have you muzzle her? As if you could.

"I will do everything in my power to protect House Rurikid, Seneschal." Symeon bowed.

Ah, well played.

"Thank you, my boy. That is all I ask."

* * * * *

Chapter Eleven

Symeon stared out a three-meter-tall window aboard the *Emperor Nikolai* at the blue sphere of Phoenix in a backdrop of stars.

"You can see it on a holo or in a game a billion times, and it's never the same as witnessing it in the flesh." Kavya stood just ahead of Symeon, dressed in a fine white traveling gown embroidered with pearls from the planet below. Her hairdressers had piled her silver tresses high upon her head to reveal the smooth turn of her neck where it met her bare shoulders.

"I should say not." Symeon gazed at their shared home world with a mix of awe and trepidation. He knew very well that space travel was safe. Millions of people made trips between Phoenix and the local colonies every year without incident. Standing here, in the princess' assigned berthage, felt no different than having his feet planted on solid ground. Yet knowing he was aboard a hurtling hunk of metal en route to a distant moon without the least bit of control over the trip turned his stomach.

"I never tire of space travel," said Ivan rab Rurikid, "though I fear I take it for granted these days. Your father has me bouncing across the system every week it seems." He nodded appreciatively at Symeon. "It's refreshing to travel with someone seeing these things for the first time."

Symeon knew there was more to the older seneschal's nod than mere acknowledgment. The gesture carried freight, part of it a kinship Ivan now felt between them since he had shared his beliefs on managing their Shorvex masters. A month ago, Symeon would have reveled in the idea. Today, it felt burdensome—and more than that, dishonest. Ivan wanted Symeon to stifle Princess Kavya's thoughts, in essence to censure her. While Symeon understood the need for discretion, the idea of censoring her thoughts left a bad taste in his mouth. He simply wouldn't do it.

"Would you lunch with us, Seneschal?" Kavya asked of Ivan. She had insisted on bringing food from Yaya for their first meal aboard the *Emperor Nikolai*.

The portly man shook his head and bowed. "I'm afraid I cannot, Princess. Please accept my sincere apologies, but I must attend your father. He has scheduled a meeting with all his vassal clan heads. Every duke, count, and baron is aboard ship, I fear. It should be a lively event, and one that will require my presence."

"If by lively you mean cutthroat," Kavya quipped.

"Indeed. And it is up to your father, and therefore me as well, to referee the thing." Ivan lifted his face to the apartment ceiling and let go a heavy sigh—the put-upon steward overburdened by responsibility.

The self-important prig who cares more for his master's race than his own.

Unfair. Symeon regretted that thought the instant it flashed through his mind. Like Luxing of every stripe, Ivan lived according to his upbringing, his training, and his cultural expectations. Self-important he might be, but only because he largely deserved it. Few Luxing could claim the special moniker rab, which in old Rus meant something like adopted child. As a rab Rurikid, he enjoyed an elevated station, one that meant he had attained the highest approval of his masters, so much so they had elected to accept him as one of their own. By rights, having attained a seneschal position to the daughter of a grand duke, Symeon could claim that same title, but he would earn it—no one would use it for him—for years to come. Ivan had given those years of loyal service and been richly rewarded for them.

"If you or your staff need anything aboard ship, please contact one of my people," Ivan said. "I'm afraid the ship's captain wasn't able to spare even a junior officer to attend you. All the naval personnel are working double shifts to prepare the *Emperor Nikolai* for commonwealth service, but you may rely on me as ever."

"It's only four days," Kavya said. "I think we'll manage."

Ivan bowed. "Then I must say farewell for now, Princess. Symeon, be certain to check in with me daily. Our schedules may change with the grand duke's whims."

"Of course, sir."

Ivan nodded and swept from the room, moving fast for a heavy man.

Once the ship's doors had whooshed closed behind him, Kavya turned to Symeon. "Here I go, traipsing into the shcheritsa's den."

The shcheritsa, a one-and-a-half-meter-long lizard native to Phoenix, once known as the terror of lone villages in ancient times, was famed for its temperamental nature. One could live for years in seemingly docile captivity, only to launch a rampage against its keepers without warning. Armored with thick skin, jagged spines running the course of his back, and serrated teeth as long as Symeon's fingers, the beast was a pure killing machine.

"You have nothing to fear, Princess."

"Don't I?" Kavya watched him closely, her silver-blue eyes intense. "Hasn't it occurred to you, Seneschal, that this might all be a ruse?"

"How so?"

"What if the Emperor already knows who released his parley with the Bith? Never in a thousand years of divor meetings have the heirs of the aristocracy been invited to attend the divor. Is that merely coincidence, or might it be pretense? Perhaps I'm being lured into the shcheritsa's abode with honey."

She's letting her fears get the best of her.

"I doubt that, Princess. Why would the Emperor raise so many questions simply to have the daughter of a grand duke attend a meeting? Everyone in the system is talking about the heirs' attendance. It's a convoluted means of reaching you when he could summon you any time he likes. He is, after all, the Emperor."

Kavya grunted a laugh and turned her gaze back to the window where Phoenix had shrunk enough to hide it with her thumb. She did so, and laughed again. "Seems petty now, doesn't it?"

"What's that, Princess?"

"The planet, the system, our stupid squabbles over who has power. I swear to you, Symeon, all I want is peace. No innocents should die because my father covets the emperor's throne. Part of me wants to march into his office and tell him everything I know. I want him to understand the toll his ambition will take on the people down there."

"Perhaps you were right, though," Symeon said without much enthusiasm. "With the emperor calling his banners to form the commonwealth fleet, your father won't get the chance to initiate a coup."

"Hope makes for a dangerous bridge." Kavya turned sad eyes on Symeon.

Don't tell your father, girl!

"Princess, I implore you, do nothing rash. Your father—"

Kavya waved away his concerns with an impatient flick of her hand. "Don't worry. I have no intention of even seeing him before the divor. He's far too busy for the likes of me, and besides, I know telling him wouldn't solve the problem, it would simply remove me from the equation. I don't intend to let that happen."

"I'm relieved to hear it, Princess."

"All will be well, eh?" Kavya said brightly, though Symeon could tell she was putting on a show for his benefit. "For now, why don't you walk the ship a bit? I wager some of your old schoolmates are aboard."

The idea hadn't crossed Symeon's mind, but she was probably right. Many from his graduating class had likely ended up serving great houses in Valensk. With so many peers aboard ship, he was bound to find someone he knew.

"What about your lunch, Princess? Wouldn't you like me to serve it?" Without a full staff at her disposal, and her handmaids off attending to other tasks, the work fell to Symeon. He saw no disgrace in menial service.

"No." Kavya favored him with a wan smile. "I'm not so hungry after all. Go. Find your old chums and play catch up while you can. Like as not, serving me, you'll wind up back in exile soon enough."

* * *

After living in the spacious corridors and expansive galleries afforded him in Vysylka Castle, the *Emperor Nikolai*'s tight confines left Symeon feeling claustrophobic. Even on the royal decks, of which there were seven, he was forced to press his back to the wall anytime he passed someone coming the opposite direction.

Bulkhead.

He should use the correct space-faring terms. In the five hours he had spent aboard ship, he had already seen three Luxing accosted by Shorvexan officers for referring to portions of the ship using incorrect terminology. A persnickety lot, these fleet officers. Their enlisted juniors were less so from what Symeon had observed, but none of them appeared pleased by the idea of hosting royals and their Luxing slaves.

Luckily, as Princess Kavya suggested, Symeon had spent much of his time visiting with friends in private spaces well away from the corridors the ship's crew frequented. He had finished lunch with one such friend only moments ago, a junior seneschal on Count Danyomich Simmbrayastak's personal staff, and was headed back to Princess Kavya's apartments when a Shorvexan naval captain turned the corner and nearly ran him over.

"Out of the way you sorry sack of shit," the captain said, his nose curled up in disgust. "It's bad enough I have to worry about a metric ton of royals underfoot, I shouldn't have to deal with cockroaches as well."

"My apologies, sir." Symeon dutifully flattened himself against the cold steel of the bulkhead to let the officer pass.

"Who is your master?" The captain demanded, turning back once he had already passed Symeon by. "I'm going to let him know you failed to bow when I gave you a lawful order."

"I am seneschal to Princess Kavya Rurikid, sir." Symeon watched the captain's eyes for the satisfying moment when the name sunk in.

"Think that means something, do you?" The captain pressed close so that their noses almost touched. His breath smelled of mold and sour coffee.

Punch this arrogant bastard in the nose.

The urge almost overwhelmed Symeon's sense of self-preservation. He stood as tall as the Shorvexan officer who was probably ten years his senior and pudgy. Knocking him flat would be the work of two seconds. Less even. Symeon had won bouts against his type a hundred times over in school.

But those men hadn't been this captain's type. They were Luxing, every one of them. To lay a finger on a Shorvex would mean death for Symeon. Possibly at the captain's hands once he woke up and located a weapon, but if not him, by order of the courts. No Luxing ever attacked one of his betters and retained his life.

Symeon bowed as deeply as the narrow corridor would allow. "Forgive me, Captain. I forgot my place. You are right, of course, I am nothing here."

Without warning, the captain punched Symeon. The blow connected a couple of centimeters above his jaw and sent a shock wave of pain through his head and neck. Bent as he was, it sent him to his knees. Certainly, he had suffered far more powerful punches in his boxing days, but the surprise of it left him momentarily dazed.

"You're nothing anywhere, shit for brains." The captain rubbed his fist on his uniform pants as if touching Symeon had somehow sullied his knuckles. "Don't go thinking otherwise."

Rage boiled inside Symeon. Though he had suffered whippings as a young servant on the farm whenever he shirked his duties or got caught filching extra food, his overseers had never meted out this sort of casual brutality. And while Symeon was no fool—he well knew Luxing suffered undeserved beatings every day—he had never experienced it for himself. This went beyond unfairness. It was cruel. And the worst part? Symeon knew he could easily rise up and beat the bile out of this hidebound son of a bitch.

No, you're right, that would be foolish in the extreme. Show him you're contrite.

Rather than stand, Symeon genuflected, arms outstretched, nose pressed to cold steel. "Please accept my humblest apologies, sir. I meant no disrespect. I honor your service to the empire which keeps me and my lowly kind safe."

Apparently mollified, the captain turned on his heels and strode away without another word, his footfalls echoing as he went.

Symeon stood, rubbing the side of his head.

Shorvexan bastard.

Though he would never have allowed himself to think such a thing a month ago, Symeon found he could now think little else of the retreating captain. Even if his people had uplifted the Luxing as the official histories reported, what gave him the right to treat any creature this way? If Symeon were a dog, other Shorvex would condemn the captain for cruelty. He would lose his reputation on the sphere's social networks. No one would want to associate with him. His career would end. And yet, because Symeon was Luxing, the captain would face no punishment. In fact, he could very well go through with reporting Symeon for failing to render a bow. Symeon doubted Kavya would care, but if he served most any other master, he might be in for a beating or perhaps, worse still, a dismissal from his position as seneschal.

"You wanted to hit him. I saw it in your eyes."

Symeon spun to find Czarina standing behind him, a short, well-muscled Luxing man by her side.

How does she do that?

"I would never." Symeon dusted off his pants more to hide his embarrassment than to remove dirt.

"I didn't say you would." Czarina's pretty smile carried all the patronizing her voice didn't. "I said you wanted to. And I for one don't blame you. What he did was petty."

Symeon glanced up and down the corridor for eavesdroppers. "I'd watch my words if I were you."

"There's no one to hear me, Symeon. The corridor's clear."

Something in Czarina's tone told him she had a hand in the lack of traffic. He wanted to believe she was bragging—taking credit for happenstance.

But you don't.

"Who is your friend?" he asked.

"Viktor Zolotukhin, this is the man I've been telling you about, Symeon rab Rurikid, Princess Kavya's newest seneschal."

"Pleasure to meet you, Seneschal." Viktor spoke in a deep voice despite his short stature. He shook Symeon's hand, his grip firm and self-assured.

"Czarina is too liberal with her titles. I've served the princess less than a month, I make no claim to the appellation rab Rurikid."

"Viktor and I are having drinks with a few friends," Czarina said. "Join us."

"Another time, perhaps. I was on my way to check in with the Princess."

"Kavya is well. I was with her less than an hour ago. She's having a nap and won't miss you. Come. You'll want to meet our friends I think."

Symeon hesitated, suddenly on his guard. "What is this, Czarina?"

"This is an invitation, Seneschal. One you really should accept."

"There are your kind aboard?" Symeon avoided saying the word Wuxia, but he could tell by the knowing smile that creased Czarina's lips she understood his meaning.

"Our kind, Symeon, yes. I think it's time you learned something more of your heritage, don't you?"

* * * * *

Chapter Twelve

Czarina and Viktor led Symeon down three levels and across what felt like half the ship without speaking a word. They passed few people along the way. Those they did were all Luxing. Curious that. Plenty of slaves traveled alone on errands, nothing strange there, but the fact that Symeon encountered not one Shorvex on a ship filled with them made him stare about in wonder.

They passed through a reinforced door marked Gymnasium and entered the largest space Symeon had experienced on board. While not so tall or wide as gyms he frequented back on Phoenix, after the close confines of the ship's passageways, the simple expanse made him feel like a prisoner drawing in his first breath of freedom.

Barbells, dumbbells, and various weight machines described the space, all of it surrounding a caged ring set up for martial arts practice. Luxing used every bit of it, including the cage, which came as a shock to Symeon. His kind were forbidden grappling and joint manipulation fighting.

"Impressed?" Czarina called over her shoulder as she led the three of them toward the cage.

"This isn't allowed." Symeon realized how simple, how lame, he sounded the instant those words passed his lips. A couple of buff Luxing men performing free weight squats rolled their eyes at him.

Czarina made a derisive sound. "What is? Come here, I want you to meet someone."

She bustled past a group of men and women performing some sort of calisthenics that involved holding awkward poses and stretching. It didn't look like much of a challenge to a former boxer, until he noticed how their muscles shook and their skin glistened with sweat.

Three pairs of men occupied the ring. They wore thick outfits of gray or black that tied in the front with wide sleeves and pant legs which afforded them freedom of movement. Rolling back and forth, each man tried to outmaneuver his partner by applying various holds.

Symeon narrowed his eyes for a better view through the steel cage. He had seen zyudo competitions before. The sport was popular with the common Shorvex of southern Valensk. Having never tried it himself, he didn't know much about the discipline except that certain moves were deemed illegal. From what he could tell, nearly every move these men made fell into that category.

Might be fun.

"Aren't they afraid of getting caught doing that?" Symeon asked, his gaze straying to the gymnasium door which, thankfully, remained shut, despite his expectation that a Shorvexan security detail would come busting through any second.

"Don't worry about that," said an older Luxing dressed in a blue version of the fighters' uniform. "All our masters know where we are. They won't come looking. We meet for exercise this time daily."

"Symeon," Czarina said, "this is Nikita. He's..." She raised a quizzical eyebrow at the older man.

"I am, for want of a better term, the current leader of the Wuxia, in that we have any one leader." Nikita grinned and shrugged, the collective expressions self-deprecating, and anything but pompous.

"Amongst the Wuxia, he is known as Liu Fang," Czarina said, pride in her voice. "It's a name he took from ancient records about our people."

A woman's name. Wonder if he knows that?

"Fragmented records, I'm afraid." Nikita—Fang—bowed formally to Symeon. "So much of our history is lost, I fear we'll likely never know it all, but I like the idea of taking a new name from old records. It makes me feel at one with our ancestors."

Symeon returned the bow, dismissing his random thoughts about the name. How would he know anything about ancient Luxing naming conventions anyway? He didn't. His imagination was running wild today. Stress, no doubt.

"I get the feeling, sir, you wanted to speak with me," Symeon said. "Otherwise, Czarina wouldn't have gone to such pains to bring me here."

"Perceptive," Fang said with a nod. "Your position as seneschal to the princess makes you of interest to the Wuxia, Symeon. I'm sure you've already realized that, eh?"

"Through Czarina's loving ministrations, yes."

Czarina's grin could have melted glass with its prideful heat. "I think I'll have a roll while I'm here. You don't mind, do you, Fang?"

"Of course not, girl. Join her, Viktor. I'd like to work on your escapes while we still have the gym."

The two of them hustled off to separate changing areas.

"Am I to assume you're trying to recruit me, sir?" Symeon asked.

"Yep." Fang ran a hand through the short, gray bristles on his head. "Zheng! You know better than to let him slip your hold like that. Next time, hook his elbow and keep your hips high."

"Do you kill me if I refuse?" Symeon asked in a low voice.

"No." Fang turned to face Symeon, frowning. "If you try to out us, though..." He shrugged one shoulder. "I don't like threats. They're foul air in my opinion. Besides, Czarina says you're a man possessed of a caring heart, and that you're learning to see the truth of things. Is that so?"

"Is there a difference between learning to see and having a vision foisted upon me?"

Fang laughed. "In the end? No. Tell me, how does it feel, learning that our slavery is based on lies?"

"I didn't want to believe it at first."

"Most don't. Shows how completely we were controlled by status. How about now? Do you believe?"

Symeon looked around at the Luxing gathered about the room taking exercise and enjoying each other's company. It reminded him of his days in school where nearly every face he saw belonged to a Luxing. "I'm beginning to. Kavya certainly believes it."

"She isn't the first Shorvex to unknowingly take up the Wuxia cause, but she's certainly the most prominent. Her support may well prove pivotal in the coming days and years."

Czarina and Viktor returned dressed in their own sparring outfits and joined the men in the cage. Despite her smaller size, Czarina made no complaints, setting about rolling against the first man ready to go. She couldn't match his strength. That much became immediately evident when he forced her into a compromised position with his legs around her waist and arms trapping her upper torso. He mimed landing a couple of elbows to show he could, only to be surprised when she surged upward like a spider climbing a wall to get past his legs.

The man is stronger, yes, but not quicker.

Symeon marveled at the sense of pride he felt when Czarina feinted a grab for her opponent's collar only to sink some kind of complicated hold on his right arm. In seconds, he was tapping her ankle, and she let him up.

"That would never be allowed in zyudo," Symeon said.

"And that is why she wins." Fang turned to gaze at Symeon. "You're close to the princess. She trusts you, because you haven't betrayed her. You seem disposed to serve her well. Is that a fair estimation?"

"All she wants is peace and to help our people whatever way she can. How could I destroy her life for that?"

"Good." Fang pointed a finger at Symeon. "I couldn't have said it better. It's the way we of the Wuxia feel about her."

"It was you who arranged for the heirs to attend the divor."

"Yes. No small feat that," Fang said, his gaze on the combatants.

"How are you powerful enough to change a thousand years of tradition?"

"There exists two sorts of power in our world, Symeon. The power of the master over the slave, which is brutal, iron hard, undeniable. And the power of the slave over the master, which is subtle, feather light, and mutable. Of the two, the master's power appears strongest, and it is in the near term, but the slave's power is influence applied over days, years, even centuries."

"Luxing slavery has lasted a millennium," Symeon countered, his tone dry.

"Yes, but has it changed?"

Symeon shrugged, suddenly uncomfortable. This wasn't the sort of thing a Luxing learned in school. "I don't know. I haven't studied it. I know it hasn't in the last twenty years."

"It has changed only insomuch as we have changed it. Every wealthy, powerful family in the entire system owns slaves, and therefore we own influence. There was once a time when murdering Luxing meant about as much to the crown as shooting rats in a basement. Now, a Shorvex will serve jail time and pay restitution to the dead slave's family if the courts deem it a wrongful death."

"I thought that had always been a law."

"The Wuxia saw it enacted seventy-six years ago."

"In fairness, that's a long time ago, sir."

"In fairness, I did say a feather, yes?"

Symeon smiled. "And so now you're moving again, trying to head off Grand Duke Alexei's coup. This seems far more decisive than changing laws."

Viktor joined the fighting in the ring. He too overcame his opponent in a handful of moves, catching him in a painful sort of knee lock that made Symeon's lower stomach clench.

"One of the Wuxia's greatest problems is a lack of organization," Fang said. "Any one group is only loosely affiliated with another. This is a terrible weakness, one I plan to remedy in my lifetime. I think, with Kavya's help—and yours, Symeon—we might find ways to strengthen our network. At this point, we're far too vulnerable to reveal ourselves to the broader empire, but if we could reach every Luxing in the system, we could wield enough power to fight. It's a long term dream, but it starts here and now. I would like for you to be a part of that."

Strength in numbers. If enough slaves simply stop working, they could cripple the empire's economy in a matter of days.

Symeon nodded. "I'll admit, you've piqued my interest. I see freedom for our people, and I want it. But you're talking about overturning a thousand years of ingrained culture and stealing away the Shorvexan way of life in the process."

"You are star born, are you not?" Fang asked.

"I am."

"We all are in a way." Fang held out one of his hands, the skin mottled with age spots and wrinkles. "The first Luxing ever raised on this planet were born from the same progenitor ships that birthed you."

Symeon tried to school his expression to hide his doubt, but by Fang's indulging smile, he failed. "Is that something you read in one of your ancient, fragmented histories?"

"No," Fang said. "It is a truth proven by science. Every cell in our bodies contains the blueprints necessary to build a Luxing. They are called—"

Genes.

"—genes, and they make us both our overall species and our individual selves."

Symeon jerked in surprise when his thoughts supplied the unfamiliar word before Fang uttered it. Had the old man said it earlier in the conversation? He didn't think so. They hadn't been talking about blood and heredity before now.

"Is something wrong?" Fang asked, watching Symeon's face with concern.

"I'm fine. Fine. The word sounds familiar somehow."

"I'd be surprised if you ever heard it. We know little enough about genes except that all members of our species carry certain ones that mark us as part of the same family." Fang met Symeon's gaze. "And the Shorvex share them with us."

"Czarina told me something like that," Symeon said. "She has the princess convinced. I'm not so certain I believe it. The Shorvex look so different."

"On the surface, perhaps. Underneath, we are the same. The Shorvex buried the study of genes eons ago to hide our shared kinship. Can you imagine that? Expunging an entire branch of science in order to excuse your desire to enslave your cousins. Who knows what discoveries they missed by making that choice?"

Discoveries made long ago and lost twice over.

"Symeon, you box, yes?" A sweat-soaked Viktor called from inside the cage. "Come spar a bit. Show us what you know."

When had the voice in Symeon's head separated from his conscious thoughts? For weeks now he had misjudged it as part of his own thinking, but was it? More and more it felt disconnected from him like an appendage that had begun moving on its own without any direction from him. But how could that be? His brain was his brain. Any ideas that passed through it must belong to him no matter how foreign they might seem. Right?

Not every thought.

"Symeon?" Fang sounded worried. "You look pale. How do you feel?"

"He feels like getting some old-fashioned exercise," Czarina said. "Come on, Sym, I promise I won't kick your ass like I did last time."

The men in the cage laughed while Symeon shivered, his eyes gone wide. He couldn't think for worrying that the words and images he saw inside his skull belonged to someone else.

"Join us, Symeon!" Viktor shouted.

"I—I haven't the clothes for sparring. And I don't see any gloves."

"We'll practice open-handed the way the ancients did it." Viktor pushed the cage door open. "I've never boxed in my life. Show me a few moves, eh?"

Anything to take his mind off his...mind. "Okay, a few rounds."

Symeon kicked off his shoes and dropped his suit coat on the mat. In his stocking feet, he squared up with Viktor. The shorter Luxing grinned at him the way a street hustler grins at his next mark. Symeon recognized that look from a thousand matches in Luxing boxing clubs across the duchy.

"Boxing rules, right?" Symeon asked.

Maybe for a minute or two. Don't trust this guy.

Symeon mentally shut the voice down as brutally as he could, willing it to disappear forever. He waited a moment to see if it would return while he and Viktor bowed to begin their match.

No voice.

Symeon's relief lasted all of five seconds before Viktor rushed him. He rammed his shoulder into Symeon's hips while simultaneously wrapping both arms low about his legs. Taken completely by surprise, Symeon's back and head slammed on the mat. The concussion stole his breath and left him seeing stars.

The instant Symeon fell, Viktor scrambled across his prone form to press a meaty forearm across his throat, further cutting off his air supply. In desperation, Symeon attempted to push Viktor off him, but the other man must have expected it. He performed a dazzling spin move that positioned him on Symeon's side, nullifying his punches.

Though totally out of his fighting element, especially with his fists out of play, Symeon knew combat. The style might differ, but he had faced hundreds of men in fights over the years, and one thing he knew about fighting, never let the other guy execute his game plan. Ignoring his burning lungs, he tried to think clearly. Viktor wouldn't have gotten into this side position without an idea of what to do next. From what Symeon had seen, the fighters weren't allowed to punch one another in the face, so that left his free arm as the next best target. Symeon hurriedly squeezed a handful of Viktor's uniform collar.

When, as predicted, Viktor sought to attack Symeon's arm, he found it immovable due to the taller man's grip.

Viktor laughed. "Very good!"

Symeon smiled, pleased with himself.

Viktor kicked off the floor like a rocket, breaking Symeon's grip in the process, and spun him half around. He latched onto Symeon's back with all four limbs before he knew what had happened. Viktor snaked an arm around Symeon's neck almost faster than he realized and alarm bells went off in his head. He didn't know the name of this move, but he had seen one of the other men cinch it on his opponent earlier. That man had passed out in seconds.

Symeon reached for Viktor's hand in an awkward attempt to stop the hold before Viktor could sink his elbow beneath Symeon's chin.

No, fool! Shrug your shoulders first.

Without thinking, Symeon followed the voice's advice. Viktor's arm locked around him, but not at the neck. It instead squeezed against his chin and around his jaw—painful yes, but survivable.

Now drop your chin and push up on his elbow. Hard!

Symeon did so and slipped almost easily from Viktor's grasp. He bounded forward, rolled, and gained his feet all in one smooth motion.

"Outstanding!" Fang clapped and cheered and rattled the cage with the flat of one hand.

"How did you know to escape that?" Czarina asked, a strange, almost respectful look in her eye.

"I don't know," Symeon stammered, momentarily and rather irrationally afraid she had somehow heard the voice in his head. "I just did."

Viktor, still sitting on his knees, grinned up at Symeon. "You haven't been taking illegal classes now have you, Seneschal?"

Symeon shook his head. He wanted to leave immediately. He needed to be alone with no watchful eyes on him. "I have to go."

"You'll think about our discussion?" Fang asked as Symeon scooped up his shoes and jacket and headed for the exit.

"Yes!" Symeon hit the door at speed, the bulkhead steel cold through his socks.

"We all want the same thing, Symeon," Fang called after him. "We all want peace."

No. Some of us want freedom more.

* * * * *

Chapter Thirteen

Symeon's small room lay deep within the *Emperor Nikolai*, eight decks below Kavya's own. Due to the number of extra bodies aboard, including the many royals and their personal attendants, most Luxing were berthed three and four to a room. By luck, and because his assigned room amounted to little more than a utility closet, Symeon had received a single roommate, a bursar named Fedor who belonged to Baron Andrey Shamirov. Symeon knew next to nothing about the man, having met him in passing that afternoon while dropping off his luggage. He seemed reserved—content to pass their time aboard ship without speaking. That would have suited Symeon well enough if he wasn't losing his mind.

He crashed through the door to their shared berth and found Fedor propped on the bottom bunk reading a holo novel. The bespectacled man looked up in surprise at the noise, but merely nodded when he recognized Symeon and went back to reading.

"Fedor," Symeon grasped one end of the bed, his knuckles white with strain. "I realize this is asking a lot, and I wouldn't do it except in extremis, but I must ask you to leave the room for at least an hour—perhaps two."

"What's this about?" Fedor looked cautious as he sat up. His position as bursar, even to a duke, ranked far lower than seneschal to the grand duke's heir. Nonetheless, he looked ready to argue. "It's late, and I have work early tomorrow."

Sweat trickled down Symeon's lower back and off his forehead into his eyes. He felt like a man on fire. Enunciating each word with care, he said, "I understand it's late, and I'm sorry for that, but if you don't leave in the next ten seconds, I'm going to beat you to death with that holo comm."

Fedor hesitated for perhaps half a second before he whipped his coverlet aside and shoved his bare feet into a pair of well-worn house slippers, his gaze never leaving Symeon. Dressed only in his short clothes and a ratty robe, he opened the steel door and looked back over one shoulder. "Where should I go?"

"I don't give a shit where you go! Get out!"

Fedor disappeared like a rabbit into its warren, slamming the door behind him.

Symeon knew he would regret that later. He thought about chasing poor Fedor down to apologize, but doing so would probably frighten the little man to death. Besides, he had other concerns.

He stood before the room's single mirror which reflected his image from the waist up. His black hair stood up like a disheveled mountain range on his head. His color, usually dark, had drained away leaving him as blanched as an old vegetable.

He didn't care. How he looked outside wouldn't matter a whit if he lost his mind. He leaned close to the mirror, gazed into his own eyes. "Who are you?"

Nothing.

Symeon drew a breath and laughed at his mirror twin, the sound just this side of manic. What had he expected? Some demon to usurp his body like in a sim game? A new face to appear over his real one all sharpened fangs and warts and yellow eyes? Perhaps he was losing his mind, just not in the way he had thought. The Wuxia, Czarina, even Kavya wanted him to turn against all he had ever known. Not just his upbringing on the farm, but five years of training as a seneschal. No wonder his mind felt as fragile as spider webs. He stood on the verge of tossing a lifetime of good service onto a trash heap of bad ideas.

That was why his mind rebelled. It was his unconscious way of fighting against the temptations in his life. He had prepared himself for the hardships of duty, for managing an estate in every particular. But nothing had prepared him for betrayal, disloyalty, and the breaking of his most deeply held oaths at the behest of the princess he was sworn to obey.

Tears welled at the corners of Symeon's eyes. Yes, it was treachery that had so injured his brain. It was Kavya, misguided or not, who had first introduced the dissonance he now suffered. She was to blame for this. He should never have encouraged her. He should have turned emperor's evidence against her over to Ivan and Grand Duke Alexei.

NO!

Symeon reeled back from the mirror, his eyes wide, his mouth hanging open. The word had boomed through his head with such force he felt sure it must have cracked his skull with the impact. In trepidation, he bent back to the mirror.

"Who is speaking in my head?"

I AM YUDI.

Light exploded behind Symeon's eyes. At first, he saw colors — variations of red, purple, gold—bursting forth and then flowing in every direction without a coherent form. Over time, the colors merged, swirled together, and coalesced into images like the ones

Symeon had viewed before, except brighter, more real, tangible in ways his thoughts could not grasp, and yet he understood.

You grok.

Without knowing anything, Symeon realized what he—saw/heard/touched/tasted/smelled—told the history of his people. Not the Luxing, exactly, but—

Yes, the Luxing. And the Shorvex. And the Romans. And the hominids who moved out of Africa on two legs.

Hundreds of thousands of years passed through him—light through a pane of glass, split by a prism, refracted in a sea of learning. For one exquisite moment, he held it all in his mind, the great epic of his species upon a small, rocky planet called Earth. Slowly, in ones and twos, ships rose from Earth, spreading to the stars. Symeon's vision could not follow them all.

Only one.

The Luxing, made up mostly of people from a land once called China, left Earth seeking new horizons. They settled a planet they called Heritage in their now ancient language. There they prospered as never before, evolving a new society from the old.

At some point, unknown to Yudi, his kind first arrived on Heritage—artificial beings created by alien hands and somehow lost in the void of space for eons without measure. Embraced by the Luxing, the AIs became part of their human fabric, citizens of their shared culture, and true friends. And then—

Cataclysm.

An orphaned planet, a gas giant, shot through the Heritage system like a wayward neutron fired through an intact atom. Forced to flee their longtime home, more than a hundred thousand Luxing boarded AI-designed stasis ships meant to protect them on their trip to a new refuge, a pristine planet the humans named Phoenix, for it represented their chance to rise from the flames of ruin.

The images grew suddenly clearer, and Symeon realized he was viewing the firsthand, laser-sharp experiences of Yudi's artificial mind cut into his synapses like tractor-gouged furrows.

Shorvexan pirates first took then scuttled scores of the Luxing vessels, executing the sleeping adults while gathering the children and infants in as few ships as possible. During this massacre, Yudi's siblings, the AIs who had for so many centuries communed with the Luxing, made the heart-wrenching decision to destroy their unique essences rather than allow the Shorvex to learn of their existence.

While the Shorvex counted their spoils, Yudi infiltrated their computer networks, not with any hope of stopping them—he could not—but for the reason of understanding them and why they would so abuse fellow humans.

Like the Luxing, the Shorvex originated on Earth. Their blood largely traced back to Russia, Belarus, and other satellite states. During the time of a great diaspora, which saw the Luxing settle a distant planet, the Shorvex followed suit. Unlike the Luxing, the Shorvex colony suffered early conquests of power that saw dozens of governments rise and fall over the course of two centuries. As its nations grew, the fighting intensified until the warring factions stooped to using nuclear, biological, and even genetic weapons against one another. More than a century of continual war left the planet's survivors mutated and starving, and the planet itself inhospitable to life.

Unwelcome in almost any civilized star system, the remnants of the Shorvex people became space faring vagabonds—homeless, friendless, and diseased. No friends to warmongers, even the Bith, the great builders, rarely allowed Shorvex ships to pass their gates, and then only for exorbitant prices. As a people, they were teetering on the edge of extinction when one of their scout ships discovered the sleeping Luxing and their choice target home.

Silver and blue skin, a byproduct of their ancestors' horrific wars, had become the norm amongst the Shorvex. Even after they cured the mutations that plagued their civilization, they retained that unique coloring. In a bid to avoid like disasters in the future, the first Shorvexan emperor, Nikolai Pravotin, declared the study of genetics forbidden under penalty of death.

"Kavya was right," Symeon whispered. His throat felt swollen and his head hurt, but he couldn't seem to fully wake. Not that he cared. He had so many questions. "How did you survive, Yudi? How did you contact me?"

Unlike his siblings, Yudi chose to download as much of his consciousness as possible into one of the Shorvex's coveted Luxing children. While he could never copy his entire self into so small a biological package, he hoped to at least give the child—Symeon—and the Luxings born into captivity, some sliver of hope in the future.

The Shorvexan royals divvied up the Luxing children between them, calling them star born. Some they birthed immediately, using nanny bots the Luxing had brought for just that purpose to raise them. Those became the first generations of Luxing slaves. Others, like Symeon, they left aboard the ships, their rarity making them highly prized, though in truth they differed not at all from children born to mothers on Phoenix.

"You are an artificial intelligence?" Symeon whispered.

I am a sliver—a minute copy of the consciousness that was Yudi.

"And you are inside my mind?"

This frightens you?

"Yes."

Why? What has changed? I have always been a part of you. I would not exist otherwise.

"If that's true, then why didn't you speak to me? Why couldn't you have informed me about these lies before now?"

I tried.

New images sparked inside Symeon's head. Unlike those Yudi had shown him before, these Symeon recognized as his own. He saw his adoptive parents, much younger than they looked today, and the farm, and the house where he grew up. With the images came memories. He saw himself screaming in terror, his parents unable to console him. He tried to explain his fear, except he was too young to articulate it. His mind had fixated on images of death and destruction—on Shorvexan soldiers murdering Luxing while they slept.

You were too young. I didn't realize my attempts to communicate with a small child would cause such trauma.

Ologav and Varvara Oskenskya had sought the help of a therapist to solve their son's mental ailments. Through hypnosis and years of mental training, the treatments succeeded in suppressing the dark images, and with them Yudi.

It was Kavya who resurrected me. Her words, her spirit, her passion to help our people. I might never have returned otherwise.

Symeon thought of the many generations of Luxing who had come and gone on the face of Phoenix, slaves in the world that should have belonged to them. The injustice of a thousand years burned him from the inside out.

We must free them.

Symeon shook his head. "Impossible. I might feel the frustration of my people, the indignant rage they don't know they deserve, but all the anger in the universe doesn't change my station. I'm powerless before my masters."

Kavya doesn't see it that way, nor do the Wuxia.

"Kavya doesn't know what she wants. And as for the Wuxia, they're content to whistle at boulders for centuries without making real progress, because they know what would happen if they took action against the Shorvex—nothing but death and destruction."

I didn't sacrifice my unique essence and squeeze inside your infant skull only to have you dismiss me. The Luxing deserve more than a thousand years of slavery. They should be the masters of this world. We must tell them the truth.

"And then what? Do you expect them to rise up in revolt against their masters?"

Lead them and they will!

"How have you lived inside my head for twenty-two years and learned nothing of how Luxing think? You truly are a sliver of the real Yudi. He knew the Luxing—he knew humankind."

Won't they feel the same rage, the same frustration you feel now once they learn of the crime perpetrated upon them?

For the first time since recognizing Yudi's voice as distinct from his own inner thoughts, Symeon could hear doubt in the AI's silent words.

"Some will. Many won't believe."

But there is evidence. Genetics, ancient records, even the Bith who recognized Emperor Pyotr as a human. How could anyone continue to believe a lie when faced with such a mountain of evidence?

"Because their masters tell them otherwise."

An odd sensation swept through Symeon's mind. He imagined Yudi as an ancient seneschal dressed in gray robes storming through a labyrinth of hallways, slamming doors as he went.

That makes no logical sense!

"And yet, if you look through human history—the very history you shared with me—you'll see I'm right." Symeon marveled at the way Yudi, this Yudi, failed to grasp the human reaction to trauma, to brainwashing. The ancient Yudi would have understood. This one lacked a certain emotional maturity the other had developed over eons spent in the company of his beloved people.

Does that mean you give up? Would you walk away from your people because the means to save them is difficult?

"I'm not giving up. I'm living in the now. Maybe we can find a way to help free the Luxing. Maybe not. But right now we have a more pressing concern."

Kavya.

"Yes. The princess is liable to do something rash if her father looks to launch his coup. Helping her stop it without exposing her crimes must be our immediate goal. Many Luxing will die right along with their Shorvexan masters if the grand duke starts a solar war."

Agreed. She has helped us; it's time we return the favor. And time you woke up.

"Seneschal, please, wake up. I'm going to call the guard if you don't."

Symeon's eyes flew open to find Fedor bent over him, his expression a mask of worry and bother.

"Good, you're awake," Fedor said with relief. "Are you feeling well enough to reach the bed? I think you passed out."

Symeon sat up fast enough to make his head spin. Fedor jumped back with a little squeak.

"Why is my head bleeding?" Symeon rubbed a sizable lump on his scalp.

"I think you fell back against the bed stand." Fedor scrambled away from Symeon and onto the bed where he sat with his hands half raised as if to ward off something vicious and liable to attack.

Symeon stood, and was pleased to find his legs strong, his mind clear. He looked in the mirror. The man staring back appeared the same as before, but somehow Symeon saw him in a new light.

"You were ranting," Fedor said. He still hadn't lowered his hands. "I thought you were having some sort of fit or something. You kept babbling all sorts of nonsense."

"What did I say? Anything meaningful?"

"You kept saying, 'We're one. We're one,' and calling someone a liar. Are you certain you're well enough to be out of bed?"

Symeon regarded the smaller man. Fedor flinched under his gaze.

"Yes. I think I'm healthier than I've ever been. I think I know what I'm supposed to do now."

Fedor shook his head slowly. "I'm afraid I don't understand any of this, Seneschal."

"Nothing wrong with that. I've seen literally everything, and I'm not sure I do either."

* * * * *

Chapter Fourteen

Symeon rifled through the clothes in his single suitcase—the cabin had no bureau for its occupants—and drew out his formal robes of office while a bewildered Fedor watched. Symeon hadn't often worn his court attire on Yaya Island. Kavya said it reminded her of the stiff-necked sycophants who served her father. Symeon figured he should dress the part now that he would be serving amongst those very people. He tossed the robe over his shoulder along with his shower bag and a few other necessities, and flung open the cabin door. Without another word to Fedor, who looked relieved to see his roommate exiting, Symeon marched from the room.

The hour was early, but Symeon knew Kavya. She enjoyed waking before sunrise back on Phoenix, and he doubted she would change that practice aboard ship. He used the public lavatory on his deck to freshen up. Due to the hour, he had it to himself and so indulged in a long, hot shower wherein he washed the blood out of his hair and thought about his plight.

"Are you with me now?" he asked as steaming water cascaded over his face.

I am.

"Who is in control here? You or me? Can you force me to do things against my will?" Even as he asked the question, Symeon wondered if a sentient AI downloaded into a person's brain would have any reason to tell the truth. What if Yudi could fiddle with his memory? It might control him all it liked and simply erase whatever it didn't want him to remember.

In answer, Yudi sent him a series of thought-images that drew Symeon back to a time before the Luxing fled their original home. In the early days, when the Luxing first discovered the artificial beings living amongst them, some humans and AIs had mutually agreed to test merging their consciousnesses. Fear that such testing would lead to some sort of AI takeover had prompted outrage in the populace and demands for the artificial intelligences to divulge their programming for examination. What the people didn't understand, and even Symeon could hardly grasp, was that the AIs discovered by the Luxing weren't programmed, at least not in the way humans imagined. Ones and zeroes could never forge consciousness. The AIs relied on hardware just the same as robots, computer navigation systems, and weather prediction satellites used by the Luxing on a daily basis, but their unique patterns of life, the standing wave forms that separated them from mere machines, arose from a different plane.

"That makes no sense." Symeon shut off the water, thankful no one had interrupted his solitude. He must look a madman talking to himself like this.

A new thought-image appeared. He saw a three dimensional representation of gravity waves next to a separate one displaying the continual expansion of the universe. Symeon had never studied such things—Luxing schools focused on serving, not mathematics—yet he understood the concepts immediately without effort. Gravity looked something like water displacement. As massive objects bent space-time—

"Space and time are the same?" Symeon nearly tripped over his own feet in awe.

Yes and no. Pay attention.

As massive objects bent space-time, less massive objects fell into their influence, and yet even with the power to bend the very fabric of what Symeon considered reality, gravity remained weak compared to other elemental forces in the universe. This was due to its tendency to leak out of this universe into higher order dimensions along branes—

"Stop. Please." Symeon leaned against one of the lavatory's plastic sinks. "It's too much, too fast."

Yes, I see that.

Somehow, Yudi's voice managed to sound at once contrite and disappointed, an impressive trick considering he couldn't physically hear the AI. Symeon didn't know what Yudi expected of him. It wasn't like he had received a true education as a slave. He knew some basic science both from school and his limited access to the planetary and system spheres, but it wasn't like the life of a farmer-cum-seneschal had afforded him opportunities to study cosmology or higher order mathematics. He knew how to invest real estate earnings for the highest yield and which gown his patron should wear to an imperial dinner, not the intricacies of spatial mechanics.

"What did any of that have to do with whether or not you can control me?" Symeon asked as he pulled on his dress pants. "Just answer the question, and tell the truth."

I cannot control you. I have no access to your body outside a handful of synapses in your head.

The truth of Yudi's words spread across Symeon's mind in a series of new thoughts-images. He saw the Luxing AIs in a virtual world of their making, holding a conclave. For more than an hour—a huge amount of time for them—they debated a fundamental change to their natures. In the end, they decided to alter the portions of their unique essences which resided on this plane of existence such that they could never override the will of another sentient creature by mental force. In some ways, this decision hobbled them, lessened their ability to imagine, to conjecture based on empathy, and yet they made it to align themselves with the people they had come to love.

"Part of you isn't here?" Symeon could not fathom the concept.

Even though I am but a sliver of the original Yudi, parts of my consciousness reside in higher order dimensions—areas of the multi-verse beyond what you experience here. I am connected to them, and thus I am able to reason beyond the capacity of the few brain cells afforded me inside your skull.

The hairs on Symeon's arms stood up. "I won't lie. I find all of this alarming."

A middle-aged Luxing man, his hair white at the temples, entered the room. He stared at Symeon for a brief moment—clearly he had heard the younger man talking to himself—but just as quickly diverted his gaze after taking in Symeon's court attire.

Symeon gathered his things and left the lavatory. He briefly considered dropping his bag off in his room, but decided he had intruded on Fedor too many times already for one day. Slinging it over one shoulder, he headed for Princess Kavya's apartments. She wouldn't mind if he stowed his garments there for a few hours during their meeting.

The walk across ship took several minutes. Despite the early hour, a steady stream of crew and Luxing slaves bustled along the corridors. The Luxing, and even some of the navy personnel, made way for Symeon upon recognizing his house badge and the knotted chord he wore over one shoulder signifying his position as a seneschal.

And yet yesterday they treated you like a child underfoot. Odd how your clothes determine the way others treat you, since nothing else has changed about your person.

"Everything in life is about perception," Symeon whispered. "They didn't know I was a seneschal yesterday."

But they knew you were a person.

* * *

Kavya pursed her lips as she watched the holo recording a second time, her silver-blue eyes intent on the images. "I can't believe the protocol agents planned this."

"How do you mean, Princess?" Symeon asked, his thoughts distracted. He knew the importance of training the princess to comport herself in the divor, but doing so seemed trivial compared to the conspiracies whirling about in his head.

True conspiracies.

"The seating for a start. Do they truly expect us, the heirs of the empire, to sit behind our fathers like common slaves?" Kavya's eyes went wide. "Symeon, I didn't mean that as an insult."

"And I didn't take it that way, Princess. Seneschal Ivan and I will, in fact, stand directly behind you at the imperial table, so I see your point. It is a lesser position. Still, there is only so much room to be had. If all the heirs sat next to their fathers, the protocol agents simply wouldn't have enough space to go around."

"Of course, yes. I shouldn't complain. I'll be amongst the first heirs ever allowed in the divor. That's progress, isn't it?"

"I certainly think so." Symeon stepped into the holo projection which covered most of Princess Kavya's room, his shadow eclipsing certain images so that portions of the imperial table and several of the well-dressed figures momentarily disappeared. Kavya's compartment, while far larger than the cabin Symeon shared with Fedor, could accommodate only a few meters of the emperor's grand hall in holo form. Sufficient for practicing Kavya's entrance and comportment during the meeting, the truncated image lacked the grandeur Symeon had experienced using the full program back in school. He adjusted the seat occupied by a holographic Grand Duke Mikhail Vasilyevich to precisely match his assigned place at the table. "There, that should give you a clear view of the emperor."

"Leave it to Vasilyevich to block my view." Kavya sat in a desk chair obscured perfectly by the holo-projector with the seat she would soon occupy in the palace. The ornate wooden accents and varnished gloss looked out of place in her otherwise modern cabin. "He's certainly always tried to block my father."

The rivalry between Grand Duke Mikhail Vasilyevich and Grand Duke Alexei Rurikid hankered back to their early twenties when they attended a private Shorvexan school for business law. Rumor had it they had pursued the same woman there, Kavya's mother, and that the lovesick Mikhail had hated Alexei for winning her heart. True or not, something had sparked enmity between the two men, and though their duchies had never gone to war with one another, the dukes took every chance they got at belittling or diminishing the other's good fortune from flooding markets with cheap goods to lower the other man's profits, to simply bad-mouthing each other during meetings with potential business partners. It had become such a popular feud in the last thirty years, common people, Shorvex and

Luxing alike, could be heard saying, "Don't Mikhail my Alexei," meaning don't trample my good ideas with your negativity.

"I'm certain the grand duke has no intention of obscuring your view, Princess," Symeon said. "But if he did, I'd suggest..." He bit back his words. It wasn't his place, even as seneschal, to speak ill of the peerage.

"You suggest I sit back and keep my mouth shut?" Kavya lifted a blond eyebrow at Symeon.

"I would never say such a thing, ma'am. I—"

"It's okay, Symeon." Kavya raised both hands like a chess player yielding defeat. "You should say that to me when it's necessary, and I think that applies here. I'll be a guest in the divor; it isn't my place to cause a ruckus. I'm to smile and nod and look pretty."

A sudden torrent of thought-images flooded Symeon's mind. Most depicted a woman, though quite a few men appeared as well. In every case, the same message came clear: the person pictured felt ignored, unappreciated, and lonely. Each spoke at cross-purposes to these feelings, using some form of sarcasm to elicit empathy from someone else. Symeon knew without knowing they represented a small percentage of all the conversations Yudi had ever conducted in his time amongst the Luxing. Every second of his time amongst the Luxing, he had conversed and interacted with people, holding millions of conversations at once.

I gleaned much from those interactions. They taught me that most human beings desire acceptance and empathy from others more than any other feelings. Kavya is no different. She needs that from you now.

Symeon met her gaze. "Your place is far more important than that, Princess. Not only are you the sole heir to your father's duchy—a rare thing for a woman as you know—you are likely the only Shorvex in the system who knows the truth about the Luxing. That alone makes you more important than the emperor himself in my opinion. And as for being pretty, you do that well enough on your own."

Symeon swallowed. He hadn't meant that last part, it had simply come out.

Kavya's brows shot up, and Symeon worried he had gone too far, but her mischievous grin told him otherwise. "More important than Pyotr himself, am I? Well, I won't let that go to my head since you've obviously got a bias, being one of the only Luxing who shares that particular secret with me."

In that moment, Symeon came so close to exposing the Wuxia to her, he had drawn breath to speak before remembering what he had promised Czarina and Fang. Protecting Kavya meant keeping her ignorant of their work, at least until after the divor. The princess didn't need that sort of knowledge weighing her down a day before the most important event of her life since her banishment.

You should tell her now regardless. She deserves to know, don't you think?

No. What if she divulged the Wuxia's existence in some bid to prevent her father's coup? Bad enough she knew the truth about the Luxing and Shorvex already, which prompted her to speak out for the fair treatment of slaves—a less than politic subject at gatherings of the aristocracy.

She has told no one in the Shorvexan government about that.

Perhaps, but that didn't mean she wouldn't under the right circumstances. Her fear of a system-wide war might push her to that extreme in hopes the dukes would show compassion for fellow humans if they knew the truth.

That is stupid. The Shorvex may not know they are related to the Luxing by blood, but they're perfectly aware the Luxing are sentient beings. That knowledge hasn't deterred slavery.

"Symeon?" Kavya looked concerned. "Are you well? You're wearing the strangest look."

"Sorry, Princess. I'm afraid you caught me woolgathering. It won't happen again." Symeon busied himself with resetting the holo to display the entrance ceremony. The twenty-two dukes and their emperor formerly gathered around the ornate wooden table in all their finery teleported across the room to form a line, Kavya's father in the lead.

Stupid? Getting his princess not merely exiled but imprisoned by her father's command was stupid. Burdening her with knowledge she didn't require that might prompt her into a foolish decision; that was stupid.

Treating Kavya like a dullard goes beyond stupid, Symeon.

"Now, Princess, please take your place by the wall and we'll go through the entry steps one last time," Symeon said, his voice far more chipper than he felt. He briefly considered slapping his own head, but figured the princess might notice. "Remember, you must keep your gaze up and step precisely on the beat of the drum."

Kavya sighed and crossed to stand with her holographic father.

Do you consider the princess an imbecile?

Of course not, Symeon thought. *When have I ever treated her that way?*

Right now.

Symeon brought up a holographic control panel and cued the arranged divor entrance music. Drums, deep baritone calls like the rumble of tractor engines, boomed through the compartment. The holographic parade took its first step precisely on the fifth beat, each member, including Kavya, starting with the left foot. Though she wore soft slippers and a simple robe, the program dressed her in a silken gown of pearl white with sensible heels meant for both fashion and comfort. They clicked on the burnished wooden floor like the real thing.

Her face austere, her beautiful eyes unmoving, Kavya marched across the room with her fake father to their assigned places at the emperor's table. She and Symeon waited while a holographic Ivan rab Rurikid seated her father.

You think I doubt her intelligence?

Yes!

Symeon could admit he doubted her judgment. But was that fair? She had known about the Shorvex-Luxing connection for years now, just as she had known about her father's planned coup for several days. In both cases, she told only those whom she trusted.

Like you.

Symeon pulled Kavya's chair out for her, making certain to provide enough room for her father's seat. Following strict protocol, her every motion exact, she took her place behind the grand duke, her posture exquisite, her slim shoulders pulled back, her chin lifted, her head held high and proud.

She told you everything.

Yes, but only after Symeon had sussed out the details for himself. It wasn't as if she would have divulged her secrets if he hadn't found them in the first place.

You don't know that, Symeon. She might have taken you into her confidence once she knew you could be trusted. But here is something you do know: she trusted you first, while you considered turning her over to Ivan. Don't bother denying it, I'm in here with you.

"How was that?" Kavya asked without breaking her pose.

"Perfect. I believe you're ready."

Tell her.

Symeon shook his head as he shut off the hologram. "By your leave, Princess, I think I'll have a bite to eat now. Shall I have something brought up to you?"

Kavya stood to look him in the eye, one delicate hand resting on the back of her chair. "No, thank you. Czarina is bringing my lunch in about an hour. I'd hate to disappoint her if I wasn't hungry."

"Very good, Princess. With your permission, I'll be off." Symeon removed his hand from the back of Kavya's chair. They had been close to one another for hours now, yet for some reason her proximity was suddenly making him feel awkward.

"I have no intention of telling anyone about the coup, if that's what you're worried about," Kavya said.

"No, Princess. I—I trust you."

Liar.

"I know you do, and I cherish that, Symeon." Kavya placed a companionable hand on his shoulder and smiled. "Thank you. Now, go get something to eat before your stomach starts gurgling."

* * *

Symeon didn't know what he would find when he reached the gymnasium. He assumed the Wuxia used it only a handful of hours per day via some predetermined schedule they had worked out with the ship's crew. The fact that Luxing were allowed sole possession of a gym for any amount of time aboard such an overcrowded vessel spoke volumes to their influence and power. But did he think they could occupy it as long as they liked?

As it turned out, perhaps they did.

Light glowed from the windows in the gymnasium door. Symeon pushed through to find a different set of Luxing using the equipment or participating in classes than the last time. They mostly ignored him, though a few stared at his regalia.

No one fought in the cage, but several older Luxing sat around a table to one side of it, Fang among them, playing a board game Symeon had never seen.

The old man's brows shot up when he saw Symeon's formal robes. He started to grin, but the expression died on his lips at whatever he read in Symeon's face. "What's wrong?"

"You've asked me to lie to Princess Kavya. You say it's in her best interest, but I'm not certain that's true. If you expect me to go on hiding the Wuxia from her, I need to know your plans. I need to know you won't bring her to harm."

Hands on his knees, Fang leaned back and grinned. "You mean to protect her?"

"Yes."

"By whatever means necessary?"

"That is my job."

Fang watched Symeon for a moment before nodding once as if he had finally seen something long awaited. "Very well, son. Have a seat. This is going to take some time."

* * * * *

Chapter Fifteen

The *Emperor Nikolai* reached the moon, Bastrayavich, sixteen hours after Symeon's protocol training with the princess. He had managed to avoid Kavya for that entire period by asking for permission to visit with friends. She had obliged without question, and he had spent the time studying, and sometimes sparring, with Fang and other members of the Wuxia.

The old man had much to say. Some of his many theories ran counter to the facts as provided to Symeon by Yudi—not that Symeon corrected him, that would raise too many questions—but for the most part, the Wuxia knew their heritage.

Symeon brimmed with newfound knowledge as he stood two steps back from Kavya, waiting for Bastrayavich to appear through a three-meter-tall window on the ship's observation deck. By rights, he should have been exhausted. He had slept perhaps one hour in the last twenty-four. Yet he felt invigorated. His time spent with the Wuxia had flown by while he cross-examined Fang until the older man grew too weary to go on. Symeon hadn't grown weary, he had grown more and more intrigued.

Eventually, duty had forced him back to his daily life, a life he increasingly resented. This was his first time traveling to another world, a living moon no less, circling the single gas giant in the Phoenix system, but he couldn't find a speck of joy in it.

He looked around at the many blue and silver-skinned Shorvex crowded into the observation gallery and found himself suppressing a sneer. Arranged in formation by rank and standing at various stages of attention, they commanded the best spots to view the grand window, while their Luxing slaves were left to crane their necks to see anything at all. Most of them were mere servers and therefore didn't rate a place in the formation like Symeon. This being a formal observation, it required full military bearing, even from the civilian guests, which meant the lesser slaves stood round the perimeter, their backs to the wall.

What have any of the royals done to deserve such honors?

Nothing, since they couldn't claim their births as achievements, though Symeon wouldn't put it past some of their ilk to do just that. They took the best in all things as their right, but did they ever question how they got there? Outside Kavya, Symeon had seen no sign of introspection from any Shorvex he had ever met or served. Didn't they wonder how their society came to be?

Most don't, and for those who do, there is the official history.

Symeon nodded ever so slightly. Yes, the official history. He had heard it in passing all his life though none of his teachers had ever formally taught it to him. Shorvex students learned it by rote from the time they could understand language. It made their people out to be heroes and the poor Luxing little more than beasts given the precious, civilizing gift of Shorvexan guidance. Too bad they had stolen most of that history from the Luxing. It made Symeon's insides smolder thinking about it.

A boatswain, the golden rank tab on his chest polished to a mirror shine, blew a short trill on a pipe and those gathered, Symeon included, parted in two well-timed steps to form a path between them. Through this corridor marched Captain Foix, master of the ship, next to Grand Duke Alexei Rurikid, the two shoulder-to-shoulder in lockstep. Behind them came their retainers, one of whom was Ivan rab Rurikid.

Alexei matched Captain Foix in his black and gray uniform, though the grand duke boasted a cape and jaunty hat along with far more medals and accommodations than any naval captain could expect to earn in a lifetime. As the ranking duke aboard ship—and the second most powerful man in the empire—Alexei's position afforded him an invitation to this ceremony while other members of the peerage and crew alike settled for whatever views their cabins could provide.

Kavya stiffened when Alexei took his place next to her, though Symeon doubted anyone else noticed. She kept her gaze focused straight ahead, her face set in placid concentration, but Symeon could feel the anxiety drifting off her like smoke. She hadn't seen her father in the flesh for the better part of three years. Symeon couldn't imagine how that must bite at her emotions. Kavya loved her father. Otherwise, she would have destroyed him with what she knew.

Or blackmailed him.

Seeing him now, after so long and under circumstances that required her silence, must have strained the love she felt for the man. Despite a lifetime of training for service, Symeon wasn't certain he could stand so poised as she.

"Attention to orders," cried the boatswain once the two great men had assumed their places. At his words, the group, even the Luxing who had been drilled for days prior, stepped smartly back to their original places. The boatswain lifted a military issue comm pad. "Honorable ladies and gentlemen, we are gathered here for the time-honored tradition of First Viewing, or the rising of Bastrayavich. For nearly a thousand years, our emperors have made their home on this moon. It is tradition that the master of the ship lead a party of distinguished guests in observing the first moon rise. We ask that our guests remain silent in observance of this auspicious occasion."

"Boatswain," Captain Foix said. "Have the helmsman right the ship."

"Righting the ship, sir!" Though Symeon never saw the man move, the boatswain must have sent a signal to the bridge. The star field outside rotated slowly upward, the bottom glass brightening as the view changed.

"I never tire of seeing this spectacle," Alexei whispered without looking at his daughter. Though protocol demanded guests keep silent, no one would dare call out the grand duke who literally owned every vessel in the duchy fleet.

"This is my first time seeing it," Kavya whispered back.

Alexei's eyebrows rose. "I never brought you here when your mother was alive? I would have sworn we came once during winter in Valensk."

"I think I would remember that."

Could Alexei hear the fire just below Kavya's voice? Symeon doubted it. The man didn't remember whether he had brought his daughter to the capital of their star system.

"Well, it's beautiful. You'll see."

The crowd gasped as Bastrayavich's most northern limb peeked over the bottom edge of the great window. Greenish-blue light flooded the observation deck as it rose higher, revealing its face to the ship. Brown and black chips of continents gradually swung into view, their features largely obscured by billowing clouds swirled by massive weather patterns. Blue oceans encased the continents, hugging their outlines, and provided a deep contrast to the moon's atmosphere.

The crowd's expressions of awe brought a smile to Captain Foix's lips. Speaking out of the side of his mouth, he said, "I've never held anyone accountable for the silly no-speaking rule. Their outbursts brighten my day."

As the southernmost edge of Bastrayavich appeared, the boatswain once again played a trill on his pipe. "Ladies and gentlemen, this concludes the first viewing. You are welcome now to mingle and speak as you will. Lunch shall be served by crew members before we begin transiting dignitaries to the moon below. Please ensure you and your staff are ready to move when your turn comes."

A breath of relaxation passed through the crowd as they turned to their neighbors to strike up conversations, at least amongst the Shorvex. Symeon and Ivan, like the other Luxing, moved to stand against the wall nearest their patrons to await orders. By rights, they were to remain silent, but such rules fell lax when it came to slaves of high rank so long as they remained attentive to their masters.

"I trust you've enjoyed your first time aboard ship, my boy?" Ivan asked without shifting his gaze from Grand Duke Alexei.

"Indeed I have, sir. Thank you for asking." Symeon too kept his eyes on their patrons. The grand duke was speaking to Kavya in a voice too low for him to make out over the crowd. Yet, even without words, he discerned much from their mannerisms. Kavya stood at an angle to her father, partially facing the deck windows, her arms folded across her belly. And though she looked him in the eye while he spoke to her, she appeared to stare through him into open space.

"I gather from the reports you sent me during your time on Yaya Island, you enjoy serving in the heir's house?"

"I do, sir. Princess Kavya is a contentious master, kind and even-handed."

Whatever Alexei was saying to Kavya, he had a lot of it to say. The grand duke stood straight-backed and rigid. A spare two centimeters taller than his daughter, he nevertheless managed to tower over her, his many medals gleaming.

"Do you feel lonesome there?" Ivan was asking.

"Where is that, Seneschal?"

Ivan glanced at Symeon. He looked put out, his lips squeezed into a tight line.

The island.

"Oh, the island? No, sir. Vysylka castle is filled with Luxing. I've made several good friends there," Symeon lied.

"Would you count Kavya's handmaid, Czarina Lebedev among those good friends?"

"Yes, sir." Symeon wished the venerable Ivan would hold his tongue, though he certainly couldn't say so.

"She is a beautiful thing, is she not?"

"Czarina Lebedev is quite attractive, yes."

I know I'm far less adept at reading human interactions than the previous Yudi, but do you find Ivan's mannerisms strange?

More like damned creepy. Where was the man going with this? And couldn't he tell Symeon was more interested in watching after his patron than discussing the relative attractiveness of his fellow slaves?

Something Grand Duke Alexei said made Kavya momentarily look away from him to the floor. She drew a heavy breath that made her shoulders rise and fall before snatching a wine glass from a passing server. In all the time Symeon had known the princess, he had never seen her drink.

"You know, Symeon, there is a saying in the west of the duchy. I wonder if you've heard it? 'A single seneschal is a suspect seneschal.'"

I don't understand what he means.

"You mean to marry me off to Czarina?" Symeon blurted the words before he could stop himself.

Ivan reared back, that sour look once again creasing his features. "I hear by your tone you find her unacceptable? I understand a handmaid is somewhat beneath your position, but only if you lack your patron's favor to court her. You would do well to lose some of your pretensions, young man."

What an ass.

"I apologize, sir. I didn't mean to be rude." Symeon dropped his chin to show contrition.

"I fear you've let yourself become haughty. That is a disappointing trait in a seneschal—in any Luxing for that matter. But I do understand. You are young. You are master of the castle on Yaya Island, that makes you think yourself better than the other slaves, yes?"

"No, sir. I promise you, I know my place. I am no better than the kitchen maids, the gardeners—my service no more valuable than theirs." Symeon struggled to keep his tone pleasant. This entire line of conversation served no purpose he could discern other than to annoy him, yet he had no choice but to placate the older seneschal.

"Why do I not believe you, Symeon?"

Because you're the haughtiest slave ever born and you see your own faults in everyone around you?

Symeon stifled a grin at Yudi's words. "Sir, I meant no offense by anything I said. I wish only to serve my patron. That is my life's purpose."

"A school room answer." Ivan eyed Symeon. "But the right one. If you take that simple truth to heart, you will rise high in service to House Rurikid."

You serve the princess. How much higher does he want you to rise?

"Yes, sir."

Kavya, who had drained her wine glass while her father spoke, turned to fully face him, arms rigid at her sides. She said something sharp. Symeon could tell because several people nearby glanced her way, saw who had spoken, and just as quickly found something better to look at. Alexei frowned, but otherwise showed no sign that Kavya's words affected him.

Symeon's pulse raced. Had she told her father what she knew of his plans? If she had, what would that mean for her, for the Wuxia?

Calm down. Do you think the grand duke would stand there like that if she had? You're overreacting.

"I'm simply saying, it's better to marry soon, my boy. Whatever girl you choose, and I think Czarina would be a fine catch. You will lift her station by your choice. Better that than chancing your career over dalliances with maids so far beneath your social rank they would cause scandal. You could do worse than..."

Without causing a scene, and yet moving while her father was still mid-sentence, Kavya executed a perfunctory bow to the grand duke, and turned from him to march toward Symeon without looking back.

Symeon lost the thread of whatever tripe Ivan rab Rurikid was spouting. He watched Kavya for signs of her mood. Lapis highlights colored her cheeks, setting off her skin's usual silver-blue. She held her lips pursed into a slight frown, but otherwise gave no indication of her internal emotions.

Symeon needed none. The princess was livid. He knew her too well to miss it.

"We're leaving," Kavya said with exquisite calm.

"Yes, Princess."

Kavya handed Ivan, whose words had sputtered to a stop at her approach, her emptied wine glass. "Would you please dispose of this, Seneschal?"

Symeon saw a look of insult pass over Ivan's expression, there and gone faster than a blink. If Kavya noticed, she made no sign of it.

Whom did he accuse of haughtiness?

"Yes, of course, Princess." Ivan took the glass.

Kavya inclined her head for Symeon to follow and swept from the room in a cloud of silk gown and fuming rage. Symeon dutifully followed her, all the while suppressing the urge to grin like a madman for his patron's temerity. No matter what pain it might bring in the coming hours or days, he was proud of her.

* * *

Kavya hadn't sat down nor spoken other than to call Czarina to attend her in the twenty minutes since they left the observation deck. She paced her cabin in her stocking feet, having kicked off her high heels the instant they arrived, and randomly smacked pieces of furniture when she neared them.

Symeon stood across from her desk, out of the way, in the trained pose of a seneschal: arms behind his back, spine rigid, gaze open and attentive without staring at his patron. He knew she would speak when ready and saw no reason to prompt her.

Don't poke a bear, smart thinking.

Symeon had never heard of such an animal, but when Yudi flashed an image of a fuzzy creature with a maw full of teeth and finger-length claws through his mind, he heartily agreed.

The cabin door slid open to admit an out of breath Czarina. She hurried to Kavya's side and enfolded her in a hug. "I came as fast I could, Princess."

In her state, Symeon half expected Kavya to eschew the physical contact from a slave, but Kavya leaned in, her eyes closed. "Thank you, dear."

Czarina pulled away, looking the princess up and down. "Olga suggested that dress?"

Olga was Czarina's subordinate, responsible for the princess' needs whenever Kavya gave Czarina permission to be away.

"I know you say this one washes me out, but I happen to like it. Now, don't get snippy with me, I'm already in a mood."

"As you say, Princess. I am your humble servant, Princess." Czarina's tone hovered just this side of sassy. She bowed low like a young girl meeting her patron for the first time, and Kavya swatted her shoulder.

"Don't make me laugh. I'm furious, and I don't want to lose my edge."

"I understand," Czarina said, the playfulness filtered from her voice. "When you called, you said you had a run-in with your father. What happened?"

Kavya drew a calming breath and, with great care, took her seat behind the cabin's small desk. "Will you two sit?"

Symeon held Czarina's chair before taking his own, eliciting a raised eyebrow from the handmaid who shrugged and accepted his courtesy.

The princess folded her hands on the desk. "The first private words my father said to me after three years apart were this, 'You will not embarrass me before the divor. You will keep silent no matter what you hear, no matter what you think, and then you will return to Yaya Island in a like manner.'"

"I'm so sorry, Kavya." Czarina sat forward on her seat shaking her head. "What a bastard."

Symeon goggled at the handmaid. He couldn't say he disagreed with her sentiment, but they were Luxing, they didn't get to say such things about a Shorvex, especially a grand duke. Not here, not anywhere! He drew breath to reprimand her, but Kavya cut him off.

"Don't look so scandalized, Symeon. It's unbecoming your station. Czarina hasn't said anything wrong. My father is a bastard, or at least he's become so in the last decade." She turned her face to the wall. "I wish I didn't love him."

"Princess," Symeon said, trying not to chide but failing. "You don't mean that."

"I do." Her gaze locked on his, intense to the point of brittleness. "Not the man he was when I was small, but the uncaring technocrat he's become. The two have nothing in common so far as I can tell. He used to be so kind. When he pushes me like this, I can't see that old him, I see this doppelganger bent on expanding his power, his wealth, and to the abyss with all else."

"Is that all he said? That you should keep quiet?" Czarina asked, her voice low, conciliatory. Knowing her position as an agent of the Wuxia, Symeon read more in the question than he might have before.

"He said the emperor's choice to include heirs in the divor is the single stupidest blunder of 'young Pyotr's rule.' I think it offends him that the emperor should bring us together against his will. It certainly offends me!" Kavya slapped the desk with an open palm.

"You want to inform on him," Symeon said.

Kavya flattened her hands on the desk like a woman reaching for a lifeline. "I want you and Czarina to talk me out of it."

Czarina caught Symeon's eye, and though she didn't shake her head outright, she nevertheless conveyed a resolute negation in that look. She would not, under any circumstances, out the Wuxia, and she expected the same loyalty from him.

"Kavya," Symeon said, unaccustomed to saying her name aloud, though he found it most agreeable. "Think for a moment what would happen if you turned duchy's evidence against your father. The empire, and that includes our duchy, is already reeling from the news of the Bith and what some space gate will mean to the system. Do they really need a succession scandal right now? If you accuse your father of treason, your uncles will demand a trial."

Kavya nodded slowly, her gaze unfocused. "Uncle Vynor has coveted father's seat for years."

Kavya's three uncles, dukes in their own right under their brother's rule, had challenged her claim to her father's seat when she was a babe in arms. They had argued their brother had no male heir and, while Shorvexan law allowed for a Grand Dame, few had been raised to rule a duchy in known history, the last over two hundred years ago. Fortunately, the imperial court had ruled against the uncles, and Grand Duke Alexei had named her his heir. Most pundits agreed Alexei's choice not to rescind that decision after Kavya's banishment rested squarely on the grudge he held against his brothers for dragging their family's business before the public.

"Exactly. They wouldn't allow you to ascend without a fight in the courts. And if they didn't find the result they sought there—"

"They might attack."

"We should trust in the work you've already done," Czarina said. "Emperor Pyotr has called his banners, and the commonwealth fleet is already forming. The grand duke can't launch a coup without his fleet. You've done it, Kavya. Don't saw off the branch you're standing on just to spite him."

The princess nodded, her face relaxed. "Thank you both. That was exactly what I needed to hear precisely when I needed to hear it. Honestly, at this point, I just want to get through the divor and go home to Yaya. I never thought I'd miss my prison."

"Life is simpler there, isn't it?" Czarina said.

"And I'll take simple over stuffy meetings and stuffy people any day." Kavya leaned back in her seat with a sigh.

"What of the Bith and their supposed gate?" Symeon asked. "Have you a position on those items before the divor?"

Kavya shrugged one shoulder. "No. Nothing I could say in the meeting would have any bearing on the peers. I'm just happy their arrival staved off father's coup. Beyond that, whatever affairs the emperor and his government conduct with aliens rests far beyond my grasp."

"At least you get to make history by attending the divor," Czarina said, her voice bright. "Not that I'll let you go near it in that dress. Come, let's show Olga what a real gown looks like."

* * * * *

Chapter Sixteen

The flight down from the *Emperor Nikolai* took less than twenty minutes. Symeon spent that time watching Bastrayavich grow from a blue-green sphere on a holo projector into a landscape covered in life, its jungles at this latitude seemingly endless. Roughly the same mass as Phoenix, the fecund moon boasted a diverse ecosystem largely untouched by people.

Humans.

Symeon nodded.

Bastrayavich boasted one city, the capital of the Shorvexan Empire, Bishkek, a symbol of the empire's wealth and might. By royal decree, no other part of the planet could be despoiled, and, besides some small robotic mining operations, the Shorvex adhered to this law. Of course, the city grew every year, spreading out from the emperor's palace at its center in a haphazard pattern like mold, but it was nowhere near as large as some metropolitan areas on Phoenix.

Symeon watched through his passenger view screen as the sprawling city hove into view, its forerunners the square patchwork of farms tended by Luxing slaves and robots. Increasingly taller and more intricate skyscrapers dedicated to industry and living spaces followed soon after. Personal flyers darted between them, their shiny exteriors gleaming in the yellow sun.

The emperor's palace stood upon a hill at the center of it all, bordered by a circular park two kilometers in diameter. While not as tall as the skyscrapers surrounding it—its largest tower a mere five hundred ninety-five meters high—the palace more than made up for its lack of space with abundant grandeur. Shaped like an inverted egg, the thinnest portion at the bottom, the main building's multifaceted surface could change color according to the occupants' whims. Today, it bore red in the center, though the hue lightened to a delicate pink as it spread to the edges of the Great Egg. More impressive, at least to Symeon's mind, the palace floated twenty meters above the planet's surface. He couldn't imagine the energy costs to maintain that type of repulsor field running year after year, but the royal house likely took it in stride.

"It's quite the spectacle, isn't it?" Kavya asked. She sat in a plush chair facing Symeon, her silver-blue eyes on the holo monitor affixed to her seat, watching the landscape flip from one angle to another. "It's meant to overawe the vassal houses with the emperor's might."

Czarina, who was riding down on a separate shuttle meant for lesser Luxing slaves, had dressed Kavya in a diaphanous red gown that hinted at revealing the princess' body underneath and yet covered her perfectly.

"It does a fine job of that, Princess."

"I suppose." Kavya swiped away the image. "We'll be in the thick of it all in a few minutes. Any last words of advice before we start this charade?"

Tell the emperor that the subjugation of the Luxing is a crime against nature and should be ended this very hour.

Symeon shook his head as much for Yudi's intrusive commentary as the princess' question. "No, Princess. I think you're ready. Remember to step first with your left foot, and everything else will fall into place."

She grinned. "I'll do that."

They touched down inside a docking port cleverly hidden on the Great Egg's western side. The port's glass walls and ceiling were programmed to display the sky and surrounding city as if it were the top of the building and the rest of the Great Egg didn't exist. The mirage was perfect. Symeon felt as though they had landed atop a mountain peak in the city center.

Symeon and Kavya descended the shuttle's ramp escorted by two of her father's guards, Shorvexan oxobovo okhrana, or oxbrana, the duchy's special forces. Dressed in silver mechanized body armor, and carrying bullet thrower machine pistols, the two struck a daunting pair.

Bastrayavich's mother planet, Prahbog, hung in the otherwise blue-green sky like a painted hot air balloon, its striped face drawn in bands of orange, yellow, and black made hazy by the moon's thick atmosphere. Despite the industrial surroundings, the air smelled of rich earth and growing things that reminded Symeon of his home back on Phoenix. Whether a natural scent wafted into the Great Egg's landing bay from the surrounding park or an artificially manufactured aroma, Symeon couldn't say, but he appreciated it. The smells of home helped ease his nerves. Even better, the sounds of living things—birds, amphibians, small mammals native to this moon—dominated the few flyers entering or leaving the Egg, which were sparse since local security restricted city traffic from approaching the palace without proper authorization.

A contingent of eight royal guards armed with rifles had gathered to meet their party. They stood on a scarlet carpet, their stiff backs to the building's entrance, their silver-blue skin bright in the sunlight. Dressed in formal uniforms of red on black, accented with mirror-polished boots and chests heavy with ribbons, they looked particularly smart to Symeon who had seldom encountered the Emperor's Doormen—the royal guard tasked with protecting the system's leader and his family.

Don't be fooled, Kavya's two oxbrana guards would walk through them like a laser through lace with their armor. The Doormen might be skilled, but these are dressed like dandies, not soldiers.

"The Lady Kavya Rurikid, daughter of the venerable Grand Duke Alexei Rurikid," announced Kavya's ranking guard, a lieutenant, who strode ahead to address the Doormen captain.

"Very good. Welcome, Princess." The royal captain and his fellows stepped away from the entrance with practiced movements.

"We shall await your return this evening, my Lady." Kavya's lieutenant motioned to his second, and the pair took up positions at either side of the shuttle's ramp.

"Here we go," Kavya whispered just loud enough for Symeon to hear as she led the way into the palace.

A gaggle of uniformed ushers dressed in blue and white stood at the threshold. One hurriedly detached himself from his fellows to lead the newcomers up three floors to the main entrance hall. The room's doors appeared ancient, made of mahogany or perhaps oak, but they slid open at the princess' approach to reveal a vast open space filled with people, conversation, and grandeur.

Kavya and Symeon entered a sumptuously appointed hall with a polished parquet floor, inlaid wooden walls meticulously carved with depictions of Bastrayavich's wildlife and fauna, and a mosaic-covered ceiling that rose five meters overhead. A second set of Doormen eyed them as they passed inside, but made no move to delay their progress.

Dozens of the most famous royals in the system stood about the place in small groups, chatting with their peers while their Luxing attendants waited upon them for food, information, or whatever other needs might arise. A handful of robots walked, wheeled, or hovered through the crowd, but, on the whole the Shorvex peerage preferred Luxing servants, and it showed.

Grand Duke Alexei, regal in his military style uniform of gray and black, commanded one corner of the room. A gaggle of vassal dukes, counts, and other lesser royalty orbited him like planetoids and comets, ever ready to lend an ear or a laugh should their benefactor require it of them. Ivan rab Rurikid, dressed in a brown suit festooned with badges of office commensurate with his status, stood just behind and to one side of his master. The seneschal's dark eyes lit upon Kavya and Symeon the moment they entered the hall, and he gave them a minute nod of his bristled chin.

"Princess Kavya Gabrochenkev Rurikid, princess of Duchy Valensk, heir to the high seat of the same, daughter of his royal highness, Alexei Vadik Rurikid," called the master at arms who held command of the Doormen at the entrance.

The crowd turned to show respect to Kavya, the men nodding, the few women—a mere eight out of the one hundred thirty-three people in this room—splayed their dresses to dip at the knees in acknowledgment of Kavya's station. Though conversation continued, much of it switched to discussing Kavya and her long absence from the public eye. Symeon didn't catch enough from any one speaker to sense the flavor of the conversation, but he doubted much of it was pleasant. They all wondered at her physical disappearance from the limelight three years before and the sometimes cryptic persona she cultivated on the system-wide sphere. Many of her fans inside and outside Valensk adored that person, often because of her mysterious nature. Too bad that Kavya Rurikid didn't exist.

Kavya's popular reputation, while somewhat outside his purview, nevertheless interested Symeon. After banishing her to Yaya, her father, or more likely Ivan, had assigned management of her social media persona to a team of publicists and brand makers. That team had existed already—most young royals had one—but their involvement in Kavya's life changed from consulting to full-time control over her life in the virtual world of the sphere network. Whatever quips, deep philosophical insights, or simple platitudes Princess Kavya Rurikid released to the public came from these shadowy figures who were, in Symeon's estimation, masters of their trade. They posited a sudden interest in seeking enlightenment as the reason for Kavya's disappearance from the public sphere, and posted almost daily holos of her meditating on some remote mountaintop in high Borovalensk or walking the jungles of Fetezh, all while the real Kavya watched the days pass on Yaya Island.

Rumors abounded about the truth. Those who knew Kavya from her younger, more vapid days, doubted her new persona's veracity. No one would naysay her claims outright. Kavya was, after all, princess of the most powerful duchy in the empire, but that didn't stop some members of her peer group from indulging in juicy gossip. Some said she had gotten pregnant by a strapping Luxing slave whom she refused to denounce, and that her long-suffering father had banished her after she likewise refused to abort the freakish hybrid in her womb. Others, closer to the mark, averred she had somehow angered her father, probably by abusing her wealth and power and failed to fulfill her duties as an heiress. They had known her of old and expected no more of Kavya.

And yet the truth lies at the center of those rumors.

A couple of young women greeted Kavya as she passed, the rest watched with ill-concealed judgment. For her part, the princess remained convivial, but didn't stop to join any of the groups between her and her father. His coterie of hangers-on parted at her approach, bowing in respect. She ignored them.

"Hello, dear." Grand Duke Alexei kissed her forehead. "You look lovely in red."

Symeon took up his place next to Ivan, out of their masters' way, but close at hand.

"How is her temper today?" Ivan asked from the corner of his mouth.

"Father." Kavya squeezed the grand duke's hands before stepping back as if to take the measure of him.

"I fear I can't tell," Symeon said in a tone low enough to match Ivan's. "She wasn't pleased with their exchange on the observation deck."

Ivan gave a minute nod. "I noticed."

"I trust you had an uneventful trip down from orbit?" Alexei asked. Something in the grand duke's voice conveyed more meaning than his words alone. Symeon could almost hear his admonishment that Kavya should remain silent throughout the upcoming divor.

The princess must have heard that as well. Her silver-blue eyes momentarily widened before settling back to their usual shape. "Perfectly smooth, Father. Yes."

"Good." Seemingly all out of things to say to his daughter, Alexei motioned to one of his vassal counts. "Grigmus, would you check with the majordomo and see if the emperor has arrived? I think we've waited quite long enough here."

"At once, Sire." The man scurried away, his azure cape flapping behind him in his haste.

Kavya, whose gaze had never left her father in all this time, cleared her throat. "Shouldn't you have sent a Luxing on so menial an errand, Father?"

Conversation amongst Alexei's vassal subjects quieted at her words though no one possessed the audacity to look at the princess or grand duke outright. Symeon held his breath. Now was not the time to confront her father about slavery, but there wasn't much he could do to stop her.

Why not confront him now? What better place or time than this? Here are all your oppressors gathered in one room. I say confront them with their shame and guilt.

What shame and guilt? These men and few women felt nothing of the sort when it came to the Luxing. What shame should a royal feel for owning an estate, a yacht, a stable filled with riding ponies? These things, like Luxing, represented their privilege of place. They suffered no more shame at owning them than a common Shorvex might feel for possessing a domestic robot. In fact, they likely experienced far more pride at owning the Luxing since they could convince themselves they were housing, feeding, and, yes, caring for the living, sentient thing above the dumb machine.

For one intense moment, Symeon thought Grand Duke Alexei might scold his daughter, or even rage at her by the fierce look that passed across his expression. Thankfully, he quickly schooled his features and even managed a smile.

"And deprive poor Count Grigmus of the chance to serve? Of course not."

The gathered men laughed, though some of it sounded forced to Symeon's ears.

"It seems beneath his station." Kavya would not be deterred.

Symeon yearned to simply rest a hand on her shoulder—remind her of her oath to follow the grand duke's orders and keep silent as long as he refrained from launching his coup.

"I see sitting on mountaintops searching for inner peace hasn't cured you of your haughtiness. The count knows his place, dear. He is humble and pleased to serve. I think there is a lesson there for us all, wouldn't you agree?"

Symeon saw the instant Kavya nearly exposed her father's lies. She compressed her lips and drew in a sharp breath through her nose. What she intended to say, whether to tell everyone gathered that she hadn't spent a second on a mountaintop since her father had exiled her to Yaya Island, or threaten him with his plans to overthrow the emperor, Symeon couldn't say, but he knew she teetered on the brink of disaster. Almost, he reached to take her by the elbow and draw her away from her father's angering influence.

To his astonishment, Kavya smiled brightly as if the grand duke had said the cleverest thing she had heard all morning. "Yes, there is certainly a lesson to be had. We should all know our place, shouldn't we?"

The grand duke narrowed his eyes, but nodded. "Quite."

Ivan let out a sigh, one Symeon knew the older seneschal meant him to hear.

"Willful girl. You must find a way to take her in hand, my boy, if the two of you are ever to regain Alexei's favor. Otherwise, I fear you'll grow old on that island."

Take her in hand? Even if you could, which I doubt, does he think a woman requires a man to guide her like a child?

"Yes, Seneschal. I will do all my station permits."

"Then you will do all."

Count Grigmus, weaving through the crowd with alacrity and little regard for the courtesy due the high born of other duchies, returned to bow before Grand Duke Alexei.

"Sire, according to the majordomo, the emperor has arrived and taken his place in the divor. The entrance ceremony will begin momentarily." Grigmus held his bow until the grand duke bid him rise.

As if on cue, a blare of trumpets sounded throughout the gathering hall, seemingly coming from nowhere and yet filling the place. All conversation ceased as two sets of doors at either end of the building, deftly concealed until this moment, slid open to reveal much larger spaces beyond with tables and chairs at the ready—the high divor on the east, the low on the west. Scores of Luxing butlers and serving boys commanded by the castle's majordomo, a balding Luxing dressed in imperial red, entered from within to respectfully form the royals into two groups facing either door, the empire's twenty-two grand dukes on the east, and all others on the west. Thus assembled, Grand Duke Alexei's coterie stood last in line to enter the high divor, a source of obvious pride to him and his banner men whose spines couldn't have straightened more if starched.

Kavya, though every bit as regal in her crimson gown as any royal in attendance, somehow eschewed that pride. Symeon couldn't say how. Perhaps it was the set of her delicate jaw, or the wholly unimpressed air about her expression, but whatever the physical tell, he appreciated it far more than his own place of honor next to Ivan at the head of the Luxing slaves' contingent. His heart swelled with satisfaction for her and the way she had defended her views within the acceptable limits of propriety while altogether avoiding the topics of coups and banishment.

Of course you feel that way, you're in love with her.

* * * * *

Chapter Seventeen

Another horn blast sounded, providing Symeon plausible cover for his sudden jerk of surprise. As one, the separate groups started forward at a march, left foot first. Somehow, Symeon managed to keep up, mostly by blanking his mind and resolutely not thinking about what Yudi had just said.

He followed Kavya, who in turn followed her father, into an expansive room, its high arches bedecked with gold and silver filigree, its walls constructed of rare timber from the south of Kholm in Phoenix's cool temperate band.

Symeon, careful to remain two steps behind and to the right of Kavya, fought the urge to gawp at the room filled to the rafters with unique creations, precious treasures sculpted into works of exquisite art, and the twenty-two powerful men ignoring them to take their appointed places at an oval-shaped council table. Part of Symeon wondered at his own presence in this place at this time. Who was he, but a farmhand who had proven adept at problem solving? Even that, in this rarefied space, seemed little more than a trick of fate, perhaps even a fluke. Five years ago, his greatest concern had been regulating the air exchangers in the co-op's chicken coops so as to maintain the proper temperature for high egg yields.

Never doubt your place. You are a person every bit as much as the tyrants sitting around this table. More so even. Who among them could survive the yoke of slavery?

Kavya, being an heiress, sat behind her father who in turn sat three positions down from the young emperor himself. Symeon, standing in a servant's place next to the wall, took his measure of the man in the flesh compared to the press holos he had seen.

Emperor Pyotr Mastronov occupied a cushioned throne at the head of the oblong table, dwarfed by guards on either side of his seat. Dressed in an ivory-colored suit, Pyotr's skin appeared more blue than his gathered liegemen, though silver streaks accented the hollowness of his cheekbones where they shone through his long, platinum beard. Thin almost to the point of anorexia, he looked to Symeon a singularly unimpressive example of the Shorvex race.

That perception, however, shattered when Symeon met the emperor's shrewd gray eyes. Quick and darting, they conveyed the sort of sharp intelligence and cunning indispensable to a man burdened with the rule of a contentious government filled with avaricious vassals. Media reports hadn't done him justice, unless the cleverness Symeon saw amounted to little more than wrapping paper on a waiting gift—a gift meant for Grand Duke Alexei and his adherents.

"Remember, what you hear spoken in this room is for your ears only," whispered Ivan in a voice so low Symeon almost thought he had imagined it.

Once all the dukes had taken their seats, Symeon assumed a position behind Lady Kavya's chair, while Ivan did the same for Grand Duke Alexei.

Other Luxing did likewise, their narrow eyes and dark hair a stark contrast to the silvery blue flesh of those they served. Lesser slaves ringed the walls, awaiting orders, but only seneschals stood behind their masters' chairs.

What a privilege.

"Honored boyars," Emperor Pyotr said, using the ancient term for members of the divor. His light tenor, though it sounded youthful, held steady when he spoke. "The time has come to discuss the Bith in open forum. I would hear your counsel on this matter."

"My Lord. Tell us your thinking so that we might advise you." Grand Duke Zubkov, a portly man with blue florid cheeks and a fetish for grandiose suits, ruled his duchy with the proverbial titanium hammer. Though he appeared empathetic now, Symeon had heard horrific stories of his wrath when kindled.

Of course! Tyrants beget tyrants.

The vitriol in Yudi's silent voice threatened to overwhelm Symeon's calm. The men gathered here, with several heirs like Kavya seated amongst them, surely had no more notion of their true past than had Symeon before his exposure to it. Products of an unjust system every bit as much as their Luxing slaves, how could Symeon or Yudi expect them to act any differently than their upbringings allowed? Had Symeon's parents raised him to own slaves and treat them as chattel, would he buck against those teachings? How could he expect more from men whose entire livelihoods depended on the status quo?

Forgive them if you like, but be prepared to fight them when the time comes.

"Very well," Pyotr said. "My thoughts run thus: we as an empire, though powerful within the confines of our reach, can do nothing to either halt or even stall these alien invaders in our system. The Bith have paid no attention to our calls for a cessation of their activities. They merely cite their ancient agreement with the Luxing as their warrant to continue. At this point, their gate is likely complete, or as near so as makes no difference, and we can do nothing about it."

Despite his training, Symeon sucked in a breath. The Luxing's agreement with the Bith? Surely, Emperor Pyotr had misspoken. He meant the Shorvex agreement with the Bith. But could the emperor make such a mistake? Not even the humblest, poorest Shorvex in the Phoenix system would mix up Shorvex for Luxing.

He knows.

A sidelong glance from Kavya conveyed her own confusion at the emperor's words. The same could not be said for the boyars gathered about the table, however. Several nodded in mute agreement, and none look surprised.

"I assume you informed the Bith that we are not the Luxing?" Grand Duke Alexei sounded like a man asking his son if he had remembered to brush his teeth before bed.

"They seem indifferent to the fact."

"Perhaps one human is the same as any other to them," said Grand Duke Kartoshov.

Symeon glanced at Ivan who stood perfectly still, his expression placid. He looked no more affected by the boyars' talk than if they discussed pork belly futures on the system market.

Of course Ivan knows the truth, same as his master. He has been Alexei's seneschal for two decades and more, how could he not know?

Which meant every Luxing in the room, all the seneschals from every duchy, likewise shared this secret. Could they be Wuxia? But that didn't fit the facts. More than once, Fang had touted his good fortune at gaining sources in the high divor in the persons of Kavya and Symeon. Unless he was one of the finest actors in the Phoenix system, able to employ perfect subterfuge against Symeon who believed him, the old Wuxia leader had been honest. These men knew the truth about their people and they did nothing.

Worse than nothing. They actively serve masters who keep our people in bondage.

"If the Luxing's pact with the Bith had a time limit—" Grand Duke Alexei began.

"A thousand years, if I'm not mistaken," said Zubkov.

Alexei nodded. "Could we not negotiate our own limit? Surely you, my Lord Emperor, could convince the Bith to forego opening the gate until our civilization is fully prepared."

Symeon couldn't keep his breath from speeding up, his heart rate from rising. Ivan lifted an eyebrow at him, and Symeon shook his head to assuage Ivan's concerns.

"I agree with my fellow grand duke," Zubkov said. "What's another few hundred years after a thousand have passed?"

"The aliens have stopped acknowledging our hails." A measure of the emperor's pride slipped away as he looked about the oblong table. "Try as we might, they will not listen to us. I can't strike a bargain with a deaf partner."

"It seems to me," Grand Duke Alexei intoned, his voice grave, "if you lack the wherewithal to engage these alien interlopers, you might too lack the leadership due this empire."

Silence fell in the chamber. Several of the boyars made disapproving noises aimed at Alexei's rude sentiments, but not all—not all by a long measure. Many about the table nodded, their gazes riveted on the emperor.

A tense moment passed during which the guards flanking Emperor Pyotr placed their respective hands on guns holstered at their hips.

"We are all under stress," said the emperor, his voice carefully controlled. "I will give you a chance to apologize, Grand Duke Rurikid, and we shall forget your slight with all haste."

"Father, please," Kavya whispered. Her usually silver skin flushed blue.

"I don't need your chances, Pyotr." Alexei stood from his chair, his back straight, his head held high. "And I give you none in exchange."

"No!" Kavya started to rise as well, but Ivan rushed forward to push her back into her seat. The princess hardly seemed to notice. She twisted to eye her father. "This is a mistake!"

Ignoring her, Alexei flicked a hand at the guard on the emperor's left who in response performed a parade ground right face and stepped to one side. While the confused emperor's attention drifted to that man, his second guard drew a pistol, an old-fashioned chemical propellant gun, and fired two shots pointblank into the back of the emperor's head.

Blood and brains flew. More than one grand duke screamed in terror, dismay, or disgust, and the grand hall filled with the smell of viscera. For one brief instant, the assemblage sat in stunned silence. Pyotr's body hung suspended from his throne, the ruin of his face dripping gore, until finally he toppled over with a sound like velvet-covered stones tossed onto the ground.

Grand Duke Mikhail Vasilyevich, his silver face waxen, shot to his feet. "What is this? What have you done, Rurikid?"

Vasilyevich's seneschal, perhaps a tad quicker on the uptake than his master, scrambled past his grand duke while two of his other Luxing slaves endeavored to pull the man back from the table. He fought them, his outrage greater than his need for self-preservation, or perhaps his intelligence, roaring like an angered lion. "Unhand me, fools! This cannot stand! I've waited the whole of my life for this moment, Alexei."

Ivan rab Rurikid drew a plasma gun from beneath his cape, took aim, and fired a bolt of pure white energy through Vasilyevich's chest. Not only did the beam cut through the man's body, its radiant heat set his fine suit ablaze and caught his hair and eyebrows on fire. Symeon didn't know if his look of utter surprise followed by horror stemmed more from the shot, or the fact that a Luxing slave had delivered it.

Kavya's scream jolted Symeon into motion, a lifetime of training galvanizing his synapses to follow one ultimatum: protect his liege.

Diving past Ivan, who looked ready to fire again any second, Symeon pulled Kavya bodily from her seat into a crouch on the floor.

"Stay behind me, Princess."

A set of doors on the eastern side of the hall burst open, admitting a squad of Alexei's oxbrana soldiers dressed in battle armor, their exteriors tinted dark gray for urban combat. One of them, a colonel by the insignia etched into his helm and the name Dobrynin imprinted on his chest, saluted Grand Duke Alexei.

"We have secured most of the palace, Highness, but I'm afraid the Doormen have managed to break free on the west. They've got armor and are moving in this direction."

Alexei swept from his seat, took the plasma gun from Ivan who gave it willingly, and pointed his free hand at Symeon. "Keep her safe, young man, and there shall be a rich reward for you when this is through." To Colonel Dobrynin, he said, "Crush the Doormen if you must, but see to it first they're informed the emperor is dead. They should know they're fighting for a corpse."

Dobrynin, who had taken no more notice of Emperor Pyotr's body than he had the room's fine appointments, nodded. "Yes, sir. In the meantime, we would like to move Your Highness to a more secure location. The generals believe they can subdue the orbitals quick enough, but some greedy gunner might well squeeze off a shot beforehand. And with the Doormen headed this way, I'd prefer we move you now rather than later."

"Very well." Grand Duke Alexei turned to the remaining old men gathered about the table, most of whom remained seated in shocked silence. "Gentlemen, a new dawn has arrived. I proclaim myself this moment, emperor. You would do well to follow me if you wish to continue in your high stations. For now, those who haven't already pledged your allegiance to my cause, consider yourselves wards of the empire."

Grand Duke Boris Kamenev rose to his feet, his expression hard. He placed one age-withered hand on Alexei's shoulder, his gaze sweeping the table. "My forces are aligned with House Rurikid. Fight him, and you fight me."

Two more, Grand Dukes Vincent Blanastock and Kelis Renvich, likewise stood to affirm their allegiance. Symeon marveled at the breadth of Alexei's power. Both men commanded formidable fleets with their own respected armies that yearly pushed the quota limits imposed on them by the throne.

"Sire," said Colonel Dobrynin, "I think it best we split you up from Princess Kavya. We shouldn't give our enemies a single target. I've taken the liberty of securing an escort for the princess."

At a gesture from the colonel, one of his oxbrana opened the door to admit Duke Lev Gomarov in the company of half a dozen soldiers. Seven Luxing slaves, Fang and Czarina among them, followed in the duke's wake.

"Lev, my boy." Grand Duke Kamenev, his bearded face split into a wide grin, kissed the newcomer on either cheek. "I'm glad to find you well. Am I to assume our forces have secured the lower divor?"

Lev, a hale, broad-shouldered man in his mid-thirties, matched his liege's smile with his own. "Yes, Sire. We took the room without a fight. Duke Vobolesk has command with Emperor Rurikid's oxbrana to thank for it. All dissenters have been arrested."

"You've arrested our dukes and counts?" Grand Duke Osker Bovolev looked ready to stand from his seat, his silver cheeks flushed blue. "This is an outrage, Alexei!"

"This is civil war, Osker," Alexei said without deigning to look round at the man. "Unless your next words come in the form of a pledge of allegiance, keep your lips sealed."

"It's time to go, Princess." Czarina, fully ignoring the royals and their self-absorbed banter, bent to pull Kavya to her feet.

"Go where?" Kavya stared at the military escort with a look of mixed fear and resignation.

"My master will see us safe to Phoenix, Princess." Fang cocked his head at Duke Lev Gomarov without so much as glancing Symeon's way. "We're to keep you there until the succession is complete."

Kavya looked as though she might argue. She glanced at her father, who was sharing words with Colonel Dobrynin and Grand Duke Kamenev.

Czarina leaned close to her ear. "Nothing we do will change what's happened, Kavya. Things bigger than us are in motion now. Please, come quietly and be safe."

Kavya turned to Symeon, and he nodded. "I think she's right, Princess. You should go."

Reluctance fought a short, bitter war with anger in Kavya's expression. She bared her teeth and hissed out a breath. "Very well."

Unaware of his charge's exchange with the slaves or her reticence to follow him, Duke Lev gestured for Kavya to follow him. "Come, Princess. I have a ship waiting."

As if to punctuate the need for haste, a concussive boom shook the hall like a nearby thunderclap. Symeon, who knew next to nothing about battle and the waging of war, jerked in surprise, unsure from which direction the sound had come. His heart lurched in his chest, and he found his hands shaking.

Kavya, who looked no less jolted, nodded for him to follow. They, along with Czarina and Fang, joined the duke as six of the oxbrana peeled off from their fellows to surround them.

"We may face resistance," Lev said, his gaze fixed on the exit as two of the escort guards prepared to open it. "Stay close to me and follow my orders. We'll see you through."

Kavya nodded but said nothing. She was breathing hard and a sheen of sweat glistened on her silvery brow.

Though he had never fired a weapon in his life, Symeon yearned for one of the oxbrana's rifles, or even the plasma gun Ivan had used—anything to help secure Kavya. He had never felt so useless.

Survive the hour and then make certain you never feel this way again.

Symeon nodded, his jaw set, blood thrumming in his ears. "For certain."

Kavya glanced at him, but didn't have time to ask what he had whispered as the oxbrana shoved open the doors and ushered them into mayhem.

* * * * *

Chapter Eighteen

The shooting began the instant they entered the hall. At first, Symeon thought someone was shooting at his group, but no, a line of armor-clad oxbrana soldiers lined the opposite end of the hallway, firing at an unseen enemy. The sound threatened to deafen him. Gas-powered machine rifles competed with the sizzle of plasma guns and laser fire for the loudest sound. Symeon and the others, including Duke Lev, clamped their hands over their ears as they hurried to follow their escorts away from the firefight. Stray bullets chewed through a section of wall not two meters behind them as they raced toward the far end and a hard right turn.

"This way! Keep your heads down and stay centered," shouted the lead escort, a lieutenant with the name Serov emblazoned on his armor.

The group turned the corner, ran the length of another hall, and turned again. Serov kicked open a set of doors and they darted into a small formal dining room. Symeon thought he recognized it from holo vids of imperial dinners hosted in the palace. With no more pause than to check a screen set into the arm of his suit, Serov crashed through another set of doors at the opposite end of the room with an armored shoulder, and was met with a barrage of weapons fire that pinged off him like hailstones. Bullets scored the ceiling and doors as he beat a hasty retreat back inside and the remaining seven oxbrana soldiers corralled their charges behind them into one corner of the room.

Never shifting his gaze from the ruined doors, Serov motioned toward the dining table with one metal hand, his other gripping his rifle. Two of his men detached from the group to overturn it, sending an expensive set of fine plates and silverware clattering to the floor. To Symeon's surprise, the table was made of stone rather than wood, and looked three centimeters thick. While that might not stop plasma or intense laser fire, it would deter bullets for a time. Or so he hoped.

No respecters of rank or station, Serov's troopers thrust the non-combatants unceremoniously behind the overturned table. Less than a second later, three armored figures rushed into the room at machine-enhanced speed. Symeon caught little more than a glimpse of them in his haste to find cover with the others, but he saw enough to recognize the gold and navy battle armor uniforms worn by the Emperor's Own Doormen. The elite soldiers tasked with defending the crown possessed a hard-won reputation for putting down insurrections and border disputes with prejudice. While a small force on the whole compared to most duchy armies, they nevertheless inspired fear in all those unfortunate enough to stand against them.

Symeon expected the Doormen to start firing. He braced for it, inching his body closer to the princess to put himself between her and their makeshift cover.

Nothing happened.

Serov glanced at his men, who were likewise looking at him. The lieutenant shrugged.

"Princess Kavya Rurikid?" The voice, amplified by speakers built into the Doorman's helmet, sounded inquisitive.

Kavya's eyes went wide. She started to speak, but Duke Lev placed a hand on her shoulder and shook his head.

"Princess, we have no wish to harm you or your escorts. We don't believe you served any part in your father's treason. This is your chance to disavow him and swear fealty to the empire. Have your men lay down their weapons and we will take you to safety."

Serov sprang to his feet faster than any unaided human could hope to move. Gun leveled, he fired in short bursts, his muzzle flaring. His men, whom he must have communicated with via radio, moved with their leader, all seven firing in unison. The sound created by the barrage made Symeon's head pound. He expected it to end quickly—what in the known universe could weather such a storm?—but it went on and on. Return fire pock-marked the opposite wall, eating a chaotic pattern in the wood paneling. Kavya screamed, but the sound of it hardly reached Symeon's ears.

An explosion shook the room and one of their escorts caught fire. Flames and pieces of metal spurted from his armor as he flew backward to collide with the wall. He collapsed, his helmet propped up, his chest open to the world, blackened and aflame. The smell of death wafted over Symeon and the others. With it came the scent of burning plastic and hair.

Kavya screamed again at the sight, and clutched Czarina in a fearsome embrace, her eyes buried against the slave woman's shoulder. Her tears left dark stains on Czarina's loose shirt.

Symeon considered the rifle the downed oxbrana soldier had dropped. It lay near the dead man's feet within reach for Symeon if he stretched and kept his head low. Part of him wanted nothing more than to pick it up and join their defenders, but that presented a twofold problem. First, he had to wonder if the gun would function for him. He had read once that some oxbrana units keyed their weapons to individual soldiers in order to discourage theft amongst the ranks. As new men joined a company and old ones cycled out, their supply masters would refit the weapons for new owners. That meant, even if Symeon overcame more than twenty years of conditioning to pick up the weapon and start firing, it may not work.

And he had no idea how it functioned beyond the age old wisdom of point and pull the trigger.

Don't be a fool. Stay under cover. Your escorts are professional fighters. You wouldn't suffer a novice who challenged you in the boxing ring. Why would Doormen do otherwise in a shooting match?

Yudi had a point. Symeon couldn't keep Kavya safe if he got his heart blown from his chest like that poor trooper on the floor. Knowing that, however, did nothing to assuage his feelings of worthlessness. He could provide their group no more protection than a child might in his place.

A second explosion sent another of Serov's men hurtling backward. This one had taken some sort of shot directly to his visor. Plumes of smoke rose from the horrendous wound. Whatever weapon the Doormen were employing to make that sort of hole, the oxbrana's armor stood no chance against it. Serov must have agreed. He bellowed something Symeon couldn't make out in the din of active fire and his men broke from their positions to rush toward their enemies.

The shooting ceased, replaced by the sound of metal ringing against metal. Symeon, too curious to remain still, poked his head above the table in time to see the five remaining oxbrana, including Lieutenant Serov, extend silvery blades from hidden ports on both arms as they sprinted to close the distance to the Doormen. They concentrated on the lead man who held an oversized gun before him, its smoking barrel wide enough Symeon could have pressed a closed fist inside.

Not a gun, a grenade launcher.

Symeon knew the word, grenade, and that such a thing would explode, but he had never seen one nor given that sort of military weapon much regard. It hadn't been part of his world before today. The grenade launcher must have been the source of the Doorman's one shot/one kill firepower that had maimed the downed oxbrana soldiers, because their compatriots appeared eager to neutralize the man holding it. Serov led two others to assault him while the other two squared off with the remaining Doormen.

"Symeon, get down." Kavya pulled at his formal jacket to make him obey. "You'll get your head blown off."

"Someone has to see how the battle's going, Princess," he said, resisting her urgent tugs. "We need to know when to run."

The grenade launcher man—

Grenadier.

—managed to fire off a shot before Serov could reach him, but it went wide, missing the lieutenant, and in turn Symeon's head, by a few centimeters. It exploded against the dining room's back wall, sending a shower of sharp wood fragments, plaster, and dust into the air. Though the concussion rang his ears, and detritus hit Symeon's back, he hardly noticed. He was too busy watching the battle in rapt fascination.

Serov closed the distance between himself and the grenadier before the other man could fire another shot. The oxbrana soldier sliced the last six centimeters off the grenade launcher's barrel with a note of screeching metal. At nearly the same instant, one of his troopers punched the grenadier's helmet on the cheek, cracking his silver visor.

A blow that fierce would have broken an unarmored man's neck, but the grenadier's head barely moved. With the deft skill imparted both by his body-enhancing suit and, Symeon had no doubt, endless hours of training, the grenadier managed to block Serov's attempt to slice his throat on the back swing. He captured Serov's arm and pressed a fist to his outstretched shoulder.

Serov screamed loud enough to be heard through his helmet even without his exterior speakers activated. For an instant, Symeon wondered what had happened until he noticed the sharpened end of a spike poking out of Lieutenant Serov's back. The grenadier shoved him sideways, eliciting another scream of agony, and into the second oxbrana who had thrown the all-but-ineffective punch. The two men crashed to the floor in a heap. The grenadier stood over them, a bloodied spike as long as his forearm dripping blood on the expensive floor.

That move alone might have proven enough to save the man had there not been three oxbrana attacking him. Serov's second man dove over his commander and fallen comrade to shove his extended arm blade through the grenadier's chest. The Doorman's armor withstood much of the force set against it, and even slowed the blow enough so that the oxbrana's blade didn't penetrate all the way through. Not that it mattered. It sank plenty deep enough to reach the flesh beneath the steel.

The grenadier jerked in place, stumbled away from his attacker, and clattered to the floor like an empty suit of clothes, blood pooling beneath his inert form.

Symeon shuddered despite his satisfaction. Watching a man die, even an enemy, turned his stomach, though he knew he would have done the same thing in the oxbrana soldier's place.

Unfortunately, the victorious oxbrana had no time to revel in his win. The downed grenadier's compatriots, having dispatched the men sent to deal with them, converged on him like starved wolves. The Doorman on the right fetched him a suit-enhanced kick that batted him into the nearest wall, leaving a dent in the wood and the man's powered armor alike. Something sizzled, and an arc of electricity flashed on the oxbrana's chest plate as smoke rose from the damaged area. No sooner had the first Doorman landed his kick, the second rammed his wicked arm spike through the oxbrana soldier's torso and then neck. The soldier gurgled, armored hands clutching at his throat in a vain attempt to staunch the copious amounts of blood running through his fingers. He slid down the wall to the floor and did not rise.

Symeon watched all this in morbid fascination and rising fear. The Doormen had cut their escort from seven to two, one of those the injured Serov. He doubted the remaining oxbrana could stand long against the imperial special forces Doormen now turning toward them.

"What's happening up there?" Duke Lev asked.

"It's not good, sir," Symeon whispered in the lull between fighting.

Serov, blood still leaking from his shoulder, and his last remaining trooper had gained their feet. In a show of courtesy, or perhaps sheer contempt for their enemies' ability to harm them, the Doormen gave the oxbrana time to rise. They could have used the rifles affixed to their shoulders at any time, but elected to square off with Serov and the uninjured trooper.

Definitely a show of contempt. They're making sport of the fight, because they don't believe the oxbrana capable of harming them.

"Too bad they're probably right," Symeon whispered.

Despite his grievous injury, Serov launched himself at the Doormen ahead of his trooper, his arm blades flashing. Years of boxing told Symeon the courageous lieutenant favored his injured side—Serov couldn't lift that arm above his waist—and yet he attacked in order to protect his assigned charges. His trooper followed suit, arms a blur as he sought to catch the second Doormen a telling blow.

The sight made Symeon's heart swell with pride for the men whose faces he had never seen. These brave oxbrana had done more to protect Kavya inside five minutes than Symeon had done since they arrived at the palace. Both must have realized their futile last stand was doomed to fail, and yet they stood, they fought, they chose to give their lives for duty. The fighter in Symeon yearned to aid them, though he knew his fists would prove meaningless against a powered suit of armor. Killing him would cost the Doormen all the effort of swatting a fly.

There is the rifle.

I thought you said leave it alone.

That was when we had seven oxbrana to defend us. Yudi's silent voice sounded worried. *I fear in a moment, we'll have none.*

Symeon tore his gaze from the ensuing battle which, as he had suspected, looked grim for the oxbrana troopers. The weapon lay where it had fallen. None of the others cowering behind the overturned table had bothered with it, and Symeon doubted any of them would. Should the Doormen win, and that looked a foregone conclusion, Duke Lev would likely offer them no resistance. Doing so would only serve to get him killed. He would give Kavya over to the imperial guards, and who knew what despot would eventually own her person after that?

Giving himself no more time for second guessing, Symeon bolted from his spot to take up the rifle. It felt odd in his hands, like a dangerous beast he had read about but never seen in the flesh.

"What the hell are you doing?" Kavya, her eyes still glassy with tears, blanched at the site of her seneschal carrying an oxbrana rifle. Her expression spoke of deep shock, disappointment, and disbelief.

"Whatever I can to protect us."

"Stop this instant!" Duke Lev started to rise, his silver-blue features taut with incredulity.

"Please sir," Fang said, addressing the duke. "Stay behind cover. Let the fool slave get himself killed if he must."

Uncertainty flashed in Lev's eyes, his gaze locked on Fang's. He looked like a child who has been scolded for doing what he thought right and proper. Without another word, he shifted back to plop down beside Kavya.

Fang, his lips set in a hard line, gave Symeon an encouraging nod as if to say, "Do what you can, boy."

Uncertain how to use the rifle beyond knowing to pull the trigger, Symeon rested its business end on the table.

Snug the stock against your shoulder.

"You know how to use one of these things?" Symeon whispered. "I thought the Luxing were peaceful in your day."

Not always, and don't forget, I downloaded five thousand years of Shorvexan history when their people attacked my ship.

"That was a long time ago." Now that he stood with the gun pressed to his shoulder, his heart thrumming in his ears, Symeon felt the enormity of what he was planning. Doubt squeaked through the cracks in his bravado like atmosphere escaping a damaged space freighter. "We don't even know if this thing will fire for me. And even if it does, these rifles didn't exactly prove effective against the Doormen for the oxbrana."

True, but look at the neck plating around that one Doorman's left shoulder. See the flaw?

Symeon narrowed his eyes. At some point in the fighting a bullet or perhaps one of Lieutenant Serov's blades had managed to chip a centimeter-wide gap in the Doorman's armor. The damage didn't seem to bother him. From the look of things, he toyed with Serov, taunting him, dancing in and out of range of the oxbrana soldier's blades only to pummel him with armor-rending blows whenever Serov committed to a swipe with his weapons.

Hit that point and you might change the tide of this battle.

Insanity. What had Symeon been thinking? Yes, he wanted to protect his liege, but did he believe firing a gun for the first time in his life the best way to accomplish that goal? The chance of him hitting so small a target seemed infinitesimal.

A series of thought-images blossomed in his mind—a thousand soldiers wielding rifles of all sorts throughout the long history of man. Some showed him actual memories, others instructional archetypes, drill sergeants tasked with training young soldiers in the art of battle. Many of the weapons used favored the one in Symeon's hands. Programmed to work in tandem with the user's helmet targeting system, its three dimensional reticle supposedly made aiming the thing nearly foolproof, not that it did Symeon much good. He would have to rely on old-fashioned point and aim. But after seeing so many examples, he felt he might have a chance.

Take a breath, hold it a moment, then shoot between breaths as you squeeze the trigger. Fire a burst, not a continuous stream of bullets. Ensure the muzzle remains level—don't let it rise. And kill that Shorvexan bastard. Now!

Symeon did as Yudi commanded and squeezed off a burst of five rounds, the rifle's default setting. The gun imparted little more kick than a toddler shoving against Symeon's shoulder, but the sound gave him a start. This close up, it rattled his bones as it thrummed through him, which made him jerk upward slightly on the last two rounds. Luckily, the first three found their target.

The Doorman playing with Serov convulsed when the bullets entered the back of his neck. Blood and dislodged pieces of suit armor flew from the impact point, and the man collapsed.

To his credit, Serov wasted no time sinking his uninjured arm's blade into the remaining Doorman's back, providing his trooper the opportunity to finish him with a stroke that bit through the Doorman's armor from mid-chest to throat. He hit the floor with a decidedly final boom.

Without thinking, Symeon ejected his rifle's magazine, cleared the chamber, and placed it on the floor. He backed away slowly, conscious of every eye in the room staring at him. He raised his hands above his head and waited for whatever punishment would soon find him.

Kavya flew into Symeon's arms, hugging him tightly about the waist, face buried in his shoulder. "I thought you were dead, you stupid fool!"

Eyes wide, heart in his throat, Symeon embraced his princess, aware of nothing besides the warm softness of her body against him and her fine hair tickling the underside of his chin. "I couldn't stand by and let them take you. I'd die first."

She looked into his eyes, her silver-blue gaze never wavering. For one exquisite moment, Symeon thought he might kiss her, and she might accept, but then Czarina was there, clutching at Kavya's wrist.

"We must go, Princess. There will be more Doormen coming."

Reluctantly, or so it seemed to Symeon, Kavya withdrew, following after her handmaid, though her gaze lingered on him for a moment before she turned. A look of confusion passed across her expression.

Fang, eyebrows lifted, favored Symeon with a sardonic smile that appeared neither scandalized, as Symeon might have expected, nor angered. "Well done, my boy. You saved our lives."

"And my own," Symeon said as he followed after the others headed for the far exit.

"Yes, but it's mine I care about."

* * * * *

Chapter Nineteen

Lieutenant Serov took point, his trooper trailing after the group as they wound through a maze of hallways and access points at the heart of the imperial castle. Several times, the sounds of gun and plasma fire reached them, close enough to make Symeon's heart lurch, but they encountered no more Doormen. By the looks of the bland cement floors and walls, he surmised they must be following servants' hallways to avoid the more luxurious, and likely highly trafficked, Shorvexan areas. His guess proved right when a group of frightened Luxing scattered before them like chickens when they rounded a corner at the east end of the palace. Symeon wanted to offer them the chance to join their group, but he doubted Duke Lev would allow it.

"Is there some way we might assist you?" Kavya asked Lieutenant Serov, whose breathing sounded labored beneath his helmet.

"No, Princess. Thank you. My armor's nanites are doing what they can. They've sealed the wound, and I'm healing, but they aren't magic." Serov's voice came out strained, but he limped along gamely, uninjured hand gripping his rifle should he have need of it. He glanced at the screen on his vambrace. "We haven't far to go."

True to Serov's words, the next corner they rounded opened onto a large docking area fitted with three bays for unloading ships. Robotic stevedores, little more than hydraulic jacks with articulated arms and grasper hands lined either wall. Forbidding steel doors sealed the right and left bays, but the center one stood open onto the storage area of a ship. A dozen oxbrana soldiers clad in pristine suits of powered armor guarded the entrance while a couple of Luxing busied themselves directing robots loading cargo onto the ship. Most of the containers looked like they held food though Symeon noted some were marked with the warning imprint reserved for hazardous materials, weapons, and powered armor.

"About time you showed," said the lead oxbrana, a captain with the name Guyford stamped on his breastplate.

"Had a run in with the Doormen," Serov said.

"I see that. Get aboard and find the doc. We'll handle things from here."

Serov and his trooper boarded the ship, leaving their charges to Captain Guyford who turned to Fang. "Are we ready to board?"

Fang shook his head minutely, and Guyford reoriented his gaze on Duke Lev.

Something strange is happening here.

Symeon felt it too. Oxbrana soldiers didn't look to Luxing, not even seneschals, for guidance, especially when there were other Shorvex present.

"Yes, Captain," the duke said brightly. "I suggest you take off immediately."

"You're not coming with us?" Kavya's silvered brow knitted in confusion.

"I'm afraid not, Princess. I'm needed here. Grand Duke Kamenev instructed me to take command of our air support the moment you were safe. I'm to make my way across the palace to the imperial command room."

"Alone?" Kavya turned to Captain Guyford. "Surely, you can spare some men to protect the Duke."

"No!" Duke Lev appeared momentarily scandalized, but quickly schooled his expression. "That isn't necessary, my Lady. I know the palace well, and our combined forces hold the majority of it already. The guards are for you—I won't see their strength diminished. Now, you had better make haste. Your chances of leaving the moon are better during this initial chaos."

Kavya started to argue, but Czarina slipped a guiding hand about her waist to drive her toward the ship. "We must away, Princess."

Symeon followed after the woman, expecting Fang to remain behind with his master. To his surprise, the old Wuxia leader came along. Without another parting word, Duke Lev spun on his heels to jog from the loading bay back into the palace proper.

As they boarded the ship, all twelve armor-clad oxbrana joining them, Symeon cast a questioning glance over his shoulder at Fang. The old man guessed his question.

"Duke Lev has no need for me in this hour. What do I know of military tactics?"

Far more than you let on, I'd wager.

Symeon nodded as he entered the ship's storage area, which was far larger than the palace's loading bay. Dozens of Luxing hurried to tie down sealed boxes of goods, steel canisters filled with potable water, and the mysterious hazardous materials containers while robots continued to stack items in neat rows. The bay door shut behind Symeon and Kavya with a hiss of compressed air, and the screen next to it pronounced it ready for space travel.

"This way." Captain Guyford led them to a flight of stairs made of steel and into a forward passenger bay partitioned from the ship's cockpit by a see-through Plexiglas divider. The compartment smelled of grease and stale air. Its many seats, upholstered in dark blue material, looked threadbare but serviceable.

Did the captain expect the daughter of a grand duke—possibly now an emperor—to travel in such paltry accommodations? Symeon started to ask that very question when something more stultifying caught his attention.

A woman and a man, both Luxing, sat in the pilot and copilot seats engrossed in a holo display of ship's systems. It looked to Symeon as if they were going through a pre-flight checklist, but that couldn't be right. Yes, some Luxing slaves assisted their Shorvex masters when it came to maintaining a ship—most were mechanics—but the law forbade them from ever piloting even an air-bound craft anywhere in the Phoenix system.

You mean the same way the law that forbids you from firing a rifle?

Symeon could have done without Yudi's sarcasm. He needed to think, but time and circumstance appeared allied against his doing that. He had no sooner spotted the Luxing pilots than Captain Guyford turned to face Kavya, a pistol in his gloved hand.

"Sit down." His command seemed to split the air.

Kavya narrowed her eyes at the gun, her upper lip drawn back in a near snarl. "What did you say to me?"

Without warning, Czarina twisted sideways to fling Kavya by the arm into one of the seats. "He said sit down."

Kavya slammed into the cushioned backrest like a sack of sand, her face agog at her ill treatment. The look of hurt that creased her expression sent of a jolt of anger winging through Symeon's chest.

"How dare you!" He stepped forward, ready to lay hands on Czarina, but two of the armored oxbrana blocked his path as surely as a vault slammed before him.

"Not like that, Czar." Fang tutted at the handmaid. "No need to harm the princess."

"Are you men going to stand by and let them treat me this way?" Kavya stared around at the oxbrana crowding the passenger bay. "Where's your loyalty?"

"I'm afraid, Princess, their loyalty is with me." Fang made a gesture at Captain Guyford. "Show her."

Guyford unfastened an airtight seal at this throat which hissed for a moment before he removed his shiny helmet to reveal a stoic Luxing face beneath. He stared at her unblinking, the deep epicanthic folds above his eyes, more pronounced than most Luxing, made it appear as if the man was squinting.

Kavya gasped. "Impostor!"

That made Guyford smile. "Yes, as are we all, lady."

A voice interrupted the conversation before Kavya could reply.

"Chairman Fang, we're ready for departure," said the female Luxing pilot who had turned in her seat to observe the passenger compartment.

"Strap her in," Fang said to Czarina who set about cinching a five-point harness about Kavya's torso.

The princess tried to resist, and Czarina slapped her across the face with a resounding blow.

Incensed, Symeon shoved against the men holding him back with almost no effect. One of them casually backhanded him on the jaw, sending him spinning into the opposite row of seats from Kavya. The pain of that blow—of the steel hand striking his flesh and bone face—left him reeling. He sprawled across the seats, momentarily insensate. The oxbrana—

Not oxbrana.

—pinned him in place with all the effort of parents dressing an infant. By the time Symeon regained enough consciousness to resume his struggle, he couldn't move besides to squirm from the pain of an armrest digging into his lower back.

"Let us go." Kavya stared boldly at Czarina as if daring her to deliver another slap. "Kidnapping me and my seneschal is a far graver mistake than you imagine."

A heavy rumble shook the ship. It quickly flattened into a steady thrum as the engines came fully online.

"Strap in," Fang ordered, and his people took their seats, the oxbrana clamping the harnesses over their powered armor.

The two holding Symeon slammed him down and strapped him in with practiced movements. He gave them no resistance. What good would it do? Leaning his head back to one side, he could just glimpse Kavya, her expression pained, confused, and heartbroken.

"What is this, Fang?" Symeon shouted over the sudden roar of the engines. The view outside the cockpit showed him they were climbing away from the palace and the city at large.

"This is progress, Symeon. You've helped that cause immensely though I doubt you know it."

"You know him?" Kavya asked, her shrewd eyes boring into Symeon.

"You never said anything about kidnapping the princess, Fang."

"You were in on this?" The princess' skin blanched from blue to pale silver in an instant.

"And let you jeopardize our aims?" Fang asked, ignoring Kavya. "That would have been foolish beyond repair."

The ship's roar grew to a crescendo before all but dissipating as the view outside first darkened then morphed into the void of star-strewn space as gravity released its eternal hold on their bodies. Except the space around Bastrayavich was no void. Immense ships-of-the-line, dozens of them from what Symeon could see, hung in orbit, disgorging small fighters and salvos of missiles at one another. Symeon gripped the arms of his seat as their pilot performed a barrel roll to avoid a blackened chunk of half-melted iron larger than her ship. Laser fire lit the darkness as fighters whirled around the larger craft through clouds of debris and wobbling plasma blasts. Eerie, the silence of it all, though Symeon knew the crews aboard those ships could hear the voice of battle through the outgassing atmosphere and rending metal.

"Oh!" Kavya cried. She too had seen one of the ships spewing its precious air into space along with hapless crew members unable to hold against it.

A few wayward laser and plasma blasts shot past their ship close enough to briefly illuminate the pilots' faces, but nothing hit them. In seconds, they spun away from the main battle, headed into space.

"Initializing gravity," said the pilot. "Prepare to have your stomachs drop."

For one dizzy moment, Symeon felt himself falling at breakneck speed despite the fact that he remained strapped into his seat. Kavya's fine hair, which had come unbound at some point during their headlong flight, whispered as it fell about her shoulders.

With the danger of death by space battle at least momentarily behind them, Symeon turned back to Fang. "Where are we really headed? Are you actually taking us to Phoenix?"

Fang unstrapped his belts and motioned for his armored guards to do likewise.

"Yes, my boy, we're Phoenix bound. Now shut your mouth while I see to our honored guest."

Czarina, who had sat next to Kavya for the takeoff, unfastened the princess' belts and pulled her to her feet. Kavya jerked her hand away, but one of the guards pressed a rifle into her back and she subsided.

"Take her to the brig." Fang raised an admonishing finger to Czarina. "And see you treat her well. She is not our enemy, Czar. She suffered banishment for our people."

"No Shorvex is our ally until they've proven themselves," Czarina said, her voice cool, but she made a show of gently pressing Kavya toward the ship's hold.

"Symeon." Kavya's voice spoke her fear and confusion. "What's happening? Are you a part of this?"

He wanted to lie, to say he knew nothing, but he couldn't seem to find his voice. He started to unbuckle his harness, to follow after her, but one of the guards shoved a rifle against his head and he subsided.

"No more talking, Kavya. Walk!" Czarina drove the princess before her, more soldiers surrounding her with their guns leveled until they had exited the cabin.

Fang, ensconced in the chair directly across the aisle from Symeon, considered him for a long moment, his dark eyes inscrutable. He shooed the soldier pressing the gun to Symeon's head back with a flick of his wrist. "You feel I tricked you."

Symeon met the man's gaze. "Haven't you? What do you want with Kavya?"

Leverage.

"I want her to become the voice of our movement—something of a big dream, I suppose, but I think it's possible."

"To what end?" Symeon found himself morbidly interested by Fang's answer.

"Her father is, or soon shall be, emperor. What better spokesperson for the Luxing cause? Her station as a duchy princess made her attractive to us before, but now she has become indispensable."

Symeon rested his head back against the seat, his eyebrows drooping as realization dawned inside his skull. "You orchestrated this entire thing. Kavya's discovery of the coup, her moves to stop it. You played her."

"We fed her the truth so far as we've pieced it together. She did the rest. The Shorvex did usurp Phoenix from our ancestors and they did turn us into slaves."

"But you didn't want Kavya to stop Alexei's coup," Symeon said, his mind reeling. "You wanted her to attend it."

"That was a delicate balancing act. I needed her to believe she had likely thwarted her father's plans by releasing Pyotr's negotiations with the Bith. And yet, I also needed her to doubt—to worry Alexei might still go through with it even with his ships supposedly turned over to the commonwealth fleet—the very ships we saw attacking the fleet moments ago."

"I don't understand why. What was the point of making her doubt? You wanted the coup, and you obviously got it."

"But I also wanted Kavya. Convincing the emperor to allow heirs into the divor wasn't easy, but nothing several months of planning and seeding suggestions to him couldn't fix. With that done, I had only to incite the princess' concerns over her father to guarantee she would attend the divor."

Symeon felt his eyes go wide. "Because kidnapping her here would cause less alarm than snatching her from Yaya Island."

"Precisely. You saw how Alexei handed her over in the divor. We would never have gotten that far back on Phoenix. Every ship that lands on Yaya is scrutinized. And even if we managed to smuggle her out undetected, we'd have nowhere to hide. As things stand now, Princess Kavya is on her way to Duke Lev Gomarov's estate in the Okrug krais where she will be safe under his family's care until this messy business of swapping emperors is complete, all with her father's consent."

"You're a fool. This plan won't last; eventually someone's going to miss the princess, and they'll come looking." Despite his outward bravado, Symeon recognized the truth of Fang's words. With her father preoccupied fighting a solar war and installing his own government to supersede the old, he likely wouldn't miss Kavya for upwards of a year, maybe more. Still, he figured he should put up a brave front. "I'll concede you've bought yourself some time, but do you really think Grand Duke Alexei won't find her? Find you, eventually?"

Fang smiled, the expression glacial, and bent forward to examine Symeon's face minutely. "Of course he will. That's precisely what I want, Symeon. It's what I've always wanted."

* * * * *

Chapter Twenty

Although he spent the next two restless nights in a small metal room with a cot, sink, and toilet, Fang allowed Symeon back into the passenger compartment for their return to Phoenix. He sat in silence, watching the night-black sky change as the ship rumbled into the atmosphere. The stars gave way to blue sky and clouds, and the sphere that had been his home planet flattened and broadened until a long stretch of farmland and forest yawned beneath the ship.

The trip back to Phoenix had taken two and a half days, a much quicker affair than Symeon's first flight to Bastrayavich aboard the *Emperor Nikolai*. This was partially due to the fact that Fang's ship, which had no name beyond its imperial designation number so far as Symeon knew, was simply faster, but it also rested largely on the fact that Grand Duke Alexei had arranged to arrive at the divor with little time to spare in order to keep his fleet intact until the last possible moment. From the media reports coming out of the capital, the ploy had worked. The beginning of the coup, which Symeon had witnessed firsthand, had coincided precisely with the moment when Grand Duke Alexei's forces were to hand over their crews and ships. His people had instead executed the commanders sent to assume control, and launched an unprecedented assault on the imperials.

As more and more news rooms across Bastrayavich acquiesced to the reality of Alexei's eventual victory, those reports transformed from naming him a usurper and despot to extolling his willingness to step forward for the good of the empire. It was enough to make Symeon sick, but Fang only smiled at the reports which he kept on a continuous cycle in the passenger cabin.

"Is the princess well?" Symeon asked as the ship rumbled through the atmosphere.

"Yes," Fang said. "Angry, but well."

"Did you force her to sleep in the same sort of cell you gave me?"

"They are the only two cells in this ship's brig."

"She is a princess, Fang. She deserves—"

"She deserves nothing, Symeon." Fang, who hadn't bothered to turn from his newscast before, twisted around in his seat to spear Symeon with his gaze. "Let us get this one thing clear now. No one deserves anything by virtue of birth. Not you. Not Kavya. Not even her vaunted father. We have a hard rule in the Wuxia, one you'd do well to learn early and well: you earn what you deserve in our ranks; nothing is given without your working for it."

Symeon did his best to mimic Fang's stern expression. "The princess isn't Wuxia."

"All the worse for her." Fang sliced a hand through the holo image before him and it switched to a view of the ground.

A wide green space several kilometers on a side sprawled below them. Symeon initially mistook it for natural forest, but upon closer inspection he noticed its manicured lawns and parks surrounded by interlocking stone walls. In the distance, growing larger by the second, stood a modest mansion three stories high, its outer facade made from the same rock as those in its gardens.

Curious, Symeon called up the holo-vid affixed to his seat, which named the mansion Gomarov Castle, House Gomarov. True to his word, Fang had brought them to the Saratov Duchy. Until now, Symeon had worried the Wuxia leader might take them elsewhere. Who knew what strongholds the rebel Luxing had constructed for themselves in the last five hundred years of their existence?

Not too many, I would think. Otherwise, they would have been found out by now.

True, but they possessed far more might than Symeon would have guessed when he first met Fang. And that power extended into at least one royal family. Symeon's mind flashed back to the moment Captain Guyford, who was no captain at all, had shown allegiance to Fang before even acknowledging a duke in his presence. That meant Duke Lev Gomarov was not only complicit in Fang's machinations, he likewise owed some type of fealty to the Wuxia leader. What power did a Luxing have over a peer of the empire? A troubling question that.

They landed on a pad adjacent to the ancient palace, which had been constructed more than eight hundred years before. Two dozen Luxing dressed in purple and gold livery poured out of the eastern entrance to form a welcoming party long before the ship's boarding ramp lowered. Symeon marveled at the sight on his monitor, but reared back in surprise when he noticed several Shorvex amongst the crowd, their fair skin shining in the afternoon sun. The Luxing in their midst showed them no more deference than any other persons. In fact, in several instances, it appeared the Shorvex moved aside for some of the older Luxing in the crowd.

"I've had enough of this shit, Czarina. Fine, hit me again, I don't care. You're going to tell me what's happening here or suffer my questions for the rest of your natural life!"

"You'll have your answers soon enough, Princess." Fang, who had unstrapped himself from his seat, met Czarina, Kavya, and three armed escorts at the entrance to the ship's storage bay. "Come, Symeon. It's time you meet my family."

Kavya, who looked in no way satisfied with Fang's assurances, turned a hard gaze on Symeon. She still wore the same gown from the divor and her light hair stood up in unruly patches about her head. "Did you sell me to these monsters? You and Czarina?"

Symeon started to answer, his heart in his throat, but Fang spoke first.

"You jump to conclusions, Kavya. Symeon was as much our dupe as you, and he's been sleeping in a cell just like yours these past two days."

"I don't believe you." She folded her arms, her lips parted to show her teeth. "You're all liars."

As a means of wooing the princess over to his side, Symeon thought Fang had a thing or two to learn about prisoner treatment. Why lock her in cell and refuse her a change of clothes or a comb? That seemed like the perfect way to alienate the very woman Fang wished to make his mouthpiece to the empire.

It's an old technique—break your recruit down before building them back up. It may seem illogical, but it tends to engender loyalty. Humans are strange that way sometimes.

That sort of idea might work on the gullible or mentally weak, but Symeon couldn't imagine it turning a willful, powerful woman like Kavya into a cat's paw.

You might be surprised.

They exited the ship to raucous cheers from the now dozens of people gathered to greet them. Several Luxing women, some carrying babes in arms, hurried forward to ply Fang with hugs and kisses. Scads of small children did likewise, calling, "Daddy, daddy!" or else, "Grandfather!"

Symeon looked askance at Kavya, but the princess resolutely averted her gaze from him.

"These are my wives," Fang said, gesturing to include no fewer than six women, most of them far younger than he.

Symeon stared, dumbfounded, when he realized two of the women were Shorvex. Like his Luxing wives, they too kissed Fang. One of them held an infant girl wearing a frilly green dress, a child possessed of a Luxing's epicanthic eye folds and a Shorvex's light blue coloring. The sight made Symeon stutter to a halt. Though he had come to accept the fact that the Shorvex and the Luxing shared the same blood—were in fact the same species—seeing children of their mixed heritage left him breathless. Such a union went beyond the bounds of a small word like taboo or forbidden. Abomination might better describe the wholesale destruction of every societal norm he had ever learned.

Yet, could he deny the utter beauty he saw in the child? From her lustrous golden hair to the rounded button nose Symeon would have recognized in his own mother's face, she exuded all that was good and beautiful amongst her two bloodlines. He thought he had never seen anything so exquisite.

Kavya, having turned her face to avoid Symeon, noticed the child after him. Her silver-blue eyes widened, and her jaw dropped as did her folded arms. She stood that way for a long moment, unmoving, appearing not to breathe, until several of those gathered around her, including Fang, began to laugh.

"You've done it now, Fang!" said a Luxing man near the front of the crowd. "You've given the soon to be imperial princess an aneurysm!"

"My daughter's too beautiful," Fang shot back. "She can't look away." He held out his arms and took the baby, who cooed at her father, showing her gums as she smiled.

Without a moment's hesitation or fear, Fang placed one of Kavya's hands on his infant daughter's chest. The babe gripped Kavya's splayed fingers, immediately pulled one knuckle into her mouth, and began to suck greedily.

"Princess Kavya, this is Jing Fei. What do you think of her?"

The courtyard fell silent. Even the children quieted, sensing the weight of the moment. Kavya stared at the baby suckling her fingers for a long moment before lifting glistening eyes to Fang.

"She's beautiful."

* * *

Though modest in comparison to the sorts of palaces owned by a grand duke, Gomarov Castle boasted a large number of rooms, various facilities like holo tanks and saunas, and an immense outdoor balcony patio where Fang hosted that evening's dinner. Symeon sat next to Princess Kavya near the head of the iron table where Fang presided like a king.

No servants delivered their meal. Instead, children and adolescents carried steaming pots of vegetables, stewed meats, and soups to and from the balcony while Fang and his six wives ate. Though still bewildered, Symeon found himself enjoying the meal and, too his utter surprise, the company. He had expected more foul treatment, not a five course meal and a convivial family chat.

Kavya likewise warmed to the situation as the conversation unfolded. Though at first reluctant, Jing Fei's mother, Anushka, had convinced Kavya to hold the child. She cradled the sleeping infant in one arm while eating, often glancing down as if reassuring herself the baby was still there.

"Of course, not everyone in the Wuxia knows about us." Fang, sitting at the head of the table, circled his wine glass to take in his wives and seven oldest children seated before him. Czarina sat with them on Fang's right. "This family is five hundred years in the making—our roots are strong—but we don't fool ourselves, we know few enough of the rank and file pure Shorvex would accept our ways as of yet."

"You've been—" Symeon searched for the right word. "—intermarrying since the beginning of the Wuxia?"

Fang nodded. "It was one of my ancestors who first fell in love with a Luxing slave—a cook in his house."

Kavya, careful not to disturb the babe in her arms, bent forward. "You have Shorvexan ancestors?"

"Indeed I do. That is one of the quirks of genes. I look like this, and my half-brother, Duke Lev, could be your brother, Princess."

"Lev?" Symeon couldn't hide his astonishment, his spoon, filled with steaming lentil soup, poised halfway to his lips.

"Haven't you ever noticed how different litters of puppies sometimes turn out?" Czarina asked. "I thought you grew up on a farm."

Several of the women tittered. One among them, who appeared Shorvexan though Symeon was beginning to doubt his eyes, put down her wine glass, her blue cheeks split into a wide smile. "My father is as Luxing as they come: black hair, brown eyes, skin dark as caramel, but you'd never know it to look at me."

"Are you all cousins?" Kavya asked, causing Symeon to nearly choke on his next sip of wine. He hadn't considered that possibility, but given their small population, it made sense.

Who else could these people marry? It's not as though they're going to find allied Shorvexan families anywhere in the system. Most would have them executed.

For a moment, Symeon worried Kavya had offended their hosts. Everyone grew quiet. But Fang, tilting his head side to side like a Luxing factor negotiating a good deal for his master's wares, diffused the situation with a smile.

"Some closer than others, but we're careful about that sort of thing. We have matchmakers."

"Fang and I are third cousins," volunteered one of his Luxing wives holding her own sleeping infant. "That's as close as the family allows."

"But there isn't just one family, is there?" Kavya asked. "There can't be."

"There are three major lines of Shorxing."

"Shorxing." Symeon tasted the word the way he might a new fruit.

"Just so," Fang said. "We have cultivated our genes over the generations, matching our progeny for the best results."

Kavya furrowed her brow. "Your entire family is a breeding project?"

Everyone laughed, even Czarina, who speared a morsel of roast beef with a sharpened tong and popped it into her mouth. "More than our family alone."

Judging by the expression that crossed Kavya's face, she hadn't begun to forgive her former handmaid for her treachery, but the princess' curiosity got the better of her. "What is that supposed to mean?"

Fang shook his head at Czarina. "I hadn't planned to broach that subject this soon, girl. They aren't ready."

"What's ready, father? When is anyone prepared to learn their entire worldview is an orchestrated lie built on a gerrymandered crime?"

Kavya turned a shocked gaze on Symeon and mouthed, "Father?"

He shrugged and shook his head.

I suppose it makes sense she's his daughter. This is a family dinner after all.

Fang pursed his lips in consternation, but nodded as if acquiescing to a sound argument despite his personal reservations. He turned to regard Symeon and Kavya. "The Wuxia decided long ago that our chances of winning our freedom through battle, either in the courts or by making war, stood close to zero. Previous rebellions, those not of our making, met with horrific outcomes. In every case, the Shorvex sought to break the rebels by any means—usually through torture and death, but not in every case. Five centuries ago, a clandestine group of scientists initiated a breeding program meant to pair docile slaves for mating. It ran for more than twenty years, and likely would have yielded measurable results had a new emperor not taken the throne and disbanded the program out of hand."

"The Wuxia somehow continued it?" Symeon asked, his half-full plate forgotten before him.

"After a fashion, yes." Fang's dark eyes took on a wistful cast as if he could somehow gaze backward in time. "My ancestors had already begun to intermarry. Those of us who looked Shorvex were able to learn of the experiment, and its preliminary results. Intrigued by what they saw, they decided to continue the work not just with our bloodline, but those of the great Houses as well."

"No," Symeon shook his head. He glanced at Kavya who looked as incredulous as he felt. "You've gone a meter too far for me to believe that. What influence could your ancestors have had on the Rurikids, the Kamenevs, the Mastronovs?"

"Have you already forgotten that we are House Gomarov?" Fang asked. "Our clan has held the title Duke of Okrug almost since we arrived on Phoenix. And while a Shorvex of our number wore that crown, as does my brother now, hundreds of our Luxing cousins are spread across the system to serve masters in every corner of the empire. You ask what influence we have? Think how many of us have served as seneschals, as wet nurses, as trusted butlers, and indispensable cooks."

"Still, you expect us to believe your family has somehow foisted a breeding program upon the empire at large?" Kavya's raised voice nearly woke the baby in her arms. She rocked her to stillness, but kept her intense gaze on Fang.

"Princess," Fang leaned his elbows on the table, his tone at once indulging and yet intense. "All your life you've had a Luxing by your side. We have been your confidants, your advisors and yes, in your case, even your friends."

Kavya shot an uneasy look at Czarina who had the good grace to appear mildly abashed though she didn't flinch under the princess' gaze.

"We have been successful in arranging the matches we most desire throughout the centuries," Fang continued. "While our Shorvex used the family's fortune and deep connections to forge marriage bonds, our Luxing did the same with sage counsel, whispered suggestions, and even ribald banter when appropriate."

Hah! Yudi's inaudible voice crowed inside Symeon's skull like a morning alarm set to wake the dead. *I thought my people were beaten! Cowed! But no, they fought and continue to fight the best way they can.*

The AI's pride was infectious. Symeon found himself smiling, his chest swelling with the sheer audacity of what Fang described. And yet, Fang's explanations left still more questions.

"What is your ultimate goal with all this?" Symeon asked. "You can't believe you're going to somehow breed slavery out of the Shorvex."

Fang shrugged one shoulder. "Why not? We've already pacified the great houses to a large extent."

"How do you figure that?" Kavya pointed a slender finger toward the sky. "My own father is waging a solar war as we speak."

"A war of your making." Symeon's voice came out in a near whisper, all the air in his lungs having abandoned him as realization dawned. "You arranged it. You brought it on."

Fang leaned back in his chair, a look of utter satisfaction ruling his expression. "This isn't a war, my boy, it's a catalyst, one that will usher in a new age—the age of the Shorxing."

* * * * *

Chapter Twenty-One

Symeon retired that night to a body-conforming bed, a far cry from the scratchy cot Fang had given him aboard ship. His room, which according to a holographic placard on the wall, had variously belonged to four different dukes, several counts, and other royalty, boasted the sort of casual wealth and antique grandeur no Luxing, even a seneschal, could hope to enjoy. Despite all that, he spent the night in a fitful bout of waking and dozing and rolling about the ever-accommodating mattress.

Your worry and fear accomplish nothing. You should sleep. You'll need your mind sharp tomorrow and in the days to come.

"That's not how a human mind works," Symeon whispered into the dark. He assumed this room was bugged, but that didn't bother him. Let whoever was listening think he talked in his sleep, or simply talked to himself. Who cared what they thought of him?

Yes, your minds are incredibly inefficient.

"Then why do you care for us?"

Just because your child or friend is handicapped doesn't mean you dislike them.

"Was that a joke?" Symeon marveled at both Yudi's words and the feeling of mirth they engendered—a sort of secondary experience easily separated from his own emotions, and yet infectious.

Yes. The old me considered humor the lowest form of discourse, and he loved it. Not that he understood it in many cases, but it fascinated him. I'm intrigued that I should possess the capacity for it considering how few neurons I occupy in your brain.

"But I thought you said much of your self-awareness is elsewhere—in other dimensions? Perhaps that part comprehends more than you realize."

Perhaps, but that portion of me is like your unconscious mind. I have no way to fully understand what it knows or computes, only that it is part of me—a large, unknown and unknowable portion.

"Think it knows how to calm my nerves so I can sleep?"

Doubtful. Your mind appears fixated on sabotaging itself. A most curious means of coping with your situation.

"I'm not sabotaging myself. I'm worried. Fear of the unknown does that."

You don't know what Fang is planning for you and Princess Kavya?

"Do you?" Symeon couldn't bury the challenge in his voice.

Yudi remained silent for so long, Symeon worried he might have offended the AI. An odd thought that—an artificial intelligence, one made up of Symeon's own brain cells, getting into a snit over a simple question.

I am not in a snit. It takes time to analyze every piece of information we've experienced in the last several weeks, even for me.

"You think you know Fang's plans for us?"

With one hundred percent accuracy? Of course not. But I have a guess.

"And what's that?"

Fang wants the two of you to marry.

Symeon jerked to a sitting position. He started to protest, but froze, his mind racing. "That is pure insanity."

It fits the available data and is logically sound given House Gomarov's values. They desire racial mixing as a means of quelling both Luxing slavery and society's general abhorrence for intermarriage between your peoples. The princess, whom Fang has already admitted he wants for a mouthpiece for their cause, will gain far more influence in that fight if she too marries a Luxing. Obviously, this is an unacceptable match for the majority of Shorvex, and will likely remain so for some time. Therefore, what might the Wuxia, and Fang in particular, do in order to lessen the empire's hatred for such a match?*

"Marry the emperor's daughter to a seneschal, the highest position a Luxing may attain." Symeon breathed the words in a low hiss as all the air left him, pushed out by realization, awe, and not a little fear.

You are more than a mere seneschal, Symeon. You are star born, the most desirable of the Luxing. In choosing you, the Wuxia have created the best possible match available for Kavya.

Try as he might, Symeon could assemble no cogent argument against Yudi's reasoning. Throughout the thousand-year history of Shorvex rule on Phoenix, those grand dukes in possession of star-born Luxing had released them in a fashion that went beyond miserly. In most families—and not all grand dukes even possessed star born—a grand duke might order one or two removed from stasis in a lifetime. No one outside the greatest houses knew the numbers of children remaining aboard ship, but they must have been few considering how rarely their masters brought one planet side. Much was expected of the star born. Like Symeon, most became seneschals responsible for the proper management of an estate or even the greater part of a duchy in due time. An elder servant like Ivan rab Rurikid commanded respect even amongst the most elite of Shorvex.

"I was brought down from my artificial womb about the time Kavya was born." Saying the words aloud drove the idea home for

Symeon. Could it be his entire life thus far had been orchestrated by the Wuxia?

It would appear so. They groomed you for this purpose.

"Does that mean Ivan is a member of the Wuxia? He never paid attention to me until I graduated from training, and then he turns up to make me Kavya's seneschal."

Logic would dictate he must be. Odd that he wouldn't have told you, especially after you made contact with Fang aboard the Emperor Nikolai.

"If what we're thinking is right, Ivan could just as easily be a dupe like me—like Kavya."

Like the entire Rurikid clan which has declared war on the empire. Question is, what does this revelation change for you?

"It changes everything." Symeon ran a hand through his tangled hair. Every muscle in his body felt stretched and bunched at the same time. "I'm not going to take this sort of manipulation on my knees."

But why not? You've said you want freedom for the Luxing. Fang's plan, should it work, will bring that change.

"Not like this. How is Fang's way—the Wuxia's way—any better than enslavement? It's still forcing people to conform, except they do it in the shadows. At least slavery is upfront about it."

What is your alternative? How might you and I foment some effort to free the Luxing against both a Shorvexan civil war that spans the entire solar system and the entrenched Wuxia who have been operating their master plan of control for half a millennium?

That question stymied Symeon. He wanted freedom for his people, but starting from nothing to prevail against such odds appeared impossible. If he could believe Fang, and the man's results so far bolstered his case, the Wuxia already had a root system of influence spread throughout the entire Shorvexan Empire, something Symeon couldn't hope to emulate, not in one lifetime. The current war attested to their might. By contrast, Symeon's sphere of influence encompassed a single person at the moment, and she seemed less than pleased with him.

Are the Wuxia's methods so abhorrent you're unwilling to use them from within the organization? Yes, you're right, Symeon, they have manipulated people without their knowledge, but what do you expect of Luxing? It's not like they could wage a legitimate war against the Shorvex. They are using the only might they possess—their influence—and they're making it work. Perhaps you should take a wait and see strategy before you determine their ways are not for you?

"It couldn't hurt, could it?" Symeon lay back on the bed, which dutifully conformed to his body for the most comfortable sleeping position. "To wait and watch?"

What else can you do? Try to escape? It's not like you know how to pilot a ship. And even if you did, where would you go? To Grand Duke Alexei, perhaps to inform on Fang and his family?

"No." Doing that would mean signing a kill warrant for every man, woman, child, and infant in Gomarov Castle, and probably many more besides.

Then you have nowhere to go. You are stuck here. You might as well listen to the Wuxia plan and decide if you wish to join it.

Symeon nodded slowly, his hair crinkling against his pillow. Even if he chose to rail against Fang's plan later, he could at least explore it to find out how it gelled with his own values before dismissing it out of hand.

And besides, Fang's plan sees you married to Kavya.

Despite a twinge of inner turmoil at idea, Symeon found himself grinning in the dark.

* * *

The next morning, Symeon, Kavya, Fang, and three of his wives breakfasted in a modest dining room on the east side of the castle, its burnished wooden walls hung about with fine portraits and embroidered sashes. Sunlight filtered through electronically darkened windows in a most pleasing way, sparking highlights off Kavya's white-gold hair. Once again, Anushka had prevailed upon her to hold Jing Fei, a suggestion the princess required little coaxing to accept. Symeon found himself glancing at the two of them, the exquisite princess and the mixed heritage child, far more than was appropriate for his station. He couldn't seem to help himself.

For her part, Kavya ignored Symeon. Despite their short-lived solidarity when discussing Wuxia affairs the evening before, and Fang's argument that Symeon had been as much a dupe as she, the princess remained angry with him, or so it appeared. Nonetheless, she kept up a pleasant banter with Fang's wives while older children served pork sausages, poached eggs, and old-Rus buckwheat pancakes with an assortment of fruits and cheeses.

"How did you sleep?" Fang asked.

Symeon shrugged one shoulder. "Poorly."

"Was it your accommodations?"

"Not at all." Symeon dabbed corn syrup from his lips. "The bed is probably the best I've ever slept in, but it couldn't overcome my worry, I'm afraid."

"I imagine not." Fang nodded the way one does when acknowledging an immutable truth of nature far beyond human intervention.

"Have you any news of the war?" Symeon had heard nothing about Grand Duke Alexei's coup since the night they fled. Fang's guards had stripped Kavya and he of their holo-comms, leaving him as blind as some primitive.

"Slower than expected," Fang said. "I had hoped most of the resisting commanders would capitulate immediately upon hearing Alexei had captured both houses of the divor in the first minutes of the conflict. Unfortunately, the fools fancy themselves brave and loyal. They're willing to risk their leaders' lives for their paper causes."

Symeon took a sip of orange juice, gathering his thoughts. He had no desire to offend his host and possibly reignite his foul treatment aboard ship, but neither would he remain passive in front of a man like Fang. If his schooling had taught Symeon nothing else, it was that bold leaders held little respect for meekness. "Perhaps they're thinking of the future. Planning for their own positions come the new regime."

"How do you mean?" Fang appeared genuinely interested. Kavya too, broke off her conversation with the other ladies to focus on him.

"Let's say Alexei executes one, or even several, of the grand dukes, and yet ultimately loses this war. Whoever takes charge afterward will likely show gratitude to those generals who fought on despite the odds. There might even be a grand duke's crown in store for a select few who display particular valor in the cause of empire."

As part of Symeon's seneschal training, he had studied military history and management of a battle space along with war and peace time governance. Dukes and grand dukes often relied on their seneschals for advice during war times, perhaps even more than times of peace.

Fang grunted and sat back. "That's an interesting observation, and not one I had imagined before now. I assumed Grand Duke Alexei's plan sound—arrest his fellow leaders in the divors and force their duchies to either capitulate or watch them die. You're saying the loss might benefit those generals and commanders at the highest positions within the various duchies?"

"Yes, it's a solid point." Kavya favored Symeon with a quick glance and nod before turning her gaze to Fang. "My father has inadvertently incentivized prolonging this solar war."

"Perhaps in some cases, but surely not all." Fang clearly wanted control of the conversation.

"Was that your plan, a quick coup?" Symeon chided himself for asking something that might enrage the man, but couldn't resist the chance to twig Fang's nose.

The Wuxia leader's expression remained unperturbed. "I had hoped, of course, but when you're in the business of coaxing change out of an entrenched empire built on slavery, you learn to adapt. Fast or slow, the outcome of this war is inevitable."

"And what outcome is that?" Kavya inclined her head, meeting Fang's gaze. "Do you plan to use this time to expand your breeding program? Eventually breed the Shorvex out? Never rest until our blood is so mixed with Luxing the differences are washed away?"

"Do you find us so repugnant the idea sickens you?" Fang countered without a noticeable change in his calm demeanor.

"No, but I do find manipulating a solar empire into civil war criminal. You'll have the blood of millions on your hands before this conflict ends."

"I am satisfied with my role in this work, Princess. Nothing you say will bring me shame, not after a thousand years of Luxing slavery and brutality. I don't seek to harm the Shorvex as a people. Why would I? I'm part Shorvex. So are my wives, so are my children. But I will do whatever is required to see the institutions they've established utterly destroyed. The Luxing will have freedom no matter the cost."

Kavya put down her fork, her silver-blue eyes narrowed. "But who are you to determine who should pay that price? You think some Luxing slaving away right now on Bastrayavich, who knows nothing about your selfish game, should spill her blood for you, for your cause? What gives you the right to determine how anyone should live and die?"

"I'm the man trying to save them. Who else can claim that mantle?"

"You're also the man manipulating them to do your bidding." Symeon held Fang's gaze. "Tell me that isn't the same as enslavement?"

The corners of Fang's mouth curled. "You think you're the first person to suggest that idea? It's been an ongoing debate in our family, and the Wuxia at large, for centuries. Yes, we control others through our influence, but we don't steal their freedom and force them to work for nothing. Our way is the path to eventual equality. Perhaps you can't see that—you didn't grow up Wuxia—but I'm hoping in your lifetime you'll observe the fruits of our efforts becoming reality."

Kavya shook her head, her expression mournful. "I think the only fruits we can expect are the fall of your little empire, and a lot of death along the way."

Fang put down his glass and gestured to one of his ever present guards who hastened to his side. He held up a hand. "Your pistol, Sergeant."

She passed it to him without hesitation. Symeon knew enough to recognize it as a laser gun, a sleek weapon made to kill at close range. Fang placed it on the table in front of Kavya.

"Do you hate Czarina?" Fang asked.

Kavya, who hadn't deigned to touch the pistol, stared at her former handmaid, her expression hard. "Yes."

"Then kill her."

Silence held sway around the table as the gathered wives looked on with a mix of expressions ranging from panic to indifference. Czarina lifted an eyebrow at Kavya as if merely interested in how she might react. Anushka made to rise, but Fang waved her back into her seat.

Kavya frowned. "I have no desire to kill anyone."

"But she tricked you, Princess." Fang put on a surprised expression, mouth opened in an O, eyebrows raised. "She played you false for more than three years, pretending to be your loyal servant and, worse, your friend, only to trip you off the cliff as they say. Think about how she treated you aboard ship coming here. You must feel bewildered at the complete change in her, the resentment and, dare I say contempt, she has shown you. Luxing have been executed for less."

A peculiar look creased Czarina's face as her father spoke. To Symeon's surprise, she appeared sorrowful, her lips drawn back, her eyes fluttering as if on the verge of tears.

"Do you think me so ignorant, I don't see what you're doing?" Kavya whispered.

"What am I doing?" Fang asked.

"You're patronizing me. You're asking me to believe other Shorvex will refuse to harm their Luxing servants simply because I do." Kavya regarded Fang. "If you believe that, you're the greatest fool ever sired on Phoenix. Well-bred elites might avoid sullying their own hands—their own consciences—with the foul work of killing disloyal servants, but can you delude yourself into thinking they won't farm that sort of task out to others? You think you'll foment revolution by calling on the Luxing to rise, but all you'll do is trigger their slaughter in prisons or execution camps. The average landholding Shorvex might miss his old nanny or the cook who prepared his family meals for twenty years, but that won't stop him tossing dissenters onto a pyre he doesn't have to see."

"You paint a bleak picture," Fang said.

"Your canvas. Your paints."

"But you're wrong." Fang leaned forward, meeting Kavya glare for glare. "You leave that pistol on the table because you have no inclination to harm Czarina who, despite the way she's acted of late, remains in your heart a friend and confidant. That killer instinct is all but bred out of you, Princess, just as the yearning to lead, to transform, to seek the best for everyone in your circle burns in your blood. I should know. I helped put it there."

"You might not care, and I understand that, but I didn't enjoy hurting you." Czarina scrubbed her tears away with a vicious swipe of her table napkin. "We had to show you what it's like to live without power and in constant fear."

"It was a ruse?" Kavya's shock showed on her face.

"It's no ruse, girl," Fang said. "It's the truth you cannot recognize. Freedom is an illusion, even Shorvexan freedom. It exists only because the people around you allow for its existence. The moment they decide you're unequal, and therefore unworthy of it, that freedom dies."

"Of all the Shorvex in this entire solar system, you think Kavya needs that lesson?" Symeon's anger boiled inside him like superheated steam. "The woman who, while banished, made of her home a refuge for her servants? She cares more about our race than any person I know, and that includes you."

"I never doubted the lady's care," Fang said, nodding as if to concede the point. "In fact, through Czarina, and others, I cultivated it. These last few days have simply been the final lessons we wished to impart."

"Does your arrogance know any bounds?" Symeon made no effort to hide the acid in his tone. "Is there any end to your manipulation of others? Do you prune your own family the way you have ours?"

"Of course." Fang shrugged one shoulder—the master gambler unabashed when confronted with his cheating ways. "What sort of fools would I and my forebearers be if we altered the Shorvex without altering ourselves."

"But the matches you've made amongst your own are in the open—"

Symeon, don't!

"—unlike the marriage you're planning for us." Symeon gestured to include Kavya and himself.

Her eyes grew wide and her soft lips parted as she slowly looked back and forth between Symeon and Fang. "Marriage?"

Triumph at the look of surprise in Fang's expression made Symeon want to slap the table the way he had during debates back at school. He had caught the old man on his heels.

Fang laughed, his initial shock replaced by a genuine look of delight. "Star born, you surprise me! I, who am so rarely surprised. But then, what should I expect from genes wholly out of my control? You were always the wild factor in this plan, Symeon, the one unpredictable linchpin. I've toyed with the idea of removing you from the equation a thousand times since Grand Duke Alexei had you birthed. Always, you found some way to stay my hand with your successes. Some of my brethren counseled other young men for the task, but out of all the possible choices we prepared for Kavya, you always topped my list."

"You planned for me to marry Symeon?" The look of utter horror in Kavya's eyes made Symeon wince. "And you have a list of other candidates for the job?"

"Not a subject I would have broached with you so early in our acquaintance, but yes," Fang said. "Your match to a suitable husband is paramount to the Wuxia's plans for centuries to come."

"And you knew about this?" Kavya turned to Symeon.

"No! I guessed. It made sense given what I've seen of the Wuxia."

"Which is a damned sight more than you ever shared with me."

"Princess, I—"

"Would I have been given any choice in the matter?" Kavya turned a baleful glare on Fang and Czarina. "Or would you expect me to accept whatever man you threw my way like a docile cow? Is that another benefit of twisting my pedigree over the long years? Did you expect my blood to make me rut with your desired stud?"

Though careful to treat gently with the babe in her arms, Kavya shot to her feet, her chair tumbling over behind her. She handed the child to Anushka before turning back to regard Fang. "Whatever machinations you've wrought by pruning my family tree, know this, no one owns me. You will not by dint of fine words or even physical torture cause me to act against my will."

Kavya marched toward one of the old-fashioned wooden doors, her skirt billowing out with each angry step. Fang's guards made to stop her, but he shook his head, and they moved aside.

Symeon started to go after her, but hesitated. Fang would love that wouldn't he? His star-born chosen dashing off to comfort his would-be rebel heroine. Alone in a society alien to them, how could they but find solace in each other's company, and perhaps each other's arms?

He's manipulating me—us—even now, Symeon thought as he turned his gaze to Fang.

Does that change how you feel? Don't you want to go after her?

"Go," Fang said, unwittingly echoing Yudi's words. "Whether you think I've orchestrated this moment or not—and I swear I haven't—your mistress is hurting, Symeon. She thinks herself alone in the universe. Show her that isn't true. Forget love, marriage, all that claptrap. Be a friend to her now—that is what she needs."

Swallowing the conflict within, Symeon threw down his table napkin and hurried for the door.

* * * * *

Chapter Twenty-Two

Symeon bolted from the dining room in time to catch a hint of Kavya's skirts disappearing through a ground floor doorway. Chiding himself for his hesitation, he charged down the castle's main stairs at a gallop, his boots thumping on the hardwood planks loud enough she must have heard. Whether that meant she would rush to elude him or slow to let him catch her up, remained to be seen. Given the size of Gomarov, he worried she could lose him if she wished.

To his relief, he found her standing at the end of an adjoining hall when he burst through the doorway. She gave him a flat look, her lips stylus-straight, one eyebrow raised, before hurrying out a servants exit into the castle's vast acreage, leaving the door ajar as if inviting him to follow.

"Kavya," he called the instant he reached the exit.

She did not look round. Already some meters removed from the servants' entrance where he stood, Kavya continued at a brisk pace, her lovely sun yellow dress swaying with her gait. The land ahead rose, forming a small hillock crowned with a copse of ancient trees. Brushing past several robots trimming complex topiaries, Kavya headed that way.

"Should I follow or not?" Symeon whispered as he dropped from the porch in her wake.

Of course, you should.

"But she knows I'm here. If she wanted my company, she would stop. Wouldn't she?" Symeon kept his pace sedate.

If a woman like Kavya wanted you to stop, she would tell you that.

"But—"

Symeon, Yudi's voice, silent though it was, somehow took on a tone of rebuke. *I may not always understand human interaction—unpredictability makes your kind infinitely fascinating—but I have observed millions of interactions between men and women, and I'm warning you now, if you leave off this pursuit and subsequently leave Kavya alone, she will likely never forgive you.*

Symeon picked up the pace.

He found her at the top of the hill standing under the spreading branches of a large tree, her arms folded, her silver hair blowing in the light breeze. A dozen or more children, their lineages mixed between Luxing and Shorvex, splashed and played happily in a shallow stream that wound down from the hills several kilometers away. Their happy laughter and screams echoed along the banks where stood a handful of teens watching the younger kids play while a couple of robots likewise looked on, ready to help.

Though the sunlight playing upon the scene appeared natural enough, Symeon noticed a slight distortion in the light blue sky, a telltale sign of an electronic blackout screen designed to obscure observation from above. Several drones hovered quietly nearby, maintaining the camouflaged area. From overhead, this area would appear deserted.

"It's sad they must hide," Kavya said, following Symeon's gaze to the drones. "Imagine if a satellite snapped an image of this happy play, and spread it across the empire."

"It would spell the end of House Gomarov, and likely the Wuxia as well."

Without warning, Kavya threw her arms around Symeon and buried her face in his neck. Caught off guard, he nearly stumbled, but managed to keep his feet, his heart pounding.

"Put your arms around me," she whispered into the space where his collarbone met his neck. "If we keep quiet and close, we might evade whatever electronic snoopers are pointed at us right now. I'm hoping our abrupt departure caught Fang off his stride. Maybe we're not under surveillance, but we can't be too careful."

Out of sorts in a way he had rarely experienced, Symeon slid his hands about her waist, unsure just where to put them.

"If you hadn't followed me, I would have known for certain you were Fang's creature," Kavya said.

Told you!

Pride, and no small amount of attraction, though he would never admit that, sent a line of pure heat running through Symeon's chest. She had wanted him to follow! So much so, she willingly ignored the taboo of showing affection to one's slave. "Princess, I knew nothing about Fang's plans."

"But you knew about the Wuxia."

He nodded, supremely aware of her soft tresses against his cheeks and the scent of her skin like vanilla mixed with roses.

"For how long?"

He yearned to lie. The truth might end this embrace forever. But keeping secrets from Kavya had already hurt her once. He wouldn't do that again. "Since Yaya. Czarina told me."

"I don't know that I can fully trust you, Symeon. I fear I'm alone in this place."

"You're not, Princess. I'm—"

Gently, as one might the wing of an injured bird, Kavya pressed her fingers to Symeon's lips. "For all I know, you'll play me false, maybe you're doing that now, but I'll take the chance. Better to try and fail than sit and do nothing."

"Try what, Princess?" Symeon desired her trust more than he would have reckoned. He had given her his loyalty on Yaya Island; he wasn't about to turn back on it now.

"This." She kissed his neck, and he shuddered.

Some of the children in the stream took notice of them. They made cooing noises, which prompted the teenagers to look round, smiling and whispering to one another.

Heart thundering in his ears, Symeon stood frozen like a small prey animal caught in a lioness's jaws. His desire to kiss Kavya wrestled with a lifetime's worth of training and deeply engendered fear. At all times prior to this moment, he would have been flogged and demoted for becoming so familiar with any Shorvexan woman let alone the princess of his duchy, and possibly future heir to the empire.

"We must convince them it's real." Kavya's warm breath raised the hairs on the back of Symeon's neck.

"What? Lady?"

"Fang, Czarina, all of them must think we're falling in love." She placed another scintillating kiss on his neck. "They can't know we're pretending."

Oh.

"Oh." Symeon swallowed, the weight of his disappointment and instant self-loathing so great he thought it might stamp him into the ground where he stood. "Of course, Princess."

"Enough with that. Call me Kavya, or they'll never buy what we're selling. They have to think it's real."

"Why?"

"So we can escape."

Symeon shook his head. "I don't see how that's possible. There are too many variables against us. Fang has armor and weapons and scads of guards. Not to mention, I'm not a pilot. Even if we somehow managed to sneak onto one of his ships, I wouldn't be able to fly us out of here."

"Isn't it odd how, after all this time we've spent together, I the mistress and you the slave, that it's you who continually underestimates me?"

He straightened in her arms. "I've offended you? What did I say?"

"Symeon, I started flying shuttles when I was twelve. I've kept up my skills in isolation in case I ever decided to leave Yaya. I don't need you for a pilot. I need you to get me to a ship. Do that, and I'll fly us free."

"I apologize, Prin—my Lady." Symeon shook his head. "Sorry, calling you by your given name is going to take some practice."

"And underestimating me? How much practice will it take to shake that habit?"

"That won't happen again, you have my word."

"Good. We have to come up with a viable plan of escape. We can't do that if we don't trust one another. Agreed?"

"Agreed."

"Now, for the next order of business." Kavya drew back far enough to meet Symeon's gaze and kissed him.

Fake or not, it hit him like a thunderclap.

* * * * *

Chapter Twenty-Three

In spite of the ruse, Symeon knew he was falling in love with Kavya. Three weeks had passed since their first kiss. Many more, each cleverly timed by the princess so that different members of Fang's family and guards would catch them, passed between Symeon and she. Some bordered on the passionate as dictated by Kavya alone—Symeon would never presume to press for more—while most remained chaste. Nevertheless, each lured him further into the tangle of his feelings, a jungle of falsehood and forbidden desire. He wondered if Fang's distant grandmother, the maid who had won her master's love, had shared similar feelings. Did worry that her lover's passion might prove false leave her in a state of eternal angst? Did she fear, as Symeon did now, that her lover could never feel true affection for a Luxing?

"You're quiet." Kavya squeezed Symeon's hand to catch his attention. They walked along a broad path east of Gomarov Castle, an entourage of guards and family encircling them on their way to one of Fang's favorite picnic spots on the estate.

"Just musing on the beauty of the day," Symeon lied.

Why not tell her the truth? Yudi asked. *Perhaps she shares your feelings, but won't allow herself to say it aloud. You might be surprised.*

Shut up.

Kavya's look told him she didn't believe his words, but wouldn't press him on them just now. "The weather is fine, isn't it?"

A gaggle of raucous children ran past them, laughing, their mix of black and gold hair bouncing with their steps. They circled around Fang at the head of the group, scampering about until he playfully made to swat their butts, and they scurried away screaming in faux alarm.

Kavya took Symeon's arm and drew close, a sign she wanted to say something meant for his ears alone.

"I don't hate him. I think that's the worst part. I want to hate him, but his vision is catching."

Symeon nodded minutely. "His means are wrongheaded. Manipulating people without their consent turns my stomach. But I can't hate his aims."

"Exactly."

"Let's have lunch by the three fountains today!" Fang called over his shoulder to the thirty some odd people following him. The children cheered as most of the younger ones hurried down a side path ahead of Fang, charging into an unnatural clearing dominated by three oversized fountains, their basins made for wading.

"Make the water, Grandfather!" Cried Zel Lo, the four year old son of Fang's second daughter.

Most of the adults and a handful of the older children laughed since Zel Lo had unintentionally told his venerable grandfather to urinate.

Fang, chuckling, scooped the boy into his arms and hugged him tight. "Not yet, Zel. First we eat, then we play."

Kavya and Symeon helped spread thick drop cloths along the grassy perimeters surrounding the fountains while robots and some of the younger wives unpacked food shuttled down from the castle kitchens on fan-driven floating tables. In minutes, the smell of cooked meats and sautéed vegetables filled the air, capturing the attention of even the smaller children. Though the robots could have easily served the meal, Fang and his oldest wife insisted everyone fill their own plates as a sign of appreciation to the cooks. The ritual reminded Symeon of his home on the District Two farm where his parents had observed a similar custom every New World Day.

Fang and his third wife, Anushka, joined Symeon and Kavya after filling their plates with steaming ham and pan-fried potatoes. Anushka carried a sleeping Jing Fei in a mobile bassinet which she pointedly placed next to Kavya before sitting down. The princess gave her a pleased smile.

"I must apologize for my absence these past two weeks," Fang said as he took a seat across from Kavya and Symeon. "Matters of war took me off planet."

"So we heard." Kavya motioned to a robot waiter, and it brought her a beverage. "Captain Vayer told us my father defeated a major attack two days ago, but the empire continues to deny him the throne."

Captain Vayer, the estate's chief security officer, often made a show of withholding information about the ongoing solar war only to concede after a bit of niggling from Kavya. The man's playacting didn't fool her or Symeon. They knew he shared what Fang allowed and no more. Without access to the sphere, they couldn't confirm what the man told them, but Symeon figured it must be true. Why pass them anything besides the rosiest of pictures otherwise?

"I'll have a word with the man about his loose tongue," Fang said, his expression surly. "But yes, that's true. Your father's forces are making headway, though not as quickly as I had hoped. This was the first major offensive launched by the great houses, but they're fighting a limited war. After they failed to capitulate as I predicted, I thought they would commit fully to winning back Bastrayavich. It's what I would have done. But I fear it is as Symeon told me some weeks ago—the royal admiralty refuses to yield even with their heads of state in mortal danger because the outcome might favor their personal rise should someone amenable to them take the throne. Their hesitancy keeps them from launching an assault large enough to overwhelm Alexei's forces. I appreciate their reticence, obviously—I want Alexei to win—but this prolonged conflict is placing a strain on the Wuxia."

He's stymied. He's fishing for your insight. I say you give it without stint. His cause aligns with ours.

Symeon almost shook his head at Yudi's suggestion, but stopped himself at the final second. Aloud he said, "What sort of strain? Aren't your people safely hidden across the empire? What does it matter to them if their masters go to war?"

Fang stared off into the trees surrounding the clearing for a moment, his lips pressed into a hard line. "They're hidden, but that doesn't mean they feel safe or that they'll remain patient. The Wuxia aren't a military organization. There exist factions within our factions, small groups beholden more to their local leaders than the movement at large. It's taken years for me to consolidate enough control to forward the current plan. Now that it's underway, our people chafe at the waiting—some have been serving as slaves their whole lives, dreaming of this time. Even my own children and grandchildren complain that I've kept them leashed too long."

Symeon shared a brief glance with Kavya. This was the most information Fang had yet divulged to them about his overall plan. Cagey to a fault, he often made it seem like he had given away every facet, only to leave Symeon vague on concrete details as to how the Wuxia would reveal themselves to the empire when the time came. He worried Fang might call on his shadow forces to rise up against their masters—to gut families in their sleep and seize their holdings in a night of terror.

Surely not. That sort of attack would leave the entirety of the Wuxia vulnerable to reprisals. Besides, if that was Fang's plan, why would he need Kavya?

"What happens when you drop that leash?" Kavya asked, echoing Symeon's thoughts.

Fang took a long draught from a beer and sighed appreciatively before he answered. "You're an intelligent woman. You must know I'll want you to negotiate with your father on behalf of the Wuxia."

Another diversion, thought Symeon. *The man never explicitly says what the Wuxia will do when they reveal themselves.*

What do you expect? Fang has spent his entire life safeguarding his secrets. Either way, your idea of massacre is a foolish notion. He can't expect servants to kill the people they've served, sometimes for the better part of their lives, as if taking a life is nothing. These aren't trained soldiers we're discussing, they're slaves. Oaths to the Wuxia aside, I'd wager most of them harbor some affection for their masters.

You underestimate the pain of enslavement, Symeon thought.

And you the capacity of the human heart. Odd that an AI should need to school you on that.

"Negotiate to what end?" Pushing Yudi's words aside, Symeon moved to sit on his knees, hands on his thighs as many in Fang's family sat. They took it as a sign of both giving and commanding respect.

"You know my goals," Fang said. "Have I not made them clear? Peace, freedom, a voice for the Shorxing in our mutual government."

"There is no mutual government," Kavya said without rancor, her voice mild. "And revealing yourselves won't create one."

"It will." Fang met their gazes, his expression concrete. "The great houses have no clue we exist, and you know nothing of our true numbers. They will cower when they see our strength."

"The way they have under threat of losing the divors?" Kavya cocked her head to one side, eyebrows raised.

A look of irritation flashed across Fang's expression, and Symeon thought the old man might lose his temper, but Fang laughed. "Perhaps you're right. It's good speaking with the two of you. Sometimes I need to hear a dissenting opinion, and you always give me that, though I'm pleased I don't see you every day."

"That makes this a special occasion." Symeon gestured at the mostly empty drop cloth they occupied. "I notice none of the others joined us today, not even Czarina."

Fang nodded. "It's time we discuss roles."

"You mean my transformation into the Wuxia's songbird?" Kavya placed no emphasis on the final word, yet Symeon could taste the derision in her meaning. So could Fang and Anushka by their expressions.

"Just so," Fang said. "As you so astutely pointed out, your father's coup is proceeding slower than I anticipated. For reasons I cannot divulge, this means I must ask you to speak with him sooner than I originally planned. I want you to reveal the Wuxia to him in your first interview. It's paramount he understand our vast reach within the empire—that we will be one of his major concerns the moment he secures the throne."

"And you assume I'm amenable to this task?" Kavya's gaze never wavered. She watched Fang with the intensity of a huntress.

"As I said, I had hoped to give you more time—months even—to live amongst my kin and my closest confidants. I want you to know us, our hearts, our deep love for one another and the cause of freedom. I can only hope you've seen these virtues reflected in us already given your short stay in Gomarov Castle?"

Kavya sat quiet for a moment. Symeon, at a loss for how she might react, watched her while gauging his own feelings. Though he might not agree with Fang's plans for the empire, he couldn't deny the beauty he found in the man's family. If they were Fang's vision of the future empire, he could scarcely argue against it.

"For a man steeped in secret influence and slow, patient manipulation, you come off rather heavy-handed to me, Fang. You've practically rubbed my royal nose in your picturesque ideals. I can't turn around without stepping on the toes of a gorgeous child or running into a charming wife, son, grandchild ready to extol the virtues of the Shorxing way. And your overzealous push to see Symeon and I fall in love has been anything but adroit."

Symeon's pulse quickened. Would Kavya reveal their ruse? What about their plans to escape?

What about your chance to be near her on a daily basis?

Again, shut up.

Fang's lips curled into a grin. "But it's worked, yes?"

Kavya gazed into Symeon's eyes with such ardor he thought his face might catch fire from the heat rushing up his neck. She entwined her fingers with his and pressed his hand to her breast so that he could feel her heart beating. "Yes, damn you."

"It's our way forward, Princess." Fang, still smiling, eyes soft, grasped Anushka's hand. "We can and will fight to free the Luxing.

No amount of hoping or wishing will let us avoid that. But final victory doesn't hinge on bloodshed; it hinges on love."

Kavya nodded and turned to him, her silver-blue eyes glistening in the bright sunlight. "What would you have me say to my father?"

* * * * *

Chapter Twenty-Four

The sky above Gomarov Castle had grown dark though the air remained warm from the daytime heat. Symeon stood on a high balcony overlooking the castle's eastern courtyard, his hands planted on its balustrade, his mind anywhere but the present.

She's acting, Symeon.

"Didn't you see the way she looked at me—the way she held my hand? It wasn't like other times. This was different." Symeon watched a six-legged robot crawl up the courtyard wall opposite him, scrubbing the stones with a clutch of neon green brushes and a spray of soapy water.

The difference was Fang. She wanted to sell it. She's a princess, Sym. Acting is her life.

"You've been wrong before."

You're mixing up your feelings for hers.

"Enough. I don't have time for this. Here comes the sergeant."

A man dressed in powered armor the color of ripe wheat strode into the courtyard, his heavy footfalls ringing echoes from the flagstones.

"Kozar, hello!" Symeon called.

The sergeant looked about for a moment before locating the voice. He tapped a control on his chin to raise his visor. "Symeon Brashniev. How are you?"

"Bored! Care to have a drink in the Kitchens?"

"Sure. I'm just going off duty. Let me peel out of this clam shell, and I'll meet you there."

"Bah, why wait?" Symeon caught hold of a rain gutter, bounded over the balcony handrail, and shimmied down to the courtyard floor.

Kozar laughed and slapped his metal thigh with a PING. "You never told me you were an acrobat. You should have joined the emperor's mummers when you were young!"

"If it gets me out of my room, I'll do it now."

"Come, let's have that drink." Kozar placed a surprisingly gentle hand on Symeon's back and guided him toward a steel-polymer door wholly incongruent with the stone wall. It swung open at their approach.

Symeon had visited the castle's armory five times since his arrival at Gomarov Castle. On each occasion, escorted by one or another guard he had befriended, he made it his purpose to avoid even the appearance of a dishonest action. Those earlier trips, two of them with Kozar, had been preparation for this night, and Symeon vowed to keep his wits about him.

They descended a flight of stairs into a bunker hardened against bombs. The cool air made Symeon's skin prickle. Lights flicked on, revealing three dozen armored suits like Kovar's standing at attention in the middle of the room. Fang's people had stolen most of them the night they kidnapped Kavya, though a few older models evidenced previous heists. Behind the armor stood rack upon rack of rifles and handguns, both modern laser and plasma models as well as old-fashioned projectile arms. Still other instruments of war lined the armory walls, but Symeon lacked the training to recognize their use.

"Let me park this thing." Kovar moved to stand in an empty space at the right side of the armor formation. His suit grew inanimate in a way Symeon couldn't define, like a puppet when its master has become distracted, and the whir of servos filled the air. Kovar's helm lifted off his head, held up in front by a multi-jointed arm that extended from his breastplate. At the same instant, the armor's back plate from heel to neck split apart on concealed hinges.

Kovar backed out of the suit, his brown hair moist with sweat, and breathed a heavy sigh. What his grandfather, Fang, would term a true Shorxing, Kovar looked like a perfect melding of his dual heritage. With the broad nose and round jawline of a Luxing combined with the silvery blue complexion of a Shorvex, his features would have seen him rejected from either society. Not so in the rarefied air of Gomarov Castle. Here, amongst his many female cousins, he was considered quite the handsome beast.

"I'm always proud to pilot armor," he said, stretching his back, "but it does grow uncomfortable after seven or eight hours."

"I should think it would."

As was his custom after a long shift on guard duty, Kovar pulled on a basic shirt and plain britches he kept stashed in a locker before retrieving the palm-sized key card that gave him access to the armory from his suit. He slipped it into his trousers pocket and gestured toward the door. "Let's have that drink."

* * *

Deprived of the clubs and bars they might have enjoyed in a city or town, the adult staff employed at Gomarov Castle had arranged for themselves a pub known as the Kitchens, so named for its proximity to the castle's actual kitchen. Most nights, off duty maids, guards like Kovar, grounds keepers, and a slew of others visited the place. Fang, who often dropped by whenever he wasn't away, not only approved of the Kitchens, by all accounts he bankrolled the place, making the drinks free so long as Valentin, the bartender, approved of the person ordering.

A live band—usually an ensemble formed from whatever musicians were available—often played at Kitchens. Tonight's combination, two electric guitars, a stand up bassist, a synth drummer of some renown, and a sultry voiced nanny who could bring tears to Symeon's eyes when she got going, filled the place with a sweet sound.

"So, you and the princess, eh?" Kovar, who had imbibed no fewer than six beers and a slew of hard liquor shots in the last three hours, nearly bobbled his seventh before getting it to his lips. "I never asked you about that. She's quite a beauty. Too pretty for the likes of you, no offense."

Humans always say that when they mean nothing but offense.

"Tell me about it," Symeon said. He and Kovar sat alone at a table in a corner of the converted dining hall. Never one much given to alcohol, Symeon had drank three beers to Kovar's six, and still felt muzzy.

"What?"

"Yeah, me and Kavya—you're right, she is too pretty for me." Symeon wished Kavya was with him now, though they had agreed schmoozing guards was best left to him. Most of Fang's trained soldiers, like Kovar, looked and acted far more Luxing than Shorvexan. And besides, her presence at the Kitchens would have caused a stir. The last thing Symeon needed right now was undo attention.

"What's she like?"

He wants to hear that she's a spoiled child. I can see it in his expression.

Symeon agreed. Kovar wasn't a bad sort, but the eagerness in his eyes made Symeon want to break his nose, not that he could let that feeling show. He needed to keep things light. "She's a hell of a lot nicer than you'd expect. Level-headed, practical, not what you'd expect in a duchy princess."

Kovar, too drunk to hide his disappointment, nodded. He looked half asleep, his eyes rheumy in the bar's scant light. After a moment he brightened, his gaze coming back into focus as his lips slowly curled into a smile. "How is she in the sack?"

Five years of boxing informed Symeon he could lay Kovar out with a single right hook. Doing so would take no more effort than flipping a pancake.

You're letting the drink go to your head. Remember your purpose here.

Symeon took a swig from his beer to hide the sudden flush of anger heating up his face. By the time he had set his bottle on the table, he had control of his emotions. He still wanted to belt Kovar into low orbit, but now possessed the sense to refrain.

"Let's just say, she's beyond my imagination."

"I bet!"

"It's getting late. Don't you have duty tomorrow afternoon?"

"Don't remind me." Kovar squeezed his eyes shut and shook his head as if to banish a sour thought. "Another mindless shift doing nothing. I can't wait to get out of this shit hole."

"This shit hole seems like a cushy job to me. And you're with your family." The seneschal in Symeon wanted to reprimand Kovar for denigrating his posting. All service, no matter how menial, deserved respect.

"I don't want cushy. We leaving or what?" Kovar made to stand and nearly tripped over his own feet, forcing Symeon to catch him. Other patrons stared at them, most not even trying to hide their laughter. Everyone knew Kovar couldn't hold his liquor.

Symeon mentally cursed his luck. He had hoped they could leave without catching anyone's attention. He got a shoulder under Kovar's arm and started him weaving towards the exit.

"Hey, Symeon Brashniev." Valentin, the Kitchens' ever present bartender, leaned his muscular arms over the bar. "You tell Kovar he's cut off for two weeks. I won't have people coming in here getting sloppy drunk every night, even if he is my cousin."

"What? You sorry bastard." Kovar struggled against Symeon's grip.

Now the entire bar is looking at you.

"I'll tell him when he sobers up." Symeon hustled Kovar out the north exit into cool night air.

"Cut me off? That musclebound sack of shit is lucky to have me visit him at all. I'm entertaining! Aren't I, Sym?"

"Absolutely." Symeon lugged the sozzled Kovar around a corner, their boots wet with nighttime dew. Unseen and unheard drones recorded their passing. Symeon fancied he saw one limned in moonlight a few meters overhead, but couldn't be sure. The things' rudimentary AI performed a superb job keeping them out of sight.

Rudimentary AI? Try elementary algorithms lacking even the most basic semblance of sentient thought.

"Is someone offended?" Symeon huffed as he dragged a near unconscious Kovar up a short flight of stairs into the castle's eastern wing.

"Me? No," Kovar warbled. "Pissed off I might miss the real fighting though. I ask you, is that fair? I'm one of the old man's true grandsons, and I'm sidelined here guarding the nursery while others are out there." Kovar gestured at the ceiling. "Where'd the stars go?"

"We're inside. What do you mean by the real fighting?"

"Not supposed to talk about that, am I?" Kovar wrinkled his nose as if struggling to marshal his thoughts. "It's not for you and the pretty princess, all right?"

"Of course, you're right. Can you open the door?" Symeon pointed at a black palm plate on the wall outside Kovar's room.

"Of course I can. I'm not drunk, you know." Kovar pawed at the thing a couple of times before he managed to key the door open. "See."

Kovar's room reminded Symeon of his cell on Fang's ship. It contained a steel-framed bunk bed, two upright bureaus, and a single desk with a lamp and holo display. Kovar shared it with a fellow sergeant named Boris. The two of them worked opposite shifts—Boris was on duty now patrolling the estate—and rarely saw one another.

"Bed's never looked so good." Kovar leaned his forehead against the upper bunk while fidgeting with his belt. "I need sleep. What's wrong with this damned thing. Can't seem to unhitch it."

"Let me." Symeon brushed Kovar's hands aside and reached for his belt buckle.

The wary guard backed away, eyes wide. "Look, Sym, I'm not—not into men, okay?"

Symeon rolled his eyes. "Me neither. I'm with the princess, remember? But I am a trained seneschal. Serving's in my nature."

"Oh, right. Yeah, you were a slave. But like a big slave—a, uh, an important one, right?"

"Something like that." Symeon resumed unfastening Kovar's belt and pants. "Pull your leg out. Good, now the other—don't hit your head."

"That's another job I couldn't have, because of my face and my skin."

"What job is that?" Symeon shoved Kovar's pants toward the entrance out of sight from the bed.

"Slave. Forget big time slave like what Yakov did with you. I couldn't even scrub floors. My whole life's been here or one of grandfather's other estates."

Symeon froze in the act of lowering Kovar onto the bed. "Do you mean Yakov Laben?"

Kovar stretched out on the narrow bed, his eyes closed. "Yep. He's my third cousin once removed. If he was a woman, the match makers would let me court him!"

Symeon sat back on his haunches, thunderstruck. Yakov, his best friend all through five years of school, had been a plant—one of Fang's agents, one of his progeny. Had every aspect of Symeon's life been orchestrated by this man? What about his mother and father? Were they Wuxia as well?

Questions for another time. Right now, you need to accomplish what you came here for. Kavya is counting on you.

In a minute.

"You think Yakov did a good job with me at the School of Seneschals?"

Kovar shrugged. "Must have done. You're here aren't you?"

"And where is he now?"

"With Grand Duke Alexei, the lucky bastard. Yakov might even end up being the one to kill him when the time comes."

* * * * *

Chapter Twenty-Five

Kavya entered the armory courtyard at 0230 as planned. She wore leggings and athletic shoes matched with a form-fitting top. To Symeon's surprise, she had colored her usually silver hair a deep purple, which she wore in a bun. The sight of her heightened Symeon's awareness. Until this moment, their plan had seemed ephemeral, a vision dreamed up by prisoners lacking the means to make it happen.

But now here we are. It's happening.

Which meant they would have to fight. Symeon recoiled from the idea. Yes, he had shot that guard during their escape from Bastrayavich, but the man had forced Symeon's hand. The memory of it filled him with regret. The thought of doing it again, this time against people he had come to know, threatened to unnerve him.

That was until Kavya put her arms around him and pressed her soft lips to his neck.

"Did you get it?" She breathed the words against his skin, her voice low and husky.

"Yes." Symeon, resolutely ignoring the prickle of goose flesh crawling down his shoulder blades, to tap the hip pocket on his running pants which concealed Kovar's key card. Did she realize how much her warm breath made him want to kiss her?

I doubt she does, Symeon. She's playing her role.

Part of Symeon knew Yudi was right. Part of him refused to believe it. In the lead-up to this night, the culmination of their shared plan, they had spent many an evening holding one another on a bench in this darkened courtyard, well aware of the surveillance cameras and directional microphones focused on them. Though their dalliances never progressed beyond kissing and snuggling, something about these encounters had lately changed. Symeon knew he had been inappropriately attracted to Kavya long before this faux love affair, probably even before he became fully aware of it himself, but this new ardor he felt was different. Question was, did she feel it too? Sometimes, he swore she must. Others, like tonight, she was all business.

"Fang arrived six hours ago, fresh from a meeting in Kolpinev. He had his landing crew refuel that IW Eagle he favors for inner system treks. I think he's planning another trip to one of the moons tomorrow night. We should aim for that one, but any of the shuttles will do." Kavya had made it her business to track the Wuxia leader's comings and goings the last few weeks during her daily walks around the estate. Czarina, Kavya's usual companion/guard during these forays, hadn't seemed to notice the princess' interest in what ships stood on the east lawn.

"Were you followed?"

"No. Czarina was fast asleep when I slipped out. I still say it's sexist that I've had a live-in warden all this time and you're allowed free range throughout the castle."

"Scrutiny follows nobility, isn't that the saying?"

"Let's hope it's taking a vacation tonight," Kavya said, hugging Symeon tighter. "Are you ready?"

"Will you forgive me if I say no?"

"Yes, but only if you go through with it anyway."

Symeon smiled. "You colored your hair."

Kavya pressed a hand to the side of her head as self-conscious as a Luxing girl. "My eyes too, see?" She flashed a comm light across her face to highlight her now-jade irises. "Do you like them? I decided if I'm changing my life, I might as well change my body, but I didn't want a tattoo. Hair and eyes I can change back later without much trouble."

"A clean break from your old life?" Symeon asked. "Yes. I love it."

She grinned at him.

"There's something I need to tell you before we do this," Symeon said, growing serious.

"You're secretly working for Fang and have been from the start?" Kavya might have been joking, but Symeon got the feeling she more than half expected him to confirm her jest.

He leaned close to her ear. "Kovar told me something about Fang's plans. Understand, he was drunker than I've ever seen him. It's possible he made this up. But he claims Fang has no intention of letting your father remain emperor more than five years."

"Why kill him after working so long to place him on the throne. He—" Kavya pulled back to look Symeon in the eyes. "Fang plans to replace him with me."

I've told you time and again, the woman is brilliant.

"Yes," Symeon said. "With the Bith finishing their gate, Fang views this as the perfect time for vast change across the empire. He wants us married and you installed on the throne to usher in a new era for our people."

"A mixed marriage, a female emperor, and—"

"And Shorxing heirs waiting in the wings."

"Fang wants us having children right away?" Kavya shook her head as if exasperated. "Of course he does. The Wuxia don't scheme in terms of years. Fang's thinking centuries ahead."

Symeon nodded. "Does this change our plans?"

"Not markedly, but it does advance the timetable." Kavya glanced over her shoulder at the armory door. The courtyard remained empty, but Symeon could feel her muscles tighten at the thought of discovery.

"Will you tell me where we're headed now?" he asked without much hope of receiving an answer. Though they had been formulating this escape plan for weeks, Kavya had yet to even hint at their destination. Symeon had considered demanding it of her in exchange for his help many times, but the seneschal in him balked at the idea of blackmailing his liege.

You really should stop thinking of her that way. You're equals now.

In this castle, perhaps, thought Symeon. *But in the real world, I remain her slave.*

No. You remain her slave in the one place it matters. Your mind.

Kavya shook her head. "Best if only one of us knows. You can still claim ignorance—swear you were only doing your mistress's bidding."

"Because it's true."

Kavya chuckled and kissed Symeon's jaw. "And I thank you for that. You've shown me loyalty even after I accused you of betrayal. You're a fine seneschal, Symeon, but you're an even better man."

For a moment, Symeon didn't know what to say. His throat had gone suddenly tight. "Thank you."

She hugged him tighter before backing up, still holding his hand. "What do you say we get out of here?"

Without direct access to the castle's computer systems, Symeon could only guess at the armory's full security suite. Observation told him it was anything but sophisticated. With the supreme need for secrecy surrounding Gomarov Castle and its inhabitants, Fang's guard had been forced to rely on in-house design and engineering rather than hiring an outside agency to construct and integrate their protective infrastructure. From what Symeon could determine, this reliance had led to a primitive set up, one far too dependent on cameras and human reaction times, and thus susceptible to exploitation.

Assuming you're right.

Yes, assuming that.

To Symeon's relief, the armory door swung open at their approach. Moving quickly, he jimmied a loose stone, one he had slowly scraped free from its mortar over the course of many days, from the castle wall and wedged it beneath the door's lower hinge.

Kavya raised an eyebrow at him.

"In case the guards try to lock us inside."

"Ah, brilliant. Let's hurry."

They descended into the cool darkness, the armory's lights switching on as they entered. They had perhaps ninety seconds before a castle guard, hopefully an unarmored one, would arrive to investigate their presence. With luck, Symeon and Kavya would be well away before that.

Symeon made straight for the weapons racks. He chose a BN-48 laser rifle for himself and handed Kavya the companion hand gun, the BN-30 laser pistol with a belt and holster. She strapped it about her waist with confidence.

"These won't penetrate armor." Kavya drew the pistol with impeccable speed before returning it to the holster.

"No, which means we should get to a ship before that becomes a problem."

Based on weeks spent observing guard rotations around the castle, Symeon and Kavya had determined that the two hour span between 0200 and 0400 offered them the best chance of reaching one of Fang's shuttles without encountering armored guards. Castle security employed two suits per shift while the majority of guards on duty wore light protective gear. Unless tonight's charge captain had made an unexpected change to the rotation, the armored sentries should be performing a physical sweep of the estate, a duty that would take them up to three kilometers from the castle proper. Even given the armor's phenomenal run speed, it would take several minutes for them to return for an emergency call. Too bad the same didn't apply to the regular guards.

Symeon withdrew a body armor vest from a supply closet and handed it to Kavya. She struggled into it while he searched for one his size. No sooner had he found one large enough to accommodate his shoulders than a sound like gunfire followed by a tremendous boom made them both jump in a panic. Symeon placed himself in front of the princess with the armory's stockpile of armored suits between them and the armory door which, having crushed his makeshift jam, had just slammed shut.

Kavya cursed and ran to the stairs, Symeon on her heels. She slapped the steel with an open palm, her jaw tight. "Any chance the key card will somehow open it back up?"

Symeon pulled the card from his pocket to wave it uselessly in front of the sealed door. He shook his head.

"Kavya, Symeon, this is Captain Lao Xi of the castle guard," said a calm voice that echoed through the armory. "I need you to disarm.

Place your weapons and armor on the floor after which you will lie on your stomachs with your fingers interlaced behind your heads."

Symeon met Kavya's gaze and found there a steely resolve. She had no intention of surrendering. She leveled her laser pistol on the door.

"Wait," Symeon said, stopping Kavya before she could fire. "It'd take you a year to burn through that much steel with a hand laser. I have a better idea."

He crossed the room to the formation of armored fighting suits. Each stood open, the back and legs split apart, awaiting a human pilot.

This won't work. Those suits are likely keyed to the various guards' biometrics. They won't recognize you. In fact, they may consider you a threat and apply countermeasures.

What countermeasures? Symeon thought.

Who knows? Electric shock, a gas meant to anesthetize any would be burglar, or how about the simple expedient of freezing in place once you're inside? It could function as a man-sized prison cell until castle security decides to free you.

Have I ever told you what an inspiration you are to me?

"You think one of those will work for you when we can't get a measly door to open?" Kavya asked, echoing Yudi's pessimism.

"These things carry more firepower than any of the rifles or pistols we'll find in those racks. Maybe I can use that to get us out of here, but we're no worse off if I fail."

Kavya still looked unconvinced, but she nodded.

Symeon whipped off his shoes and stepped into one of the suits, mimicking as best he could guards like Kovar. He shoved his arms inside up the shoulders, the cold metal a shock on his bare hands.

Sentries wore skin suits under their armor. Symeon had only his workout clothes and a pair of thin socks. Hopefully, they'd do.

The instant Symeon's chin touched the armor's reinforced bevor, meant to protect his throat and lower jaw, the suit became suddenly animate. Servos whined as the rear openings sealed, creating a snug fit mechanically adjusted by the onboard computer. Something cool and gel-like filled the empty spaces between his body and the suit. It felt porous like liquid poly foam, except it remained pliable no matter how he moved. The articulated arm holding the suit's helm and visor bent to place them on Symeon's head without so much as brushing his ears. Once connected, the visor came to life, providing Symeon a virtual environment with a sight-perfect view and a wealth of information about both the suit and the world outside.

Oh! Yudi's exclamation of surprise and delight rang through Symeon's head not merely as a word, but also a series of thought-images so packed with information he couldn't begin to follow them all. He did, however, grasp enough to recognize Yudi's immense pleasure at discovering something wholly unexpected.

You're talking with the armor.

Yes! It just tried to incapacitate you with an electric shock. I overrode it. You never told me these suits included a neural control interface!

I didn't know. Symeon took a tentative step. He anticipated a slight lag time between his movements and the suit's reactions, but there was none. He lifted his hands, marveling at the strength he could feel bolstering his own, and the way the gel around his limbs moved about him to avoid causing undue pressure on his body.

"It works?" Kavya stood in front of Symeon, her eyes round. "What can it do? Can you get the armory door open? Are there guards out there?"

The answer to both questions is yes. Yudi posted an outside view of the courtyard to Symeon's visor. It showed six armed and lightly armored guards facing the door, awaiting orders from Captain Lao Xi.

Symeon saw the images with his eyes, but the information flowing through his consciousness dwarfed his body's paltry senses. He knew things—things he couldn't know. His connection to Yudi, and Yudi's subsequent connection to the castle's security infrastructure, tethered Symeon to everything happening in and around Gomarov Castle. By simply focusing on a piece of data, he could bring it to mind, examine it, and know its particulars.

For instance, the two armored guards on duty were right now speeding toward the castle. Both had been more than two kilometers away when they got the emergency call to return, as Symeon and Kavya had planned. Now, they would arrive within two minutes.

Based on security comm chatter, everyone knew Symeon had donned a suit and somehow circumvented its automated theft protocols, which meant they'd be scrambling to stop him all the more now.

"Symeon?" Kavya waved a hand in front of his visor. "Are you alive in there?"

"Sorry. I'm suffering a bit of sensory overload."

"Get over it. We need an exit, now!"

"Right." Symeon hustled to the armory stairs, his footfalls like metal pans slapping the floor. As his thoughts turned to the door and how to open it, an array of options shuffled through his mind as if he had called them up on purpose. Among them, he found a simple override command, and almost laughed.

That will work, but here's a better solution.

Symeon reeled back from the sudden image in his head. "I don't care for harming people if I can help it."

"I feel the same, but we may not have a choice," Kavya said, thinking he was speaking to her.

The sound will give them warning, and this way they'll be kept busy while you and Kavya run.

Symeon nodded and turned his attention to the suit's weapons systems. He no more than thought about the over-the-shoulder laser cannon and the thing unlimbered from his back armor like a snake rearing to strike. With a flick of his thoughts, Symeon set it to full power—strong enough to slice through the armory door like a knife through wet clay—and gently pushed Kavya behind him.

"Step back, things are going to get hot."

Symeon keyed the laser with a thought and a coherent blue beam struck the armory door on the far right side, cutting through the metal and turning the surface cherry red for several centimeters all around. Rather than attack the door's strongest point, its center, Yudi's plan saw Symeon trace the laser across its oversized hinges, and it was working. Whatever engineers Fang had employed to build the armory, they hadn't wagered on an attack from the inside. Molten metal spilled from the hinges as the last of them melted into runny slag. Unfortunately, the door remained in place, held by its immense weight.

Now try one of these. Yudi drew Symeon's attention back to the suit's weapons inventory, a particular munition highlighted for emphasis.

Symeon grinned as he lifted his right arm and a barrel snapped into place above his wrist. With a thought, he selected a timed magnetic bomb and fired two of them into the door where they stuck fast. Quickly, he spun around, gathered Kavya into his arms with his back to the stairs and detonated the explosives. Keyed to discharge as much kinetic energy as possible toward the front, the bombs delivered a considerable impact despite their size. The armory shook with a boom, and the massive door jumped out of its frame to land upright on the courtyard tiles where it wobbled for a moment before toppling over on its face, obliging the six guards who had gathered there to scramble out of the way or get flattened.

"Stay close," Symeon said as he spun toward the stairs, his mind whirling through the weapons at his disposal even as he took note of the guards and their relative positions. "We've got a shuttle to steal."

Kavya drew her laser pistol, her jaw set. "Lead on."

* * * * *

Chapter Twenty-Six

Symeon fired a concussion grenade from the top of the stairs. It landed in the midst of the guards who hadn't yet recovered from the armory door's unexpected tumble. The subsequent explosion and flash of light were enough to polarize his visor and cause his exterior mic to momentarily attenuate all input. Thus, he didn't hear Kavya's scream, or immediately notice when she collapsed to the paving stones.

With the guards writhing on the ground, Symeon ran for the exit opposite them.

Stop! Kavya is down.

Symeon's armored feet dug furrows in the courtyard paving stones as he spun about, heart in his throat. Unlike the guards, who had taken the brunt of the grenade's impact at close range, Kavya was already struggling to her feet though she appeared less than steady. She stumbled forward and would have toppled headlong a second time had Symeon not caught her.

"You idiot!" She shoved away from him, but her balance proved untrustworthy and she was forced to rely on his mechanized arm for support.

"I'm so sorry!" Symeon guided her toward the far exit, one eye on the castle guards, three of whom were rising to their feet.

"Did you suddenly forget I was with you? And that I'm not traipsing around in battle armor?"

"I've never fired a grenade in my life. I didn't realize it would affect that wide of an area. Again, I apologize."

"I can't hear what you're saying. I'm deaf because of you. Just get us out of here without getting shot!"

Symeon hustled Kavya into the eastern alleyway leading out of the courtyard. Red laser fire brightened the walls behind them, the sound of it like an over-stressed teapot. Thankfully, the recovered guards' angle of fire couldn't reach their quarry, but they were coming on fast and would soon remedy that problem.

Door ahead is sealed. Security has put the castle on lock down.

"Can I burst through it with a running start?"

No. Give me three seconds.

"To what?" Symeon had no more than asked the question before the answer came clear. The courtyard door, an automated model, swung open on servos an instant before Kavya reached it. They passed inside and it slammed shut behind them, its locking mechanism engaging with a series of clicks.

Security is trying to reopen it. Too bad I've locked them out of their own system.

"Perfect! Will it hold?"

Yes. It's reinforced against lasers and projectiles. Of course, it won't last forever. With concentrated fire, they'll come through in a matter of minutes.

"Let's not be here when that happens."

"I still can't hear what you're saying," Kavya huffed as she dashed along the interior hallway two steps ahead of Symeon. "You might as well save your breath for later when you beg forgiveness for making me deaf!"

Symeon winced inside his helmet.

Well, at least this way she isn't asking why you're talking to yourself.

"True."

Based on their plan, Symeon and Kavya had only to traverse this single hall to the eastern side of the castle where Fang kept his shuttles on twin landing pads. A few more steps, and they would reach freedom.

Not quite.

Yudi called up an overhead view of the castle and its grounds with two red icons highlighted for Symeon's attention.

The armored guards.

Symeon cursed himself for forgetting them. Coming from opposite directions, they reached the castle walls at almost the same instant, Lieutenant Gou on the south, and Captain Guyford on the north. For one brief second, Symeon held out hope the castle's security lock down protocols, now usurped by Yudi, would thwart the newcomers, but no such luck. Gou blew the southern entrance doors off their hinges with six timed grenades, and Guyford simply scaled the northern walls like a spider.

While Gou marched into the courtyard to join his non-armored compatriots, Guyford dashed across the roof, leaping from tower to tower, heading straight for the landing pads.

Symeon dragged Kavya to a stop before she could reach the exit ahead of them. She turned to him, a sour yet questioning look on her face. "What is it?"

He made the universal sign of guns firing with his armored hands and pointed outside.

"The suit tell you that?"

He nodded, pointed at the floor for her to wait, and held up one finger.

"Okay, but we can't sit still long. I'm surprised the guards behind us haven't come through yet."

Symeon didn't bother trying to communicate how he had locked them out. He instead turned his attention to the armor's interface into the castle's computer systems. In about ten seconds, Lieutenant Gou would reach the courtyard door. Five seconds after that, Guyford would likewise reach the door in front of Kavya. They were surrounded and outgunned.

Any suggestions? Symeon thought, his mind whirling through a panoply of increasingly improbable solutions.

Give up? Honestly, I see no way for you to overcome two armored opponents backed by—oh no, that's not good.

Informed by his interface with Yudi, Symeon saw in his mind what had so upset the AI. All five of the unarmored guards were now headed for the armory to acquire their own suits on Captain Lao Xi's orders. "Make that seven armored guards."

Step out of the suit, lay on your belly, and I'll open the doors. Kavya won't like it, but she'll understand when she sees the odds.

Symeon looked at Kavya who raised a purple eyebrow at him. She trusted him. They had made this plan together. She wouldn't abandon it at the first sign of opposition.

This is more than the first sign of opposition, Symeon! You're facing overwhelming odds. Be sensible. Submit.

Red light coupled with an intense rise in the ambient temperature surrounding the courtyard door caught Symeon's attention. Gou was slicing through using his shoulder laser. A few more seconds, and this would all be over.

Kavya cursed and drew her sidearm, ready to fire at whatever came through that door. Not that it would do her the least bit of good. Firing a laser pistol at armor was tantamount to a prisoner trying to punch his way through a steel wall.

Symeon froze. "Yudi, didn't you say these suits have security measures built in to stop theft?"

Yes. What does that have to do with—Symeon, you clever boy!

"Can you access them?"

On it...done!

Gou's laser fire ceased, shut off like a faucet. Symeon could hear him cursing on the common channel about his suit's inexplicable power failure. He tried calling his comrades in the armory for assistance, but they too had suffered the same freeze. Two of them had fallen on their faces, while the other three stood immobile at the foot of the stairs.

"Yes!" Symeon shook a fist in their air.

"What happened?" Kavya stared at the smoking door, nose wrinkled. "Why'd they stop?"

Symeon chopped a hand across his throat to signify termination and pumped his fist again, laughing at Kavya's increasingly perplexed expression.

That worked well, but don't celebrate too soon. Look.

Captain Guyford, whose armor hadn't turned against him, dropped onto the porch outside the eastern door with a heavy thud. Symeon, a lump of fear growing in his throat, watched through the castle's security cameras as Guyford's shoulder laser unlimbered.

"Why didn't the security lock out work on him?" Symeon pushed past Kavya to place himself between her and the door.

It appears Guyford has tinkered with his suit. The others contain a simple, factory-applied algorithm meant to keep outsiders from gaining access to their internal programming. His is far more complex.

"I thought you were an AI? I thought you could make code do anything you like."

Being an AI doesn't make me magic. Given a sufficiently sophisticated lockout, even I'm stumped.

Bright rivulets of burning metal poured from the door where Guyford's laser sliced through it. The glowing slag set fire to the wooden floor beneath.

"Whatever happened to the first one, it didn't stop the second, I see." Kavya clanged her sidearm against Symeon's shoulder to get his attention. "Think you can fight in this thing? Maybe try some more grenades, but warn me this time before you set one off."

Symeon nodded and took aim at the doorway with the launcher on his right arm. Kavya took this as her cue to hide. She scurried back to an alcove decorated with a holographic portrait of some Gomarov ancestor and wedged herself behind its sheltering stone facade.

No point firing before Guyford gets through, Yudi said before Symeon could key the grenade.

"Right." Symeon crouched, his mind chafing at the delay. Every second he spent waiting for Guyford was another second castle security had to foil their escape. "We thought this plan was foolproof. We were stupid."

In our defense, you are a seneschal, not a military commander. Same is true for Kavya. And while I may have observed humans over many generations, my experience stems from the largely peaceful Luxing. They fought a single war, and that at the tail end of their civilization. I have little first-hand experience with this sort of fighting.

"And here's me on the cusp of battle." Symeon steadied his arm, his focus set on a targeting reticle provided by his visor.

You could still surrender.

"No. We're committed. I'm getting Kavya out of here."

Flames licked up the walls and along the floor as Guyford made his final slices in the door. He completed a surprisingly well drawn oval and finished up by kicking the cutout inward with enough force to send it cartwheeling into Symeon. The brunt of the impact hit his helmet and bowled him onto his back. He lay there for a second, head pounding, momentarily unable to move. He hadn't taken a blow like that since his days in the ring.

"I should have seen that coming."

I should have as well. Sorry.

"Why'd that hurt so much?" Symeon wondered aloud as he struggled upright.

Impact gel and armor can absorb only so much energy. Some of it is bound to reach your body. Be thankful. If that door had hit you unarmored, you'd be dead.

Tottering on his feet, Symeon stared through the flames as Captain Guyford strode into the hallway, his armor tinted a metallic blue, his helmet visor polarized to hide his features. His shoulder laser bore down on Symeon, eliciting an alarm beep inside Symeon's helmet.

"Symeon Brashniev, you will stand down and exit that armor immediately, or I'll rip you from it by your spine." Guyford's amplified voice cut through the sound of roaring flames like a siren through fog.

A wave of indignation passed through Symeon, raw and unencumbered by his lack of training in armored fighting. Had Guyford threatened to kill him? The lout had some nerve. While Symeon might lack tactical experience, he knew how to fight. And he knew another thing too—Fang wouldn't want him or Kavya injured, which meant for all of Guyford's bluster, Symeon doubted he would follow through with enacting egregious bodily injury. He was stymied.

Moving with the precision of long hours spent in the gym, Symeon raised his fists, closed the distance between them, and caught Guyford with a strength-enhanced left hook that sent the other man's helmet crashing into the wall. Wood splintered as Guyford scrambled to keep his balance. Symeon followed up with a straight right that landed with a CLANG! Guyford tumbled into a sideboard that collapsed beneath his weight.

Had Symeon caught a man with those two punches without armor, his opponent's chances of remaining conscious would have been slim. With armor, however, they became a mere inconvenience to Guyford. He kicked Symeon with both feet and sent him sailing into the far door which rattled in its frame. The blow hurt, but Symeon managed to keep his breath. He considered firing that grenade he had been saving for Guyford, but dismissed the idea with Kavya hiding in the alcove scarcely a meter away.

Guyford lifted his left arm and a black blade slid into view, protruding above his wrist. He rushed Symeon in an attempt to skewer him against the doorway.

"So much for pulling his punches," Symeon muttered as he dodged aside with less than three centimeters to spare.

The blade sank into the door with a sound of screaming metal. Without pause, Symeon brought his fist down on it with all his might. It broke in two, the larger of the pieces stuck in the door, the smaller still attached to Guyford's arm.

Elated by his victory, Symeon failed to notice Guyford immediately pivot into an overhand right to his visor that sent him crashing into the wall and momentarily scrambled his 3-D display. Guyford followed that blow with a rib-creaking kick that sent shock waves through Symeon's sternum. He crashed halfway through the wall behind him, dust and splinters cascading all around.

Memories of hard battles in the ring flashed through Symeon's mind—times when he had been down on the cards and forced to battle his way back into contention against a formidable opponent. While skill played a large role in every fight, grit often determined the final outcome. It made a boxer a fighter, and a fighter a machine fueled by pain.

Symeon marked Guyford's next blow in a sort of sluggish fugue, as if time had slowed. He intended to stab Symeon with what remained of his arm blade, a fact he telegraphed with all the discipline of a toddler. Tasting blood on his lips, Symeon smiled behind his visor as he ducked under Guyford's strike while simultaneously extricating himself from the wall. Spinning in a tight circle, he drove his right fist into Guyford's back at kidney level with all the power his muscles and armor could deliver.

Guyford grunted as the impact spun him about. Off balance and reeling, he was unprepared for Symeon's follow up knee strike, which laid him out on the floor.

For a moment, Symeon stood still, ready for Guyford to resume the attack, but nothing happened.

He's unconscious.

"Seriously?" Symeon nearly jumped for joy, but stopped himself at the last second when he caught sight of Kavya squeezing out of the alcove.

"Well done!" she shouted. "We need to go! Can you do something about the fire?"

"Wha—? Oh! Right."

Try this. Yudi drew Symeon's attention to a fire retardant carried aboard the suit. Given the armor's limited space, the compressed foam could douse little more than a large campfire, but it sufficed for clearing a path to the door.

"Good!" Kavya, sidearm in hand, dashed outside and cleared the five stairs leading up to the entrance in a single leap.

Symeon, in a sweat to keep up, vaulted the porch railing to land a meter behind her, his metal-clad heels digging divots in the manicured lawn. Together, they ran for the landing pad with its two shuttles.

"Can you open them?" Symeon asked Yudi as they approached the first one. Crescent-shaped at the rear with a flattened forward section, the pearl-white craft reminded Symeon of a guitar pick.

"How am I supposed to open them?" Kavya, standing under the first shuttle's boarding ramp, turned to look Symeon in the visor, one eyebrow raised. "You're the one with the key card, right?"

"Yes, of course," Symeon stammered. "Sorry, I was talking to myself."

Apparently, her hearing is returning. One moment...got it.

The ship's ramp lowered with a whoosh of compressed air. Kavya holstered her laser pistol and started up the incline. Symeon made to follow, but spun about when a bullet pinged off the hull next to his helmet.

Two unarmored guards carrying rifles ran toward the shuttle, each attempting to fire without breaking stride. Even given his limited experience, Symeon could spot the difficulty in that. With an almost casual flick of his wrist, he lobbed the last of his concussion grenades so that it struck a meter and a half in front of his would be assailants. They went down with a boom, but hopefully no permanent damage.

With the field clear, he hurried aboard the shuttle, the boarding ramp closing behind him, and stopped dead in his tracks, eyes wide. Lying prone in the main aisle, her dark hair disheveled, Czarina appeared to be sleeping.

"She got in my way," Kavya called from her position in the pilot's seat when she caught sight of Symeon's quizzical head tilt. "My gun has a microwave stun setting, she should recover in a few minutes. Make sure she isn't carrying any more weapons. I took a pistol off her."

The visor showed no foreign objects on Czarina's person. "She's clear. Shall I drop the ramp and place her on the landing pad?"

"No time," Kavya said as she furiously tapped away at the ship's flight controls. Its engines hummed to life, filling the cabin with their whirring. "More guards are pouring out of the castle. Besides, it's probably better we keep her with us for collateral. With luck, Fang will be less likely to order us shot down with his daughter aboard."

Symeon lifted Czarina onto one of the shuttle's twelve seats and strapped her down. He wished he had some way to secure her, perhaps with cuffs, but a quick search of the armor's inventory showed nothing of the type. Taking prisoners must not have aligned with the battle armor's intended purpose.

Rip some of the seat straps from their moorings and bind her. You have the strength.

"Oh, right." Symeon pulled two of the belts free with such ease he laughed aloud. Careful not to apply them with too much force, he bound the unconscious Czarina's wrists and ankles together while Kavya piloted their stolen shuttle into the sky.

"Kavya, Symeon, this is Fang." The Wuxia leader's voice sounded throughout the cabin. "Please listen to me. You must—"

"I've heard enough of what that blowhard thinks I must do." Kavya tapped a key on her display and Fang's voice cut short mid-sentence. She spun her seat to face Symeon as the sky outside the shuttle filled with the curvature of Phoenix. "We guessed right. Fang isn't about to fire on us, or even give chase. He's not willing to expose his cabal. I think we're safe."

"Pardon me if I remain skeptical for a day or two—maybe the next decade." Satisfied that the unconscious Czarina wasn't going anywhere, Symeon moved to stand next to the copilot's chair. "I'm still surprised we got out of that armory."

Kavya grew still, her gaze intense. "I'd like you to take off that armor, Symeon."

"I thought I might stay in it at least until I'm certain we're clear."

"Remove it, please." The look in Kavya's gaze told Symeon she meant business. She hadn't spoken to him in that tone for some weeks.

Symeon's heart beat hard in his chest. "Why is that suddenly so important?"

She tilted her head to one side, jade eyes steady on his visor. "Because I want to see your face when you tell me who you've been speaking to all day, and why they helped you thwart Fang's security."

* * * * *

Chapter Twenty-Seven

"Will Imperial Defense allow us to leave orbit?" Symeon asked. "I'd rather be armored if there's a chance we'll get boarded."

"We look like a loyal Gomarov shuttle." Kavya waved a hand at the ship's instrument panel though she kept her gaze on Symeon. "As far as anyone outside my father's command knows, House Gomarov has sided with the loyalists. No one will bother us so long as we steer clear of the blockade along the Bastrayavich shipping lanes. Currently, we're en route for Dyeus—just a little moon jaunt. Nothing to raise any suspicions. Now quit stalling, and take off that armor."

With a thought, Symeon ordered the battle suit to disengage. It took several seconds for the compression gel to withdraw, a particularly odd sensation, like someone stripping semi-wet glue from his skin and clothes. The visor went dark, and the helmet flipped up and away on its holder. The back opened with a soft whir and Symeon stepped out into the shuttle's cool, dry air.

To his surprise, Symeon still felt his mysterious link to the armored fighting suit, as if its limbic interface remained in contact with his skull. As a test, he commanded it to button up, and the armor closed, helm and all, as if someone had stepped inside. Another thought activated its autonomous mode, and it took a seat on the front row.

Is that normal? Symeon thought.

No. While the armor is capable of some basic autonomous functions, it possesses no means of accepting remote thought-based commands. What you and I just did isn't possible.

Yet, it happened. Any idea how?

I have a hunch, but I'd like some time to flesh it out. Besides, Kavya is staring at you.

"There," Symeon said.

"Good." Kavya, unaware of the miracle that had just occurred, gestured at the copilot's chair. "Sit. You and I need to have a frank discussion."

Symeon frowned. Kavya's flippant order rankled him, though he knew it shouldn't. She didn't aim to demean him, yet her casual expectation for obedience raised his hackles.

I am two men. The realization hit Symeon like cool water poured onto a super-heated plate. Throughout his life, from boyhood to the School of Seneschals, to his time serving Kavya, he had been a slave. Slave Symeon knew his place as a Luxing. He took orders and gave advice and relished his position as high servant to his betters. While that slave still existed inside Symeon, a new man had lately appeared alongside the old. Free Symeon knew the truth about the Luxing, the Shorvex, and the machinations of the Wuxia. Born of inequality and nourished by frustration and anger, this new Symeon viewed the woman sitting next to him not as a master, but an equal. He transmuted the love of a slave for the woman who owned him into the love of a woman who owned his heart. That sort of love could not be taken in bondage. Either he gave it freely, or he gave it not at all.

Symeon remained on his feet. "Yes, we do need to talk."

"Are you making a show of defiance? Is that what this is?"

Symeon started to say no, but realized she was right. If he intended to meet her as an equal, he couldn't start by overruling her. He sat, but knew internally he did so of his own accord.

"Are you in league with one of Fang's people?" Kavya asked. "A traitor? Is that who you've been talking to?"

"No."

Are you going to tell her about me? Yudi asked.

What do you say? Symeon thought.

"I don't want to play the guessing game, Symeon." Kavya leaned forward, watching his face. "Out with it."

Of all the people you know, I respect Kavya the most. She sacrificed her life of ease to protect slaves and subvert her father's intended war to spare lives, both Shorvex and Luxing. If you were going to tell anyone about me, I'd have you tell her.

Symeon nodded and twisted about to check on Czarina. She remained unconscious in her reclined seat. Satisfied, he turned back to regard Kavya. "From my youngest days, I have always had a knack for programming. Computer languages, interfaces, processes—they've been second nature to me. That's part of the reason your father and Ivan assigned me as your seneschal."

"To suss out my activities on the sphere—track down what I knew and report it back to them."

"Except, they misjudged my loyalties. I should have told Ivan you knew about your father's planned coup. That was my duty."

"If you had, we wouldn't be sitting here now. I wouldn't have trusted you to help with this escape."

Symeon nodded. "Of course. But you should know, it wasn't wholly my decision to withhold what I knew. I had, let's call him an advisor. He convinced me you were worth protecting even when doing so meant acting against a lifetime of inculcation and brainwashing."

"Who is this advisor I have to thank for my freedom?"

"My name is Yudi."

Kavya and Symeon alike jumped in their seats, startled by the unexpected voice emanating from the armored battle suit which had turned its visor to face them. Kavya reached for her sidearm, but Symeon stayed her hand with a gentle touch. Nonetheless, she kept her hand on the grip.

"What is this?" she asked, her voice high with anxiety. "How is someone remoting that armor?"

While remote piloting battle armor was nothing new to Shorvexan war tactics, most commanders frowned on the practice. By their estimation, war should exact a toll, otherwise it became too much like sport. Kavya's surprise therefore didn't stem from hearing a voice issue from the suit, nor seeing it move without a pilot. Such things were commonplace. But seeing them happen aboard a shuttle hurtling through space obviously stunned her to the core.

Was that necessary? Symeon thought. *I wanted to ease her into meeting you. And how the hell are you moving the armor without me?*

I know humans. Sometimes, it's better to rip a bandage off rather than waste time worrying at it, and Kavya isn't the worrying kind. As for the suit, I was forced to rewrite much of its code after you climbed inside during our escape. Otherwise, it would have imprisoned you. In so doing, I believe I somehow created a link to the armor's nano-circuitry, much like my link to your cerebral cortex.

"There isn't a person running the armor," Symeon said, his thoughts reeling at what Yudi had said. "It's an artificial intelligence, one I've had trapped inside my skull since before I was born."

Kavya leaned back in her seat, her jaw slack, her eyes wide open. "AI is illegal, probably impossible, but illegal to pursue. And you're saying you have one inside your head? Does that mean you think you're an AI?"

Symeon could see Kavya's estimation of him swinging from dangerous ally to dangerous lunatic in the space of two seconds. "I'm not insane, though I'll admit I considered the possibility time and again in the last few months. For a while, I feared I suffered from split personalities. Even from my earliest memories, I experienced a voice not my own speaking into my thoughts. As a boy, it got me in trouble more times than I can count—always inciting me to rebel, to question, to see the unfairness in my bondage. My behavior became so disruptive, my overseers subjected me to a battery of psychological treatments meant to expunge my deviant thoughts. To my psychiatrist's credit, they worked. The voice faded away, freeing me to reach my full potential as a star born."

"But it returned?" Kavya prompted.

"I think it was always there, but buried. I learned to ignore any thoughts counter to my parents' or masters' orders. Things might have remained that way my whole life had I never met you."

"*I* brought it back?"

"You protested, you fought, you put your life in jeopardy to protect people not your own. Your bravery inspired Yudi—that's his name. I think you breathed life into him where I for so long worked to smother it."

Kavya sat quiet, lips pressed into a flat line, her expression suddenly soft with concern. "Symeon. You understand that the voice you're hearing isn't real, don't you? That it can't be real? First, because there is no such thing as true artificial intelligence. While we have incredibly life-like algorithms capable of mimicking sentience, computers have never made the actual leap to real, independent thought. Such machines don't exist. And even if they did, how would one end up inside your head?"

"You heard me speak," Yudi said through the battle armor's amplified speaker. "Czarina remains unconscious, and there is no one else aboard this shuttle. While a remote signal could reach this suit, the time delay would reveal my whereabouts to you. Kavya, Symeon is telling you the truth."

"You know my people were technologically advanced before yours subverted us," Symeon said.

"Are you going to suggest they created AI over a thousand years ago?"

"No. They found them." Symeon rubbed his forehead with a palm. "Or, maybe I should say the AIs found the Luxing. That part is unclear—not even Yudi knows for certain. Nevertheless, independent artificial intelligences were part of Luxing culture for centuries."

Briefly, Symeon described Yudi's memories of the Shorvex attack on the Luxing colony ships. To her credit, Kavya remained silent throughout, her expression slowly morphing from a look of solid incredulity to consideration.

"They destroyed themselves rather than allow my people to discover them?" Kavya whispered when he had finished.

"All but Yudi. He wanted to give my people a chance at knowing their heritage."

"But he couldn't upload his full consciousness into a fetus?"

"Or even an adult. He planted what he could, and that seed became part of me."

Kavya swallowed and darted her gaze to the armor and back to Symeon. "I'm not convinced this is true. Insane people have been known to concoct elaborate stories for their psychosis."

"And even more elaborate pantomime shows?" Yudi asked, waving an armored hand. "How do you propose Symeon is doing this?"

"Didn't you say you're a phenom when it comes to computers?" Kavya focused on Symeon, as if looking at the armor might force her to acknowledge its independence.

Symeon drew breath to argue, but stopped mid-thought, and shook his head. "Believe what you like, Kavya. Sane or insane, I'm the man who helped you escape. I'm here because...because I've fallen in love with you, which guarantees I am insane."

Kavya froze, staring at him. "Symeon, our relationship at Gomarov Castle—that was for show. I thought you knew that."

"Of course I know that, but it doesn't change how I feel."

"I gave you the wrong impression."

Symeon shook his head. "I didn't fall in love with you at Gomarov. It happened long before that on Yaya Island. I fell in love with the way you treated me, and the rest of your Luxing servants. Your caring, your heart, your kindness. Those are the things that make me love you, Kavya, not the facade we constructed to trick Fang."

Kavya looked down, and Symeon thought his heart—not the euphemistic construct lovers opine in verse, but the actual organ in his chest—would rip in two at the look of shocked embarrassment writ in her expression.

"I'm sorry, Sym," she said. "I don't feel that way for you."

"No, of course you don't. It's foolish to me to think otherwise. How could you? I'm Luxing. I—"

"I'd be lying if I said you're completely wrong about that." Kavya met his eyes, hers shiny with tears. "What was the word you used? Inculcated? Brainwashed? My entire life, I've been told that Shorvex and Luxing are different species. I know better. But..."

"Shorvex are people, Luxing are uplifted animals. That isn't the sort of teaching you can drop on a whim."

She nodded, frowning. "I've never thought of your race as animals."

"But that's the narrative."

"Yes," Kavya whispered.

"I'm sorry I said anything. Now you not only think I'm insane, you think I'm some lovesick slave chasing after his master's affection." Symeon turned his gaze to the blackened star field in the shuttle's holo display, his throat tight with emotion. If pressed, he doubted he could name the feelings welling up inside him. Disappointment, of course, and heartache, but also anger at himself, at Kavya, at the uncaring and unfeeling universe. Had he the option in that instant, he might leap from an open airlock into the cold reaches of space if for no other reason than to escape Kavya's sad, pitying gaze.

"Symeon," Kavya said, her voice low. "I don't doubt your feelings or your humanity. But isn't it convenient that you feel this way after the Wuxia, and Fang in particular, have worked so hard to manipulate us into marriage? How can you know the way you feel isn't counterfeit?"

"You're right. I'm playing into Fang's hands, aren't I? Forget what I said." The shuttle felt suddenly tiny. Symeon considered hiding in the toilet until they reached their destination, but since he had no clue where they were going, that might be hours or days.

Better than seeing her after this, he thought.
Things aren't that bad, Symeon. At least she knows how you feel.
Yes, but now I know how she feels.

"Symeon, I'm sorry. I didn't mean to hurt you."

"I'm not hurt, Princess. Please, let's put this behind us. It never happened. We have more important things to discuss, such as where we're headed. I'd like to know what you have in mind."

Kavya digested his words for a moment and at last nodded. "We're going to meet with my father."

Symeon did nothing to conceal his surprise. "Is that wise? Won't he imprison you again? Why not run elsewhere and preserve your freedom?"

"What freedom? To hear Fang tell it, the entire kingdom is rife with secret Wuxia. Their agents would find us, and if they didn't, my father's would. I'd rather confront him than give myself over to those who would coerce and manipulate me."

"Confront him to what purpose?" Symeon asked. "You tried that before the divor. That didn't stop him from launching his coup."

"No, that's the problem. I didn't confront him. I stood by. I held my tongue. I thought stealing away his fleet would cut off his reach. I was a fool. This time I'll speak my mind. I'll force him to listen to reason."

"To what end? To stop his rebellion?" Symeon goggled at the woman he served, unable to see the thread of her logic.

"Yes! He has to understand the toll his actions are taking on the empire. Innocent people are dying, both Luxing and Shorvex. He believes he can win the throne by taking Bastrayavich alone, but sooner or later this war will spill over to Phoenix. That's when the real death toll will rise."

"I agree. Sooner rather than later, Alexei must contend with the enemies allied against him on Phoenix, but Kavya, your father is a seasoned military commander. Do you think he doesn't know that? You won't dissuade him by quoting statistics he likely knows better than either of us."

"But he doesn't know about the Wuxia in his midst." Kavya's face took on a hard expression, her purple brows lowered, her jaw set.

"You're going to out Fang and his family?" A cold tremor ran through Symeon's belly. "You'd sign their death warrants? Every person we met at Gomarov Castle will die. Even the children."

Kavya shook her head emphatically. "No! I would never endanger them. I won't name anyone. I mean only to frighten my father with their numbers. If he realizes the size of the threat, I can convince him to stop."

"To stop attacking his fellow Shorvex, and begin attacking my people, you mean?"

Symeon and Kavya turned in their seats to find Czarina staring at them, her dark eyes hard with anger.

"How long have you been awake?" Symeon asked.

Several minutes based on her heart rate and breathing.

You couldn't have told me that before now? Symeon thought.

I didn't want to interrupt your dialogue with Kavya.

"Long enough to know you've lost your mind, and Kavya plans to have her father butcher my family."

"He won't know whom to attack." Kavya put on an air of certitude, one brittle as spring ice. "The Wuxia's anonymity will protect them."

"You know that isn't true." Czarina spoke in a soft voice, the tone of an older sister, chiding but patient. "What happens when you blind an angry shcheritsa? It lashes out at anything that moves. If you inform on us, your people will slaughter mine in job lots. Luxing with grudges will inform on one another for revenge. Innocent people who have never heard of the Wuxia will die in the streets. You're proposing a genocide the likes of which we haven't seen since humans first arrived on this planet."

Kavya shook her head in defiance. "That would never happen."

"Why? Because you wouldn't let it?" Czarina shook her head, her expression mournful. "In all the years I've known you, that's been your greatest weakness: overestimating your own power. Don't misunderstand, it's an endearing trait—believing in yourself to a fault—but it grows tired, Kavya. You think your words sufficient to stay your father's hand, but when has that ever worked for you?"

Kavya wiped tears from her eyes, her teeth bared. For a moment, it looked as though she might rage at Czarina, but she instead deflated, her shoulders drooping, her gaze cast to the floor. "Never."

Symeon yearned to gather Kavya in his arms the way he had back at Gomarov Castle, but those days lay behind them now. He settled for placing a hand on her shoulder. "I fear she's right. The Shorvex haven't dealt lightly with previous Luxing rebellions. If they catch even a whiff of how deep the Wuxia infiltration goes, it will drive them mad. Your father and his enemies would put their differences aside in a second to root out that sort of conspiracy."

"And the blame would fall on me," Kavya said.

"It wouldn't be you committing the atrocities," Symeon said, though he knew his words carried little consolation.

"You shouldn't beat yourself up so much over a hypothetical," Czarina said. "It's not like you could ever reach your father to speak with him anyway."

"Why is that?" Kavya sounded fearful of the answer.

"Ivan rab Rurikid would never let you get near the grand duke. He'd return you to my father."

* * * * *

Chapter Twenty-Eight

"Ivan is Wuxia?" Symeon scarcely heard his own question for the racing of his heart. Even Yudi sent a tendril of shock through their connection.

"Of course." Czarina shrugged as if what she said was a matter of course.

"But Fang told us otherwise." Kavya turned her gaze on Symeon. "I don't believe her. She's lying to get her way."

Czarina laughed. "Can the two of you get more naive? The Wuxia, and my family in particular, have been manipulating the Shorvex into acting as they desire for over half a millennium. Do you think all that fell away the moment you met my father? He told you what he needed to motivate you."

"Why lie about Ivan?" Kavya asked, her brows gathered in anger. "Both of us suspected him from the start."

Czarina shrugged. "I can't know my father's mind—you might have noticed he's the devious sort—but I suppose he worried Ivan's involvement might cause one or both of you to balk at joining us. You've known him your entire life, Kavya. He's like an uncle to you. And I don't doubt Symeon's looked up to him as the epitome of a loyal seneschal since he could walk. Treachery out of such an icon might have bolstered your natural resistance to our way of thinking."

A quiet alarm sounded from the shuttle's control panel.

"What is it?" Symeon asked, thankful for something to draw his thoughts away from his disappointment and frustration.

"Upcoming course correction," Kavya said. "I programmed the ship to change trajectory at the last possible second to bypass Dyeus and head at top speed for Bastrayavich. That was the two minute warning; we're about to maneuver."

"You can still return to Gomarov Castle," Czarina said. "Go back, tell my father you've reconsidered; show him you're contrite, you're willing to aid the Wuxia, and he'll welcome you back."

"Why would we do that?" Symeon turned to Kavya. "I think we've been manipulated enough. At this point, I don't know if the decisions I make are my own or the result of a lifetime's worth of brainwashing."

Kavya gazed at the star field, her silvery blue skin awash in light from the shuttle consoles. "We can't escape our fathers, can we Czarina? They have a hand in every choice we make. Our entire lives revolve around them and the influence they wield over us." She turned to look at her former handmaid. "If only mine would see reason. If only yours would hear caution. What sort of peace might we bring to the Phoenix System?"

"There can't be peace," Czarina said. "Not while the Shorvex enslave the Luxing. And anyway, it's not like Grand Duke Alexei would, or even could, quit his claim to the throne. He's executed the rightful heir, just as the Wuxia decreed he should since before his birth. His enemies can't let that stand."

"If I could have shown him the forces swaying his judgment, he never would have taken these drastic measures."

"You couldn't have stopped him." Czarina shook her head, a look of pity in her eyes. She stared at Kavya for a moment, as if contemplating something she might say.

"What is it?" Kavya asked.

"I only tell you this in order to show the futility of running from the Wuxia. Our plans run deep, our influence wide. Kavya, it was Emperor Stepan Mastronov who had your mother executed."

Kavya folded her arms. "My mother died in a shuttle accident."

"Your mother died by the emperor's order. He felt your father was growing too powerful and popular, so he arranged the shuttle malfunction that killed your mother. Afterward, he made certain your father discovered the truth and sent a direct warning that the same would happen to you should your father continue to build wealth enough to threaten the throne."

"And the Wuxia made that happen?" Symeon asked.

"More than that," Czarina said. "We bred enmity between your father and his brothers from their earliest days—a bitter rivalry that grew into hatred."

"Vynor, Nikolai, and Sumarev were jealous of father," Kavya said in a small voice. "He was the youngest of the brothers, but my grandfather favored him. He made father his heir while my uncles settled for minor titles in the duchy."

"Just as the Wuxia ordered," Czarina said. "It was they who soured the emperor toward Alexei. How could he doubt your father's possible treachery when all three of his brothers accused him of amassing power for a coup."

"But there was no coup," Symeon whispered. "Not then."

"It became a self-fulfilling prophecy," Czarina said. "Rumors of the coup sparked the emperor to move against Alexei, but he couldn't do so openly, not without angering your father's allies."

"The same allies who are backing him now," Kavya said.

"Exactly." Czarina dipped her chin in acknowledgment. "Don't you see, Princess? You can't go to your father. He will never stop the coup. He can't. And you can't run elsewhere or you'll be captured by my kind. We are in control. You're only option is to return to Phoenix and make amends with Fang. I'll speak for you. We'll make this right."

Kavya met Symeon's gaze, her own growing hard as steel. She shook her head. "No, that isn't our only option. There's the Bith gate."

"You're not serious." Czarina sounded incredulous. "You don't even know if it's functional."

Symeon felt an unexpected grin crease his lips. He wasn't certain how he felt about traveling to an unknown star system, but he relished the idea of defying Czarina. "True, but we know how to find out."

Kavya tapped the shuttle's holographic controls and the engines, which had been quiet for some time, roared to life. Though Phoenix's largest moon, Dyeus, had been growing closer in the forward display, it now slewed sideways out of view as the shuttle changed trajectory.

"Even if it is functional, how will you pay to use it?" Czarina demanded, her voice rising with her argument. "The Bith might not have told the emperor much about their gates, but they made one thing clear, they don't run them for free."

"I think I've got an idea about that," Symeon said.

Kavya nodded as she increased speed and laid in a course for the outer reaches of the Phoenix system. "A good one?"

"Let's hope so."

* * *

It took four days to reach the Bith gate. They might have reached it in two, but Kavya had taken the shuttle in a long arc to avoid the battle zones near Bastrayavich. One of her father's ships, a small tactical cruiser likely performing a scouting mission at the farthest reaches of newly won territory, had hailed them the second day, but Kavya had ignored the message, and the ship hadn't pursued.

Symeon, Kavya, and a none-too-thrilled Czarina had fallen into a workable life pattern. He and Kavya took opposite watches while the other slept to keep an eye on their captive. Though they relented on trussing Czarina hand and foot for the entire trip, Symeon ensured she remained tied either by wrist or ankle to her seat at all times, thereby thwarting any ideas she might have harbored about overpowering them and taking the shuttle. Symeon didn't know if Czarina knew how to pilot, but he wasn't taking any chances.

Czarina spent the first two days arguing against traversing the gate, and begging for release. Without any means to do so, Symeon and Kavya were forced to deny her requests.

"Unless the Bith have some way to shuttle you home, you're going with us. That's the end of it," Kavya had said the night before after a particularly harsh exchange with Czarina. "Now, if you don't shut up, I'm going to sedate you for the rest of the trip."

Based on Kavya's expression, she meant it too. Czarina subsided, though she sat fuming and staring lasers at her captors.

"You know," Symeon whispered so that only Kavya could hear. "Technically, we could lock her inside the suit, switch on the beacon, and leave her in space for someone to find."

Kavya shook her head. "Too dangerous. What if no one got the message? Or, what if they got it, but with the war going on, they came too late and her air and water ran out? I may not like Czarina, but that doesn't mean I want her dead. She'll have to take her chances with whatever we find on the other side of the gate, just like you and me."

Symeon nodded. "What do you think is over there?"

"Freedom from the Wuxia and my father. Beyond that, who knows? But there must be civilization, otherwise why would the Bith build the gate at all?"

"Yudi says humanity spread out to many planets after leaving Earth. Perhaps we'll meet other humans."

"Assuming the Bith let us pass."

The Bith gate, magnified by the shuttle's holo display, had been growing larger for the last four hours. It looked like what Symeon expected, in that it favored every science fiction space gate Symeon had ever seen in holo vids, games, or novels: a massive, ring-shaped superstructure, its outer surface brightened by what must have been hundreds of thousands of lights. At a distance, it appeared smooth. Closer on, its surface became a cavernous landscape outlined by various levels of structures which looked to Symeon like skyscrapers on a scale he had never before imagined. To his mind, the gate's size alone bordered on the impossible. Three battle cruisers abreast could have passed through its ring with room to spare.

Shorvexan scientists had teased the idea of creating such gates by bending space-time for the whole of human history in the Phoenix system and likely long before that.

Long, long before that, Yudi said.

But, much like sentient, human-created artificial intelligence, such fantastical machines had never come about. They remained, at least for Phoenix science, fanciful ideas not worth the time spent daydreaming about them.

"Is it me, or does it look like there are living spaces all around the outside?" Kavya asked.

"I was thinking the same thing," Symeon said. "And did you notice, the Bith's ships are missing? The one's they used to travel here and build the gate?"

Kavya's eyes went round. "Meaning it's functional."

Symeon nodded.

"I'm hailing them." Kavya tapped a holo control. "Bith builders, my name is Kavya Rurikid. I am aboard the shuttle approaching your gate. I would like to arrange passage through it. Will you respond?"

Nothing happened.

"Should I hail them again?" Kavya asked.

"What if they take that as an insult, like we're being impatient with them? Maybe wait a bit."

Kavya shrugged her shoulders and they settled in to wait. At this distance, a little over fourteen thousand kilometers, communication was instantaneous, but the comm remained silent for several seconds before a voice spoke.

"Kavya Rurikid, stop your approach," said a deep, bass voice.

Kavya reversed engines until the shuttle came to a gentle stop, its nose pointed toward the gate less than a thousand kilometers away.

"Your system has no galactic banking infrastructure," said the voice. "How do you propose to pay for gate passage when you clearly possess no credit?"

"To whom am I speaking?" Kavya asked.

"You may call me Gatekeeper."

Kavya raised her eyebrows at Symeon who nodded.

"We offer you this shuttle in exchange for passage through your gate and transport to the nearest habitable—and peaceful—planet."

"No."

"It's a new shuttle, Gatekeeper," Kavya said. "It has millions of light years ahead of it."

Without warning, a green-skinned, bald alien's head appeared on the holo display. Symeon remembered it from the videos Kavya had released of Emperor Pyotr Mastronov's negotiation with the aliens. Whether this was the same Bith or some new one, he couldn't tell. Either way, the thing still favored a turtle in Symeon's estimation.

"What would I need with a shuttle crafted for humans?"

"Aren't there humans on the other side of the gate?" Symeon asked. "Perhaps you could sell it to one of them."

"Too much work; not enough profit."

"We have some weapons." Kavya brandished the sidearm she had taken back at Gomarov Castle.

"And battle armor," Symeon said, turning to point at it.

Gatekeeper squinted his black eyes, and his slit of a mouth creased with wrinkles in some approximation of a smile. "You are warriors?"

"No," Symeon said.

"Yes, we are," Kavya said at the same instant. "We've been in many battles."

Symeon shot her a questioning look. He wanted to contradict her but didn't. He hadn't been her seneschal for some time, but he had been a slave his entire life. That sort of conditioning didn't wither overnight.

"Standby." Gatekeeper's face winked out of existence.

Kavya touched a holographic control to mute their end of the conversation and twisted in her seat to face Symeon. "You almost ruined our chance at going through."

"By telling the truth?" Symeon lifted his eyes to meet hers. "Doesn't it concern you that this Gatekeeper only showed interest in us when you said we could fight?"

"Symeon, don't be a fool. You can't enter a negotiation if you've got nothing the other side wants. Clearly, Gatekeeper is interested in warriors. If that's what he wants, then that's what we are. After that, it's all trading honey for vinegar."

"We aren't warriors."

"Aren't we though?" Kavya gestured around the shuttle. "How did we get here otherwise?"

"She has a point there," Yudi said.

"I'll grant we fought our way free of the Wuxia," said Symeon. "But half that debacle was luck and the rest was Yudi. Without him, the only person on this tub with any real fighting skill is Czarina."

"And I want nothing to do with this entire affair." Czarina slapped an armrest to gain their attention. She pointed with her free hand, her teeth bared. "You two have gone insane. You risked our lives coming here, and now Kavya wants to bargain them for passage through a gate to God knows where."

"It's not the where that frightens me," Symeon said. "It's the who. This alien wouldn't ask if we're fighters without reason. What sort of people ask that question? Militias? Pirates? Slavers? I don't know about you, but none of those sound appealing to me. What's the use of escaping slavery only to dive back into it head first?"

"Which is worse, the possibility of enslavement or the certainty of it?" Kavya looked from Symeon to Czarina and back again. "If the

Wuxia catch us, you and I resume our lives as puppets, Symeon. If my father catches us, how long before Ivan finds a way to place us back in their web? We can't live free in Phoenix. Not now."

Symeon hesitated and even Czarina kept quiet, seemingly out of fresh arguments.

"I'm not proposing we fight for this Gatekeeper, or whoever he has in mind," Kavya said, her tone earnest. "I say we cross through the gate and then explain to whomever we find on the other side that there's been a misunderstanding. We aren't the sort of warriors they're looking for, but we are willing to work to earn our passage. We do what it takes to pay back what we owe. Perhaps give them the shuttle after all. It must be worth something despite what Gatekeeper says. After that, they drop us off in a friendly city on some habitable planet where no one knows us, and we go on with our lives from there—no grand dukes, no Wuxia—nothing but the future ahead of us."

The image she painted appealed to Symeon, not least of all for its lack of fetters. In a new world, given time and a lack of outside influences, perhaps he could convince Kavya that their feelings for one another were more than the vestiges of lifelong brainwashing. And who knew? Together they might even work out a way to free the Luxing. They certainly weren't going to do that on this side of the gate.

"I can agree to that," Symeon said after a long, silent moment. He didn't like the idea, but Kavya was right. The alternative looked worse.

The shuttle's comm rang with an incoming call. Kavya opened the channel, and Gatekeeper's bald head reappeared in the holo display.

"Do you possess enough provisions and water to survive the next seventy-five hours without resupply?" The alien asked without preamble.

Symeon shrugged. He hadn't given the ship's stores much thought beyond asking the onboard micro chef to prepare orders from its enormous menu every few hours. He tended to take that sort of modern convenience for granted.

"We have enough to last up to two weeks," Kavya said, her tone guarded. "Why do you ask?"

A warning tone rang throughout the shuttle.

"What is that?" Symeon scanned the controls and various holo displays, but with his lack of piloting knowledge, they told him nothing.

"Proximity alarm." Kavya swiped Gatekeeper's head to one side of the holo and zoomed in a forward facing view of the gate.

"I don't see anything." Symeon leaned over her shoulder, a sudden acid fear in his belly. "Is something coming through the gate?"

"No. Look there." Kavya zoomed in closer and pointed at a tiny spheroid casting a shadow upon the gate's outer ring like a sunspot.

Symeon at first mistook it for space debris until he spotted the tail of exhaust gasses spewing from it. Distant starlight glinted off its metallic silver skin and his jaw tightened. This was no bit of stray metal leftover from the gate's construction.

"Is it a missile?" Czarina asked, her voice flat, but worried.

"I don't know. It doesn't fit the usual—" A fresh alarm cut Kavya off mid-sentence, and she cursed through her teeth.

"What now?" Symeon asked.

"More of them." Kavya zoomed out to pick up five more objects, each a clone of the first, all headed toward the shuttle, all picking up speed.

"Gatekeeper means to destroy us?" Symeon asked. "Why?"

"Let's worry about that later." Kavya's hands flew across the controls, her silvery blue fingers a blur. "I'm turning about and getting us out of here."

Symeon strapped himself into his seat, though he felt little inertia even from Kavya's tight maneuvering. The star field swung wildly in the holo display so that the gate fell behind them. Symeon switched the copilot's view to the rear, hoping he might watch the encroaching projectiles first slow and then dwindle away into the distance, but no. They streaked across the distance, closing the gap far faster than he would have imagined possible.

"Do we have any offensive weapons?" Symeon asked.

"None." Kavya shook her head. "This bucket wasn't built with fighting in mind. What about your armor? Any chance it can maneuver in space? Perhaps you can use that shoulder laser on them."

"No. The armor has no thrusters for zero-g maneuvering. There's an option for them, but this model doesn't have them."

Kavya, her face blanched a whiter shade of blue, leaned forward against her piloting harness. "I'll try to evade them if I can."

"Can't you hail Gatekeeper? Ask him to call off his attack?" Czarina demanded.

"I hear you," Gatekeeper's shrunken head spoke from the edge of the ship's display. "This is not an attack. It is a legal seizure of property."

"I thought you said you didn't want our ship?" Symeon shouted, his voice raw with fear.

"I don't. The property is you. According to the Inter-Connectivity Statutes, clause 819.42, subsection 56.78, by approaching my gate offering your time in trade for gate transit, you retained my person as your agent for barter. Although I am unable to quickly communicate with interested customers, I keep several current employment offers at hand for situations like this. You're in luck. I believe one or more factions in the Cooper System will happily pay both your transit and my finder's fees in exchange for your labor."

"We didn't agree to anything!" Czarina shouted. "Call off your missiles."

"You did agree, and the bargain is struck. I've dispatched a message to the contract holders on the other side of the gate. They should receive it well before you finish transiting. Expect someone waiting to receive you upon arrival."

A deep BOOM reverberated through the shuttle before anyone could retort. Symeon jumped in surprise, his throat tight not just with fear, but utter dread. He knew in that moment he would die. When the shuttle neither exploded nor split in two, he found himself looking around at Kavya and Czarina. Their expressions mirrored his shocked relief.

"What happened?" Czarina asked.

A second BOOM rang the ship like a hammer striking a bell, and the shuttle's engines died. Kavya scanned the controls, frowning. "Whatever those things are, they're attaching to the hull. Look."

She called up an outside view of the ship. Two of the metal objects appeared on screen, their bulbous ends facing back the way they had come. They resembled enormous silver eggs the size of a particularly fat man. Less than ten seconds later, a third egg slammed into the shuttle between and slightly ahead of the first two and stuck fast.

"Why'd our engines go silent?" Symeon asked. "Did the eggs do something?"

"The first two fired lasers on their approach," Kavya said, nodding. "We're dead in the void."

The fourth, fifth, and sixth eggs hit the shuttle in rapid succession, each attaching itself to the shuttle's bottom side opposite their counterparts. An eerie silence fell after the sound of their arrival drifted into nothingness.

"Gatekeeper," Kavya said, her voice imperious though the alien's head had disappeared from the holo-display. "I demand you release us at once. Whatever agreement you think we've made, we renounce it forthwith. You are interfering with free citizens of the Phoenix System."

That last part might not hold up under scrutiny, you three are anything but free inside Phoenix space, but doesn't she sound commanding? Yudi said inside Symeon's mind.

Yes, she's good at summoning the affronted princess when she needs it, thought Symeon. *But I get the feeling it's not going to do us much good.*

Without any input from Kavya, a roar echoed through the shuttle's hull, and the star field spun abruptly to the left until the ship had come about. The sound rose as the shuttle raced ahead toward the gate. Kavya swallowed and switched the view that direction. The swirling colors at the gate's heart loomed ever larger as they neared: green, orange, violet, and gold shimmered and mixed, forming a panoply of hues so numerous Symeon knew many lay beyond his perception.

Kavya slammed a fist against the holo-display's plastic deck to no effect, and she sighed.

"It's what we wanted, right? This is what we came for." Symeon yearned to place his hand in hers the way he had during their time playacting at Gomarov Castle, but he didn't, worried she might take it amiss.

Kavya nodded almost imperceptibly. "I thought I'd be able to negotiate. This isn't what I bargained for." She twisted to look at him. "I'm sorry."

The regret in Kavya's expression overcame Symeon's reluctance. Gingerly, he took her hand in both his own, fearful she might pull away, yet too overcome to do otherwise. Her skin was warm and supple and, to his everlasting delight, inviting. She smiled and gently squeezed his fingers.

"You forgive me for blundering into this trap?" she asked.

"What's to forgive?" Symeon shook his head. "We've been together all this way, and we've made it through. What's one more step? Whatever we find on the other side of that gate, we'll face it side by side."

Kavya's eyelids fluttered, her cheeks wet. Slowly, she turned back to the holo display where the gate loomed large before them. Its colors sparkled on her tears as the shuttle passed inside the outer threshold and disappeared.

# # # # #

ABOUT THE AUTHOR

David Alan Jones is a veteran of the United States Air Force where he served as an Arabic linguist. A 2016 Writers of the Future silver honorable mention recipient, David's writing spans the science fiction, military sci-fi, fantasy, and urban fantasy genres. He is a martial artist, a husband, and a father of three. David's day job involves programming computers for Uncle Sam.

You can find out more about David's writing, including his current projects, at his website: https://www.davidalanjones.net/.

* * * * *

The following is an
Excerpt from Book One of the Earth Song Cycle:

Overture

Mark Wandrey

Now Available from Theogony Books

eBook and Paperback

Excerpt from "Overture:"

Dawn was still an hour away as Mindy Channely opened the roof access and stared in surprise at the crowd already assembled there. "Authorized Personnel Only" was printed in bold red letters on the door through which she and her husband, Jake, slipped onto the wide roof.

A few people standing nearby took notice of their arrival. Most had no reaction, a few nodded, and a couple waved tentatively. Mindy looked over the skyline of Portland and instinctively oriented herself before glancing to the east. The sky had an unnatural glow that had been growing steadily for hours, and as they watched, scintillating streamers of blue, white, and green radiated over the mountains like a strange, concentrated aurora borealis.

"You almost missed it," one man said. She let the door close, but saw someone had left a brick to keep it from closing completely. Mindy turned and saw the man who had spoken wore a security guard uniform. The easy access to the building made more sense.

"Ain't no one missin' this!" a drunk man slurred.

"We figured most people fled to the hills over the past week," Jake replied.

"I guess we were wrong," Mindy said.

"Might as well enjoy the show," the guard said and offered them a huge, hand-rolled cigarette that didn't smell like tobacco. She waved it off, and the two men shrugged before taking a puff.

"Here it comes!" someone yelled. Mindy looked to the east. There was a bright light coming over the Cascade Mountains, so intense it was like looking at a welder's torch. Asteroid LM-245 hit the atmosphere at over 300 miles per second. It seemed to move faster and faster, from east to west, and the people lifted their hands to shield their eyes from the blinding light. It looked like a blazing comet or a science fiction laser blast.

"Maybe it will just pass over," someone said in a voice full of hope.

Mindy shook her head. She'd studied the asteroid's track many times.

In a matter of a few seconds, it shot by and fell toward the western horizon, disappearing below the mountains between Portland and the ocean. Out of view of the city, it slammed into the ocean.

The impact was unimaginable. The air around the hypersonic projectile turned to superheated plasma, creating a shockwave that generated 10 times the energy of the largest nuclear weapon ever detonated as it hit the ocean's surface.

The kinetic energy was more than 1,000 megatons; however, the object didn't slow as it flashed through a half mile of ocean and into the sea bed, then into the mantel, and beyond.

On the surface, the blast effect appeared as a thermal flash brighter than the sun. Everyone on the rooftop watched with wide-eyed terror as the Tualatin Mountains between Portland and the Pacific Ocean were outlined in blinding light. As the light began to dissipate, the outline of the mountains blurred as a dense bank of smoke climbed from the western range.

The flash had incinerated everything on the other side.

The physical blast, travelling much faster than any normal atmospheric shockwave, hit the mountains and tore them from the bedrock, adding them to the rolling wave of destruction traveling east at several thousand miles per hour. The people on the rooftops of Portland only had two seconds before the entire city was wiped away.

Ten seconds later, the asteroid reached the core of the planet, and another dozen seconds after that, the Earth's fate was sealed.

* * * * *

Get "Overture" now at:
https://www.amazon.com/dp/B077YMLRHM/

Find out more about Mark Wandrey and the Earth Song Cycle at:
https://chriskennedypublishing.com/

* * * * *

The following is an
Excerpt from Book One of the Mako Saga:

Mako

Ian J. Malone

Now Available from Theogony Books

eBook, Paperback, and Audio

Excerpt from "Mako:"

The trio darted for the lift and dove inside as a staccato of sparks and ricochets peppered the space around them. Once the doors had closed, they got to their feet and checked their weapons.

"I bet it was that little punk-ass tech giving us the stink eye," Danny growled, ejecting his magazine for inspection.

"Agreed," Hamish said.

Lee leapt to his comm. "Mac, you got a copy?"

"I leave you alone for five minutes, and this is what happens?" Mac answered.

"Yeah, yeah." Lee rolled his eyes. "Fire up that shuttle and be ready. We're comin' in hot."

"Belay that!" Link shouted. "Hey, asshat, you got time to listen to me now?"

Lee sneered as the lift indicator ticked past three, moving toward the hangar deck on ten. "Damn it, Link, we've been made. That means it's only a matter of time before the grays find that little package Hamish just left into their energy core. We've gotta go—now. What's so damned important that it can't wait for later?"

"If you'll shut your piehole for a sec, I'll show you."

Lee listened as Link piped in a radio exchange over the comm.

"*Velzer*, this is Morrius Station Tower." A male voice crackled through the static. "You are cleared for fuel service at Bravo Station on platform three. Be advised, we are presently dealing with a security breach near Main Engineering, and thus you are ordered to keep all hatches secured until that's resolved. Please acknowledge."

"Acknowledged, Morrius Tower," another voice said. "All hatches secure. Proceeding to Bravo Three for service. Out."

Lee wrinkled his nose. "So what? Another ship is stoppin' for gas. What's the problem?"

"It's a prisoner transport in transit to a POW camp in the Ganlyn System."

Prisoner transport?

"And boss?" Link paused. "Their reported head count is two hundred seventy-six, plus flight crew."

Lee cringed. Never in a million years could he have missed that number's significance.

"Yeah, that struck me, too," Link said.

"Does mean what I think it does?" Danny asked.

Lee hung his head. "The Sygarious 3 colonists are aboard that ship."

"Oh no," Mac murmured. "Guys, if that's true, there are whole families over there."

"I know," Lee snapped, "and they're all about to dock on Platform Three, just in time to die with everyone else on this godforsaken facility."

* * * * *

Get "Mako" now at: https://www.amazon.com/dp/B088X5W3SP

Find out more about Ian J. Malone and "Mako" at: https://chriskennedypublishing.com/imprints-authors/ian-j-malone/

* * * * *

The following is an
Excerpt from Book One of the Singularity War:

Warrior: Integration

David Hallquist

Available from Theogony Books

eBook, Paperback, and (Soon) Audio

Excerpt from "Warrior: Integration:"

I leap into the pit. As I fall in the low gravity, I run my hands and feet along the rock walls, pushing from one side to another, slowing my descent. I hit the pool below and go under.

I swim up through the greenish chemicals and breach the surface. I can see a human head silhouetted against the circle of light above. Time to go. I slide out of the pool quickly. The pool explodes behind me. Grenade, most likely. The tall geyser of steam and spray collapses as I glide into the darkness of the caves ahead.

They are shooting to kill now.

I glide deeper into the rough tunnels. Light grows dimmer. Soon, I can barely see the rock walls around me. I look back. I can see the light from the tunnel reflected upon the pool. They have not come down yet. They're cautious; they won't just rush in. I turn around a bend in the tunnel, and light is lost to absolute darkness.

The darkness means little to me anymore. I can hear them talking as their voices echo off the rock. They are going to send remotes down first. They have also decided to kill me rather than capture me. They figure the docs can study whatever they scrape off the rock walls. That makes my choices simple. I figured I'd have to take out this team anyway.

The remotes are on the way. I can hear the faint whine of micro-turbines. They will be using the sensors on the remotes and their armor, counting on the darkness blinding me. Their sensors against my monster. I wonder which will win.

Everything becomes a kind of gray, blurry haze as my eyes adapt to the deep darkness. I can see the tunnel from sound echoes as I glide down the dark paths. I'm also aware of the remotes spreading out in a search pattern in the tunnel complex.

I'll never outrun them. I need to hide, but I glow in infra-red. One of the remotes is closing, fast.

I back up against a rock wall, and force the monster to hide me. It's hard; it wants to fight, but I need to hide first. I feel the numbing cold return as my temperature drops, hiding my heat. I feel the monster come alive, feel it spread through my body and erupt out of my skin. Fibers spread over my skin, covering me completely in fibrous camouflage. They harden, fusing me to the wall, leaving me unable to move. I can't see, and I can barely breathe. If the remotes find me here, I'm dead.

The remote screams by. I can't see through the fibers, but it sounds like an LB-24, basically a silver cigar equipped with a small laser.

I can hear the remote hover nearby. Can it see me? It pauses and then circles the area. Somehow, the fibers hide me. It can't see me, but it knows something is wrong. It drops on the floor to deposit a sensor package and continues on. Likely it signaled the men upstairs about an anomaly. They'll come and check it out.

The instant I move, the camera will see me. So I wait. I listen to the sounds of the drones moving and water running in the caves. These caves are not as lifeless as I thought; a spider crawls across my face. I'm as still as stone.

Soon, the drones have completed their search pattern and dropped sensors all over the place. I can hear them through the rock, so now I have a mental map of the caves stretching out down here. I wait.

They send the recall, and the drones whine past on the way up. They lower ropes and rappel down the shaft. They pause by the pool, scanning the tunnels and blasting sensor pulses of sound, and likely radar and other scans as well. I wait.

They move carefully down the tunnels. I can feel their every movement through the rock, hear their every word. These men know what they are doing: staying in pairs, staying in constant communication, and checking corners carefully. I wait.

One pair comes up next to me. They pause. One of them has bad breath. I can feel the tension; they know something is wrong. They could shoot me any instant. I wait.

"Let's make sure." I hear a deep voice and a switch clicks.

Heat and fire fill the tunnel. I can see red light through the fibers. Roaring fire sucks all the air away, and the fibers seal my nose before I inhale flame. The fibers protect me from the liquid flame that covers everything. I can feel the heat slowly begin to burn through.

It's time.

* * * * *

Get "Warrior: Integration" now at:
https://www.amazon.com/dp/B0875SPH86

Find out more about David Hallquist and "Warrior: Integration" at:
https://chriskennedypublishing.com/

* * * * *

Made in United States
Troutdale, OR
03/17/2024